*"You okay, sport?" Cable stooped down and tentatively stretched a hand to stroke Jeremy's head.*

Jeremy sniffed and turned his head to look at Cable. "Uh-huh." He reached up and took hold of Cable's hand and hugged it against his little chest.

Cable's tenderness brought a lump to Sara's throat. She'd never seen him like this—completely vulnerable. He had rushed to Jeremy's side as if he had a right, as if he were the boy's father.

The intimacy of the moment slammed into her with hurricane force. The three of them, bound together, heart-to-heart, hand-to-hand, as surely as any family.

She was afraid to look into Cable's eyes for fear of what she would find. Playing house was dangerous. Playing mommy and daddy would be disastrous.

Dear Reader,

Welcome to Silhouette **Special Edition**...welcome to romance. March has six wonderful books in store for you that are guaranteed to become some of your all-time favorites!

Our THAT SPECIAL WOMAN! title for March is *Sisters* by Penny Richards. A dramatic and emotional love story, this book about family and the special relationship between a mother and daughter is one you won't want to miss!

Also in March, it's time to meet another of the irresistible Adams men in the new series by Sherryl Woods, AND BABY MAKES THREE, which continues with *The Rancher and His Unexpected Daughter*. And continuing this month is Pamela Toth's newest miniseries, BUCKLES AND BRONCOS. In *Buchanan's Baby,* a cowboy is hearing wedding bells and the call of fatherhood. Rounding out the month are *For Love of Her Child,* a touching and emotional story from Tracy Sinclair, Diana Whitney's *The Reformer,* the next tale in her THE BLACKTHORN BROTHERHOOD series, and *Playing Daddy* by Lorraine Carroll.

These books are sure to make the month of March an exciting and unforgettable one! I hope you enjoy these books, and all the stories to come!

Sincerely,

Tara Gavin
Senior Editor

Please address questions and book requests to:
Silhouette Reader Service
U.S.: 3010 Walden Ave., P.O. Box 1325, Buffalo, NY 14269
Canadian: P.O. Box 609, Fort Erie, Ont. L2A 5X3

# LORRAINE CARROLL
## PLAYING DADDY

Silhouette®

SPECIAL EDITION®

Published by Silhouette Books
America's Publisher of Contemporary Romance

For The Lord and all the people He sent to bless
my life during these last four years.
The Group: Laura Virgil, Deborah Cox,
Rickey Mallory and Sheri Kenyon.
My Agent: Alice Orr, for refusing to let me give up.
My Family: Joe, Dan and Matt, for loving me anyway.
And for all the Associates at McRae's Northpark for their
friendship, support and understanding.

 SILHOUETTE BOOKS

ISBN 0-373-24020-1

PLAYING DADDY

**Books by Lorraine Carroll**

Silhouette Special Edition

*Lead with Your Heart* #670
*The Ice Princess* #705
*Playing Daddy* #1020

---

## LORRAINE CARROLL

says, "There's something about the South that brings out the romantic in everyone." Born and raised in Columbus, Ohio, Ms. Carroll was first inspired to write by her eighth-grade teacher. But her talent lay dormant until 1978, when her husband was transferred to Baton Rouge. Being surrounded by the romance and the history of that region set her on the path to writing romance fiction. She has also published several articles on television history, and has worked as a staff writer for a community newspaper.

Ms. Carroll has been married to her husband, Joe, for twenty-seven years. They have two sons, Matthew and Daniel. Her hobbies include sewing, reading, gardening and playing piano. But her favorite pastime is curling up in a chair with pen and paper and her dog Pixie Dust, and writing a love story. "It just doesn't get any better than that."

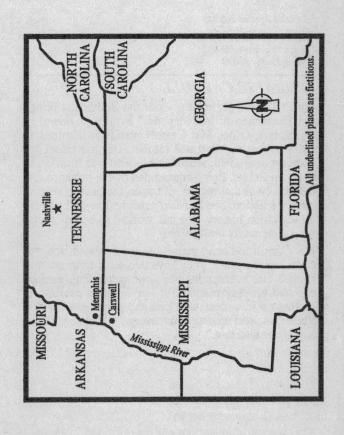

All underlined places are fictitious.

## Chapter One

Sara Nelson guided her small car into the drive of the old Victorian house, coming to a stop near the garage in the back. With a deep sigh, she momentarily rested her forehead against the steering wheel.

The last twelve hours had been the most exhausting of her life. When Mrs. Louis, her full-time sitter, had called this morning with her immediate resignation, Sara had been stunned. Who was going to take care of her son, Jeremy? There was no one else she knew who could keep him on such short notice.

Her only choice had been to make the five-hour drive home to Nashville, grab a few necessities and bring Jeremy back here to stay with her in Carswell, Mississippi.

This assignment—setting up the newest and largest Dixie Mart in the south-central region—was a chance to showcase her ability and increase her chances for promotion. Her future career advancement depended on getting the store open on time. But without a sitter, how was she going to take care of Jeremy and still get the store opened by Memorial Day?

She'd started this assignment with high hopes and a positive outlook. But now, after this unexpected change in plans, her attitude was leaning sharply toward pessimism.

And then there was Cable the Crab, her reclusive and disgruntled host. He'd been less than hospitable since her arrival, and she was apprehensive about his reaction to having a three-year-old suddenly thrust upon him. It wouldn't surprise her at all to find that her belongings had been dumped on the back porch and the locks changed.

Opening the car door, Sara climbed out, pulling the seat back forward and reaching into the rear to unfasten Jeremy's safety belt. The sleeping child squirmed, then half opened his eyes. "Are we home now?"

"Yes, sweetheart." It wasn't exactly home, but for the next four weeks the two large rooms in the big old house were all they'd have.

Keys in hand, she gathered up the sleep-warmed child, resting him against her hip while she tugged out her purse, a large nylon satchel, the bag of toys and a stuffed dinosaur. Shutting the car door with her backside, she started up the stone walkway to the back porch.

Butterflies awoke in her stomach as she neared the house. Cable McRay wasn't going to like this. The scowling hermit had already made it clear he wasn't thrilled with her presence. This wouldn't sweeten his disposition in the least.

The only comforting thought was that Ken would have called Cable by now and explained the unusual circumstances. After all, Ken Burrows was Cable's first cousin as well as Sara's boss. He was the one who had arranged for her to stay here in the first place, and today on the phone, he'd assured her that Cable wouldn't mind the addition of a small boy.

Ken had been certain. Sara was not.

Cable McRay exemplified the word *hermit* to perfection. During the two weeks she'd been living in his house, their paths had rarely crossed. But when they did, he was cold and distant, with an attitude as discouraging as a barbwire fence. He'd made it abundantly clear he wanted little or nothing to do with her or anyone else.

She'd been at a loss to understand why he'd accepted her as a boarder in the first place. Ultimately, she'd decided Ken must have resorted to blackmail. Nothing short of that could possibly influence a man like McRay.

The butterflies in Sara's stomach took flight again as she climbed the steps to the porch. Maybe this wasn't such a good idea after all. Until this moment, she'd been too busy at the store to care about Cable's sequestered life-style beyond idle speculation. She left early and returned late. She dismissed his sour attitude and terse responses as inconsequential. It was as if they had some mutual unspoken agreement to ignore each other at all costs.

That would have to change now. Not even a hermit crab could ignore a three-year-old, and there was no way she could keep Jeremy quiet and occupied every second they were in the house. There was no doubt in her mind that Cable was not going to welcome the upheaval in his home.

Jeremy clung to her neck as she fumbled with the keys, trying to find the right one and fit it into the lock without dropping her precious cargo.

Grumbling between clenched teeth at the stubborn lock, Sara puffed out a sigh of relief when the door finally swung open. Unable to catch it, she cringed as it banged against the kitchen counter with enough force to wake the dead.

Great. Not only was she bringing an energetic little boy into Cable's house, but she was going to wake him from a sound sleep as well. As quietly as possible, she shut the door.

Turning slowly, she took a step forward and froze.

Cable McRay stood in the kitchen doorway, a deep scowl creasing his forehead. Eyes black as pitch bore into hers, and the jaw beneath his scruffy beard was rigid with anger.

Sara's apprehension swelled under his fierce stare, launching the butterflies into orbit. Then Jeremy moved in her arms, and her courage took over. She wasn't about to let the Crab intimidate her. Hoisting her son farther up on her hip, she faced Cable defiantly. "I know it's late, but there was an accident the other side of Memphis that had traffic backed up for hours. So if you want to discuss this, it'll have to wait until morning. I'm tired and I want to get Jeremy into bed."

Cable's jaw flexed. "Jeremy?"

Sara frowned. Was the man dense? "My son," she said sarcastically.

Slowly, Cable's eyes focused on the child. His expression darkened ominously. Sara's heartbeat increased. She braced for attack, expecting him to order them out of his house. Quickly she sent up a little prayer. "Ken assured me it wouldn't be a problem for you. Didn't he call?" She took a firmer hold on the plastic strap that was cutting into her forearm.

"I haven't talked to Ken," he replied, bringing his gaze back to her.

Sara's heart sank as a vaguely sick feeling settled in the pit of her stomach. Great. Ken hadn't called. He hadn't warned Cable that she was bringing Jeremy back with her. No wonder the Crab had his claws in the air.

"Our agreement didn't include a child."

Oh, God, it was happening again. No matter how little she cared about Cable McRay's opinion, the fact that she was being rejected once more because she had a child caused the old pain to twist in her heart.

Summoning her courage, she took a deep breath. She'd survived it once; she could survive it again. But it was too late and she was too damned tired to deal with Cable now. He could attack with all claws snapping, but she wasn't going anywhere tonight.

"I'm sorry about the mix-up, but my housekeeper quit unexpectedly and I had to go get my son. First thing tomorrow, I'll locate a day care for him and find us another place to stay. But right now it's late and I'm going to bed."

She met Cable's stony glare with all the confidence and determination she had, despite the butterflies still warring in her stomach. She started past him. For a brief second they challenged each other, Sara daring him to stop her, Cable defying her to invade his territory further.

She waited for him to snarl, to clamp his claws around her and order her from the house. Instead, he turned without a word and walked away, but not before she caught a glimpse of raw fear in his brown eyes.

"Mommy, I'm sleepy."

Sara pulled her son close and kissed the top of his head, the contact reassuring her as much as him. They could face anything together. Even an attack of the six-foot-two-inch Killer Crab. "I know. Come on, let's go to bed," she said softly, readjusting the straps of the heavy satchels. "You can sleep with me tonight, okay?"

Sara continued on toward her rooms, wondering if it was really fear she'd seen in Cable's eyes or merely a dislike of children. Whatever it was, she was too tired and it was too late to deal with the many bad attitudes of Cable McRay.

Cable McRay had never understood the term *poleaxed* until tonight. He'd stepped into the kitchen and been blindsided, gunned down and left bleeding in the street.

Taking the stairs two at a time, he strode quickly toward his room, slamming the door shut behind him. Inhaling a deep, ragged breath, he rubbed his eyes, trying to wipe the vision of the woman and child from his mind.

His chest ached, as if every molecule of air had been sucked out of his lungs. His temples pounded and he could hear the blood roaring in his ears. The pain of old, distant memories pierced his heart, thrusting deep into his soul, leaving him shaken and vulnerable.

He'd found peace and a measure of serenity here in the rural college town. His handcrafted furniture business was financially rewarding and emotionally satisfying. But tonight, when Sara had stumbled into his kitchen with a drowsy little boy in her arms, that peace had been shattered.

Mother and child.

Instinctively, he'd tried to retreat behind his emotional walls, to pile another row of bricks on the top to deflect the winds of pain, but the memories were too intense. He'd been defeated.

Damn. He hadn't even known she had a child. Why in God's name did she have to bring him here?

Ken had better have a damn good explanation for this. Snatching up the phone, Cable punched in the required numbers, his anger mounting as he waited for an answer on the other end of the line. "What the hell are you trying to do?"

"Cable? What's going on?" The voice that came back to him was slurred with sleep, but at the moment Cable didn't care if he'd wakened his cousin.

"She brought her kid here."

Ken cursed softly. "Hey, man, I'm sorry. I really meant to call and warn you they were coming, but the day got away from me. Is it a problem for you?"

Problem? Having the scar tissue gouged out of his soul? No, that wasn't a problem. "You had no right."

"Hey, take it easy. You agreed to the arrangement, remember? I thought it was working out okay."

"You didn't tell me all of it. You didn't tell me there was a kid."

"There wasn't a need for you to know until now. Who knew her sitter would get sick and she'd have to bring him along?"

"I like my privacy."

"Yeah, well, I think you like it a little too much."

"That's not for you to decide."

"Maybe not. But it wouldn't hurt you to get out from behind that concrete wall you've put up around yourself. There's life out here, Cable. Remember?"

"I have a life and it doesn't include a woman and her child." Cable rubbed his forehead in a vain attempt to ease the pressure in his skull. "Don't do this to me, Ken."

There was a long pause before his cousin answered. "Okay. Maybe this wasn't such a hot idea, after all. But Sara's not only one of my managers, she's also a good friend. Don't toss her and the boy out tonight, okay? At least wait until morning."

Cable didn't even respond to that last comment. He slammed the receiver down and clenched his fists. He should never have agreed to this arrangement, but his cousin was a charming and persuasive negotiator. You just couldn't say no to the man. Ken had assured him the woman would be working nearly round the clock setting up merchandise in the store. He would barely know she was there. That single fact had persuaded him to agree. He could handle the intrusion, as long as she went her way and didn't get in his.

A simple plan that had gotten complicated the moment he'd opened the door two weeks ago.

Sara Nelson had swept around him like a gusty spring breeze, throwing light and fresh air into the recesses of his mind and clashing with his basic need for quiet isolation. He bitterly resented her disturbing his haven of peace.

But like that spring breeze, she'd captivated him by her intoxicating presence.

She wasn't a beauty in the classic sense, but there was an appealing, winsome quality to her features that held his attention and made him want to smile.

Tall and slender, she moved with the grace of a willow. A cap of silky, dark blond hair flirted with her forehead, framing her heart-shaped face. Her large blue eyes were the color of a high summer sky; her gaze was direct, intelligent and curious.

Too curious. Cable didn't like people poking into his life, wondering about him or his past.

Sara Nelson scared Cable to his roots.

Anxious to put distance between them, he'd dispensed with the amenities as quickly as possible that first day. Still, it had taken him an hour to defuse her vitality, which had clung to him like strong perfume. He'd decided then and there to keep out of her way.

Keeping her out of his mind, however, was another matter. Sara had impacted upon his senses in a way no woman ever had. Some mystic, subconscious antenna kept him aware of her. When she was in the house, he knew where she was every second. When she was gone, he felt a new kind of silence and emptiness. Even the old house seemed to sag and sigh sadly when she was absent.

He'd convinced himself that he could tolerate her intrusion in his life for the five weeks remaining in her stay. Fortunately for him, she spent most of her time at work, and he'd effectively curtailed her persistent attempts at friendship with cool indifference.

But he couldn't allow her to stay now, not with the boy. It would hurt too much, dredge up too much pain.

Ken was right; he couldn't throw them out tonight. But first thing in the morning he'd make sure she followed through on her offer to find another place to stay.

Cable ran his hands over his scalp and walked to the window, staring out at the night sky. She had no way of knowing what she and the child had done to him when they'd barged through his door tonight. She couldn't know that the sight of them, the mere idea of them, ripped into him like scalding claws of steel, shredding the fabric of his soul, exposing emotions he'd protected for five years.

With an irritated sigh, he turned away from the window, one hand rubbing his ragged beard. If only he could rub out the picture of them from his brain.

Despite being burdened with bags looped over her shoulder and dangling from her arm, Sara had held the sleeping child lovingly and protectively against her hip. The image had jolted him. He couldn't let the touching scene get to him.

Now that the pain and shock were subsiding, he began to recall little things about how she'd looked tonight that he'd been too stunned to realize before. Fatigue had etched the corners of her mouth, dulling the light in her blue eyes, and the energy that usually surrounded her was missing.

A twinge of guilt seeped through a small crack in his irritation. It wasn't her fault she was staying here. He had agreed to the arrangement. None of this was her fault.

He should have said something to let her know that he had nothing against her and the boy personally. He could at least have offered to help her with the bags.

It was a long drive to Nashville and back to Carswell. She must be exhausted. The child, too. But that didn't change the fact that they had to go. He'd made a grave mistake, and he would correct it first thing tomorrow morning.

"Clifford."

Jeremy reached out for the stuffed dinosaur and Sara handed it to him, smiling at the sweet picture he made.

Smoothing back his soft hair, she kissed his forehead. "Mommy loves you, Jeremy."

"I love you, too," he said, snuggling down into the bed.

She watched as he drifted off to sleep, caressing him with her eyes for a long moment.

He was her whole world, her very heart. Part of her was secretly glad that Mrs. Louis had quit and she could have Jeremy with her all the time. The enforced separations had become more and more difficult to endure.

This set-up assignment was the farthest from home she'd been since her promotion. When Ken had first offered it to her she'd actually thought about declining, but the opportunity was too invaluable to ignore. You didn't tamper with a position that would send your son to college and provide a secure future.

In the beginning, the job had been a godsend. The salary and benefits were exceptional, and there'd been plenty of time to spend with her son. But in the last two years the position had changed. She was expected to travel more, which forced her to make adjustments and compromises.

The biggest sacrifice had been time. Time away from Jeremy. Long, lonely, agonizing weeks at a stretch. She'd learned how to work hard and fast so she could get back to him, and she'd done a good job of juggling all the loose ends.

But she couldn't keep going at this pace forever. It wasn't fair to Jeremy or to herself. She had to find another solution, and the only one that presented itself was the chance at the promotion to district set-up coordinator, a position that would entail a nine-to-five workweek and no travel.

Checking on Jeremy one last time, Sara went into the sitting room and dug her portable phone out of her purse. With each punch of the buttons she fumed at her forgetful boss. The steady beeping in her ear increased her irritation.

Busy. She was willing to bet Cable had beat her to the punch and was already giving Ken a piece of his mind.

Damn. She should never have agreed to live in this house. If the local motel hadn't been filled with college students displaced by a dormitory fire, she wouldn't be in this mess.

Sara crossed her arms over her chest, mimicking her boss, as she murmured, "Cable lives all alone in a big old house, Sara. He's more than happy to let you stay there, Sara. No problem, Sara." Yeah, right.

Ken had been deliberately vague about his cousin. Had he told her what a recluse the man was, how fiercely he protected his privacy, she would never have accepted Cable's hospitality.

Angrily, she picked up the phone and jabbed the redial button. Busy.

Hospitality? Ha! That was a joke. There was nothing hospitable about Cable McRay. He had greeted her that first day with an icy glare, had shown her to her rooms, handed her a key and crawled back inside his hard shell. He was totally unapproachable, which was fine with her. She was too busy at work to spend one millisecond thinking about him.

It was too bad, though, that he was so grim all the time. She would like to have been friends. It would be nice to have someone to talk to now and again, someone who didn't work for her. But Cable didn't talk, he only growled and scowled. If he didn't frown so much he'd be a very attractive man. He had gorgeous brown eyes and dark, wavy hair that curled around his ears and against the nape of his neck.

She'd often wondered what a smile would do to his strong features and if those were really dimples she'd glimpsed in his cheeks or shadows from the weeks-old stubble he seemed to favor. Without the ragged beard, he might be downright handsome—not that it would make an iota's worth of difference in her opinion of him.

Lifting the phone, she poked the redial button again. Busy. Exasperated, she tossed the apparatus onto the wing chair.

How could Ken have thought this would work? How dared he forget to call and smooth things over before she barged in on Cable in the middle of the night? "If I had you here, I'd wring your stupid, forgetful neck!" she muttered wrathfully.

Too agitated to sleep, Sara turned her restless energy toward unpacking and trying to organize the two large rooms at the back of the house into some sort of a home. She had to admit this was better than staying at a motel. She had the use of a spacious sitting room, a narrow alcove that would be perfect for Jeremy's toys and books, and a large bedroom and bath.

After making space for Jeremy's clothes in the dresser and toothbrush in the bathroom, she made a sweep of the room, placing breakables out of reach and otherwise making the room as childproof as possible.

Even though taking valuable time to search for another place to stay was going to put her behind schedule, she was still glad to have Jeremy with her. To be able to hold him at night and be with him when she wasn't at work was worth any sacrifice. She hated every minute she had to be away from him. She had to get this promotion so she could avoid the constant traveling.

Satisfied that the room was safe for Jeremy, but too keyed up to sleep, Sara thought about the rest of her things still packed in the car. For a second she considered going to find Cable and asking him to give her a hand. Pride and the memory of his less-than-enthusiastic welcome quickly doused that idea.

He didn't want them here, especially not Jeremy. No need to stir already troubled waters. Besides, she didn't need any help. She was perfectly capable of handling her life on her own.

But darn, a pair of broad shoulders would be very welcome right now. Someone to carry the luggage; someone to give just a little help and understanding. She was so very tired.

With a weary sigh she walked to the door and pulled it open, almost tripping over the luggage and boxes sitting neatly outside the door.

Surely Cable hadn't thought to do this. Had he? He'd been blunt to the point of rudeness. Did this mean they could stay or not? Stepping out into the hall, she looked around, but saw no sign of him. Puzzled and oddly touched, she lifted the largest suitcase and carried it inside. Maybe the old crab had gotten over the shock and decided to at least be civil about this mess. Thank goodness. Now she could get her life back under control and forget about Cable McRay.

"Mommy, I'm hungry."

Opening another cupboard, Sara searched for a box of cereal. Any kind would do. "I know, Sweetie. I'll find you something real quick. Be a big boy and play with your dinosaur while I look, okay?"

She didn't have a clue where Cable kept his food. In the two weeks she'd been here, she'd always eaten out. As a result, she was in foreign territory in this large old kitchen.

Continuing her search, she grumbled as she found spices and a few canned goods, but nothing to feed a three-year-old for breakfast.

In the next cupboard she finally found what she was looking for. Oatmeal. Good, healthy food. Except it wasn't Jeremy's favorite, and it had to be cooked. She glanced around for a microwave oven. Unless it was camouflaged as a trash can, there was none to be found. That left the old gas-stove method. Now where had she seen the pans?

"Mommy, I can't reach," Jeremy said.

Sara looked back at the table and grinned. Jeremy's little chin was resting on the tabletop. He looked so pitiful and so adorable. After adjusting the flame under the pan, she went back to the table.

"That chair isn't tall enough, is it? Here," she said, noticing the Memphis and northern-Mississippi phone directory lying on the table. "Hop down and we'll use this to boost you up." She reached out to close the book, but stopped when her eyes caught the large ad that had been circled with a red marker.

The Caring Connection Day Care. Carswell's Finest Child-Care Facility, the ad proclaimed.

What a coincidence that the area phone book should be open to this page. The memory of Cable's hostile reception last night flashed through her mind. *Our agreement didn't include a child.* Coincidence? Hardly.

Apparently this was Cable's not-too-subtle reminder that her son wasn't welcome in his home. So much for thinking the Crab had adjusted to the idea of Jeremy being here.

Sara shut the thick book with a loud thud, dropped it onto the chair and plunked Jeremy on top of it. Well, that settled it. Until now she'd tolerated Cable's irascible temperament, but she refused to subject Jeremy to his crankiness. She refused to stay where they were not wanted.

Walking back to the stove, she poured the hot cereal into bowls and splashed on some milk. Picking up a spoon, she stirred briskly, taking out her irritation on the steaming oatmeal. The first thing she'd do today was go to a real-estate office. There had to be other places to stay even in a small town like Carswell.

Carrying the bowls to the table, she sat down, her mind racing. She was already two days behind schedule at work. But surely she could register Jeremy at a day care and locate another place to stay before lunch. If she could get back to the store by one o'clock she'd have the rest of the afternoon to try and correct the mix-up with the fixture shipment. Maybe by the end of the week she'd be back on track.

"I don't like it," Jeremy whined, shoving his bowl away.

Sara shifted mental gears. "Jeremy, you have to eat. I'll buy some Crackly Grainflakes while we're out, but this is all Mr. McRay has."

The screen door creaked loudly behind her, and Sara glanced over her shoulder to see Cable standing tall and intimidating just inside the kitchen. Immediately defensive, she opened her mouth to assure him they'd be gone soon, but the words lodged in her throat when she saw the expression on his face.

The scowl was still there, that deep frown that habitually creased his forehead, but the look in his eyes wasn't one of anger. It was shock, as if the wind had been knocked out of him.

She followed his gaze; he was looking at Jeremy. But he'd seen her son last night. Why would he be shocked to see him again this morning?

"I guess you found everything all right," he growled, striding to the coffeemaker.

Now she understood. He was angry because she'd helped herself to his food and utensils without permission. "Yes," she replied in a clipped tone. "I had to find something for my son to eat."

Cable stirred his coffee, then turned and met her gaze. "I don't have much."

Apparently he was a crab and a tightwad to boot. "Well, don't worry. I'll replace anything I use."

"I don't expect compensation. Use whatever you want."

Sara met his straightforward gaze but could read nothing in his eyes. She must have imagined that look of shock. Turning her attention back to Jeremy, she caught him climbing down from the chair.

"I don't like o'meal."

"Oh, no, young man," Sara said firmly. "Get back up there. Take a few bites and then you can get down."

Jeremy covered his mouth with his hands and shook his head.

"You have to eat breakfast. I promise I'll go to the store and get you something else, but right now you have to eat."

"Oatmeal will make you grow big and tall."

The sound of Cable's voice startled her, and she turned to look at him. He watched Jeremy, his eyes glazed and haunted as if he was seeing something else, or someone else, in his mind.

There was a tense moment as Jeremy stared at Cable, sizing him up. "Tall as you?" the little boy finally asked.

Cable nodded, quickly lowering his gaze to his mug.

Sara watched in amazement as her son pulled the bowl toward himself and took a mouthful of cereal. Jeremy could be obstinate when he chose. She'd anticipated a real battle of wills, but Cable had known exactly what to say to get results. How would a hermit know something like that?

"I talked to Ken last night."

Cable's deep voice again interrupted her speculation. She'd guessed correctly about why she'd been unable to get her boss on the phone. Cable had beaten her to the punch, and she had a pretty good idea what he'd said to his cousin.

"I know," she interjected, holding up one hand. "Jeremy wasn't part of the arrangement, but—"

"No, he wasn't."

Sara ignored the harsh tone of his voice. "I didn't have a choice. Like I tried to explain last night, my sitter quit and there was no one else to watch him."

Cable didn't reply, and Sara wasn't sure how to interpret his silence. "At any rate, I've taken care of it. I called Edith first thing this morning, and she's agreed to watch Jeremy for me today."

"Edith?"

Sara gathered up the bowls and her coffee cup and carried them to the sink. "The lady who cleans for you twice a week."

"I know who she is."

Retrieving the pan from the stove, she moved to the sink and began rinsing it out. "She was coming to clean today, anyway. It's the most sensible solution for the time being."

She walked back to the table and wiped off the surface, aware of Cable's eyes boring into her back. She tried to ignore the edginess it created. "I'll find another place for us to stay before the end of the day."

"Something wrong with this place?"

"No, of course not. But as you pointed out, the arrangement was for me, not for a three-year-old. Under the circumstances, I won't hold you to the agreement."

"It's a big house."

Sara stopped in the middle of the room and looked at Cable. He was standing in front of the window with his back to her. What did he mean by that? That there was room for all of them? That he could keep out of their way?

Shaking her head in confusion, she stacked the dishes in the sink and looked around. "Where's the dishwasher?"

"I don't own one."

Sara exhaled slowly, staring dejectedly at the stainless-steel sink. She hated doing dishes by hand. No microwave, no dishwasher. Living with Cable was like living in the Stone Age.

Jeremy climbed down from the chair and began walking his plastic dinosaur through the air on an imaginary road. The stuffed Clifford was Jeremy's favorite toy but running a close second was the little pink plastic brontosaurus with movable legs. He skipped over to Cable and smiled up at him, holding out his toy. "This is a big din'saur. He eats trees and bushes. I can make his legs move. Watch."

Sara glanced over in time to see Cable brace himself. From where she stood, she couldn't see his expression, but he was obviously annoyed.

"I ate my o'meal all gone. Will I be tall as you?"

Stiff and mute, Cable nodded. Quickly, Sara went to her son. No need in getting her host angry. Not until they had another place to stay.

"Jeremy, leave Mr. McRay alone." She'd started to guide Jeremy back to the table when she glanced up into Cable's face. His expression was chiseled from granite. But the eyes, usually so cold and unreadable, were filled with sadness—a sorrow so deep, so profound, it was physically painful to see.

Abruptly, he turned and walked to the door, pushing it open. He stopped in midmotion and spoke over his shoulder. "He can call me Cable." He paused a moment, as if uncertain, then said, "I dug out the phone book. My friend Geri Arthur runs the Caring Connection. She'll take good care of him for you."

Before Sara could grasp the significance of his statement, he was gone. Bewildered, she stared at the door for a long moment before walking back to the sink. That was the most she'd heard Cable say at one time since she'd arrived here. What had prompted it?

He'd said "my friend." She couldn't believe he had any, but he had at least one, and she ran a day-care facility. A place that would take good care of Jeremy. What had prompted his change in attitude? He'd sounded so genuinely helpful. Had she misread his intentions in having the phone book open? No, she decided quickly. Impossible. It didn't fit with what she already knew about Cable the Crab. Thoughtfulness was not in his nature.

"Jeremy, go brush your teeth. Edith will be here any minute, and then Mommy has to go." As Sara finished cleaning up the breakfast dishes, the memory of the deep emotions she'd seen in Cable's eyes kept intruding on her thoughts. There had been fear and a soul-wrenching sadness that still left her aching inside.

What could cause such profound emotions? Did it have something to do with him being so reclusive? She'd asked herself that question more than once since she'd moved in here. She'd wondered about Cable from the first. He seemed too young to be so withdrawn from life. Hermits were disillusioned, sour old men, Cable must be in his mid-thirties.

As far as she could tell, he wasn't physically impaired, so it wasn't disfigurement that kept him hidden away. She knew he went into town. Once he'd been gone for several days, so it wasn't agoraphobia or whatever that fear about people and open spaces was called.

What did that leave? Hatred of all humans? He had at least one friend, so that couldn't be it.

She went to her rooms to check on Jeremy. "Are you finished with your teeth?"

"Is that man as big as a din'saur?"

"His name is Cable, honey. No. But he is very tall, isn't he?" Six two, she speculated, picking up her own toothbrush. Emotional problems? Is that what made a man like Cable hide from the world and keep everyone ten feet away? Surely Ken would have told her if his cousin was mentally unstable.

Shrugging off thoughts of her landlord, she joined Jeremy in the sitting area. It was a lovely section of the house. Each morning the sun streaked through the beveled-glass panes and gently awakened her. Outside the front windows stood a huge magnolia tree, and below the bay windows in the alcove were large gardenia bushes, heavy with pungent white flowers.

She would regret leaving here. The house had a wonderful homey quality. With a little work and some modernization, it could be quite spectacular. But apparently Cable had no such inclination.

It was strange, but the house didn't fit Cable at all. He lived in it, but the place didn't feel lived in. There was no sense of the man, of his personality, evident here. She had the oddest feeling that he'd bought it, moved in and never changed anything.

He was a difficult man to figure out. Trying to get some insight into Cable was like looking at a tintype from the Old West, where the people posed with expressionless faces. There was no sign of a person's true personality, that special spark that distinguished one from another.

Cable wore his stoic mask like an old friend.

Still, last night and again this morning, when he'd looked at Jeremy, the mask had failed him. She'd seen real emotions reflected in his deep-set eyes. Painful emotions, private and not meant to be shared.

What else lay behind his stony facade? What had caused a strong, indomitable young man to bury himself behind an iron curtain of privacy?

## Chapter Two

Cable turned off the belt sander and wiped his palm across the surface of the tabletop. It didn't need more sanding. It was smooth as glass. But the vibration of the tool and its accompanying noise made it difficult to think. And right now, the last thing he wanted to do was think.

Thinking led to remembering, and remembering led to pain. Taking a deep breath, he rubbed the back of his stiff neck.

Why hadn't he agreed when Sara had suggested moving out? It was what he wanted, wasn't it? He wanted his privacy back. Having her in the house had been one thing; he could avoid her with little effort. But the boy—how could he deal with having him around all the time?

Last night and again this morning, when he'd stumbled upon the two of them, it had been like knives plunging into his heart.

These little domestic scenes of mother and child had propelled him into the past with an agonizing jolt. His other life, the one he'd had and lost, had swirled around him like a killer tornado. If he let them stay, he'd be caught in that cyclical storm over and over again.

For five years he'd led a quiet, peaceful existence with no reminders.

Until now.

Sara and Jeremy had rattled doors in his heart and mind he'd thought completely sealed. They'd brought him to the threshold of rooms he'd hoped never to enter again—rooms where the past lay buried.

Slowly, hesitantly, he slipped his hand in his back pocket and closed his fingers around a worn leather wallet. Taking a deep breath, he pulled it out, and while he still had the courage, flipped it open.

A thin film of sweat broke out on his skin. His heart rebelled at what his mind urged him to do. Why was he so afraid to look? It had been five years. He'd dealt with it and put it behind him. He didn't feel anything anymore.

So what was compelling him to look now? What masochistic bent taunted him to view parts of his life that were over and done with? What demon urged him to look again on those beloved faces, the faces of the most important people in the world?

Fear, cold and immobilizing, prevented him from searching the inside compartments of his wallet. He never looked at the memento. He didn't have to. He carried the images engraved upon his heart.

He was long past grieving. That process had been conquered, subdued and stored away in the deepest vault in his being.

Cable took a deep breath, forcing air into his lungs and expelling a ragged breath. He was being weak, foolish. *Just pull it out and look. It can't hurt you anymore.*

With trembling fingers, he slipped the faded photo out of its dark hiding place and into the light. But it took another dose of courage to focus his eyes upon it. When he finally did, his entire body convulsed with sorrow, as if he could no longer deny the awful truth.

Lord help him, this was a mistake.

The woman with her sweet face, the warm dark eyes and the mane of soft, chestnut curls smiled back at him. "Amanda." Her name was like a softly whispered prayer.

He tried to remember the scent of her, the feel of her, but all he could remember was his own emptiness.

His eyes focused on the other face, the boy with the wide grin, the tooth missing in front and the inquisitive eyes. His son, Todd.

Cable beckoned a memory—the sound of his son's laughter, the tone of his voice—and came up empty again. The one memory that filled his mind was the day it had ended. The day a drunk teenager had run a red light and taken the lives of two people he loved.

The day his soul had died.

With a quick, decisive motion, Cable shoved the photo back into the recesses of his wallet and rammed it into his pocket. He hadn't looked at the picture in three years. Why now? All it did was dredge up the pain of that day and the weeks and months that had followed.

The only thing that had saved his sanity was moving away from San Antonio and coming to Carswell. He'd slowly rebuilt his life. He'd turned his woodworking hobby into a small furniture-crafting business, discovering an ability he'd never before developed. It provided him with a modest income, but more importantly, a creative and satisfying purpose. Eventually he'd been able to forget and bury the pain of his loss.

Until last night, when Sara had crashed into his house holding the little boy. Damn her for bringing him here! He didn't need the constant reminders of what he'd once had and lost.

He'd tell her now. He'd apologize and do everything he could to find her another place to stay, but he couldn't have them here. It would be like having a piece of shrapnel rubbing against his heart each time he saw them.

Cable walked out of the workshop toward the house, determined to settle this matter immediately. Sara's car was not in the driveway. An unreasonable sense of relief washed through him at the realization. It was just as well. The delay would give him time to organize his thoughts and present them in a calm, reasonable manner.

He was nearly to the back porch when the screen door opened and Jeremy scurried out, clutching a purple bear under his arm. He stopped at the edge of the steps, his brown eyes widening in delight. "Doggies!"

Cable turned and saw Alamo, his cat, parading across the walk with her latest litter. Captivated, Jeremy dropped the toy bear and hurried down the steps. He squatted, squealing excitedly as the kittens scampered around him. After several failed attempts to catch a tiny fur ball, he finally captured a little gray one.

Jeremy hugged it to him lovingly, but lost his balance and plopped back on his bottom in the grass, still clutching the kitten. The rest of the litter pounced on him, sending him into fits of hysterical giggles.

Cable's heart contracted with the force of a fist rammed into his sternum. He wrenched his gaze away from the endearing scene and turned his back. No, this wasn't going to work. He strode purposefully toward the house, but as he neared the porch steps, he felt a tug on his pant leg. He glanced down and saw the child at his side.

"Is this your doggie?" he asked, holding the kitten up toward Cable.

"Yes." He nodded, managing somehow to swallow around the constriction in his throat. He took the small kitten from the child, then reached down and picked up the purple bear from the edge of the porch. "Is this your bear?"

The little boy frowned. "That's Clifford. He's a din'saur."

"Oh."

Jeremy wrapped his chubby arm around the toy and climbed the steps to the porch. Cable set the kitten down, and it went immediately to the child.

"He likes me!" Jeremy beamed, grabbing up the animal again.

Cable hardened his heart against the pure joy revealed in the child's face, but somewhere, a part of him refused to comply, and he heard himself ask, "Would you like to have him?"

Jeremy nodded and clutched the animal closer, looking with huge, guileless brown eyes.

Cable wasn't sure why he'd offered the child the cat or what to say next. Jeremy seemed to be waiting expectantly for something, but Cable was at a loss as to what it was. "Uh, should you be out here alone?"

"Miz Edith said I could stay on the porch so she could see me."

"Oh."

Apparently satisfied, Jeremy carried the kitten to the swing and deposited his new friend on the slatted seat.

A strange tug-of-war began in Cable's mind as he watched the little boy playing. Part of him wanted to turn his back and run. But another part wanted to stay and watch, to soak up the scene like a thirsty sponge.

For the life of him, he didn't know which inclination terrified him the most.


"I can't believe I struck out on all fronts today." Sara dropped her purse and her binders on the kitchen table with an exasperated grunt.

"I was afraid of that," Edith replied as she gathered up her cleaning utensils. "Carswell is a small college town. Housing is always at a premium, especially now with the motel filled with those students. You're lucky Cable agreed to let you stay here or you'd be making a two-hour trip from Ethelton twice a day."

"I know, but I thought I could at least get Jeremy into a day care. They all have a two-month waiting list." She sighed and came to stand by Edith. "Is he asleep?"

The woman nodded. "He should be awake soon."

"Thank you again for watching him for me today. I know this was a terrible imposition."

"Nonsense!" She reassured Sara with a smile. "I raised seven children. I learned long ago how to do five things at once."

"You're a lifesaver. I hope he didn't give you any trouble."

"None at all. As a matter of fact, I've been thinking about your situation, and I may have a solution. I could watch Jeremy for you."

Sara's hopes soared. She couldn't imagine anyone better qualified to take care of her son. Even though she'd known her only a few weeks, she found Edith to be a sweet, caring and very dependable woman. "Are you sure?"

"The timing is perfect. You'll only need me for a month. My daughter in Baton Rouge is due with her first child in about six weeks. Watching Jeremy will keep me too busy to worry about her until she delivers."

"You're an angel," Sara said, hugging the older woman.

Edith patted her back warmly. "Thank you, dear, but there is one catch. I'll have to watch him here. My place is much too small for a three-year-old."

Sara's elation plunged and she shook her head. "Cable will never agree to that. He's made it clear that Jeremy isn't welcome here."

"Did he say that?"

"He was quick to point out that our bargain was for me alone, not Jeremy."

"Is that all he said?"

"Well, then he scowled in his usual grouchy way."

Edith wagged a finger at her. "Now, don't be put off by his gruff ways. Under that prickly hide is a very kind and thoughtful man. He just takes a little getting used to."

"Right, like root canals take a little getting used to."

Edith chuckled. "Don't worry, I'll talk to him. He's not quite the ogre you seem to think."

"I never said he was an ogre," Sara amended. She was being a little unfair to her host. "More of a crabby recluse."

"He has his reasons." Picking up her things, Edith smiled patiently. "I fixed you a tuna casserole for supper. It's on the stove."

"How sweet of you."

"Well, I knew you'd have a rough day."

"Mommy!" Jeremy dashed across the kitchen, his arms outstretched.

"Hello, sweet thing," Sara crooned, bending down and scooping him up into her arms. Her fatigue and frustration melted away as she hugged him. "Did you have a nice day today staying with Edith?"

Jeremy nodded. "She made me peanut butter with no cruss. And look what Cable gave me." He pointed toward the floor.

Sara looked down and grimaced. "Oh, no!" Jeremy squirmed and she set him down. He immediately grabbed the scrawny gray cat.

"See? He likes me, and Cable said I could have him."

"Cable gave it to you?" Why would a man who disliked children do such a thing? "Oh, sweetheart, I don't know about this. I don't think we can take on a pet right now. This isn't our house, and Miss Edith doesn't have time to care for you and Cable's house and a pet, too."

"Uh-huh," Jeremy muttered.

Sara looked pleadingly at Edith, who shrugged and started toward the screen door. "He hasn't moved more than three inches from the critter since he got it."

"That's all I need," Sara said, following her. "Another complication."

"Don't worry, dear. It'll all work out for the best. It always does."

Sara wished she could feel as positive as she wiped Jeremy's face and hands a half hour later. The casserole had been delicious and filling and a welcome respite from the restaurant food she'd been eating. Even Jeremy had cleaned his plate, though it had taken some persuading for him to leave the cat on the floor while he ate.

"Can me and Doggie sit on the porch?"

Sara considered his request and decided it sounded safe enough. "All right, but it's almost dark. Don't go into the yard. After I do the dishes, I'll give you a bath."

As she began cleaning off the table, the day's tension settled heavily upon her shoulders. After striking out with the real-estate companies and the day care, she'd gone to the store, dreading the hours on the phone trying to straighten out the mix-up in the fixture shipment.

To her delight, her assistant manager, Bud Houston, had already taken care of it and had even made arrangements for correct sizes to be delivered. He was going to make one heck of a manager. The kind Dixie Mart prided itself on.

Freed from that unpleasant task, Sara had spent the rest of the afternoon reorganizing her schedule. She'd divided more of the on-site duties among her small staff and sorted out managerial tasks that could be done at the house.

Jeremy's presence would virtually eliminate the flexibility of her hours if Cable didn't agree to Edith's baby-sitting plans. And that was a mighty big if.

Edith seemed confident that Cable's kind and thoughtful side would prevail. Was she right? Could there be a different man beneath that hermit-crab shell he lived in? If so, then his bringing in her luggage last night might have been an apology of sorts. Maybe he really had circled the ad to be helpful.

Scraping the dishes, she stacked them and carried them to the counter. So if Cable was kind and thoughtful, why did he always treat her like an alien invader? Did he hate people in general, or just her and Jeremy because they had invaded his home? But then why would he give Jeremy a cat?

What did she care what Cable McRay did or said, anyhow? It was a waste of time. She'd learned the hard way that people were often not what they seemed. When it came to her assessment of others, she was always way off the mark. Particularly where men were concerned.

Sara momentarily closed her eyes as a cold draft rose from the ever-present hollow spot below her heart. She willed herself to ignore it.

This whole assignment was growing more complicated by the hour, and to add insult to injury, she had to do dishes by hand, when all she wanted to do was snuggle up with Jeremy and relax for a few moments.

With a resigned sigh, she shoved the stopper into the drain and squirted green liquid soap into the sink.

Cable stood in the front yard, watching the night sky slowly unfold. He'd learned each constellation, knew the phases of the moon, recognized the calls of the night birds and the cries of the nocturnal animals.

Listening to the night usually soothed him—this quiet, peaceful darkness where he could restore his energy, feel a connection with the universe and an appreciation for life at its most basic.

Not tonight. There was a restlessness in the pit of his stomach, an uneasy, vaguely dissatisfied feeling he'd never known before.

The woman and the boy were to blame. They were a glaring reminder of a part of his life he wanted to leave buried.

Seeing Jeremy with the kittens this morning had stirred a distant memory. It had gnawed at the edges of his mind all day, lurking just beyond his grasp.

Taking a deep breath, he cautiously lowered his barriers, allowing his thoughts to turn to the past, to Amanda and Todd. There had been a pet Todd had loved. A cat. No, a dog named... What? It was a shepherd. No, a cocker. Damn. Such a stupid thing. Why couldn't he remember?

Anxiously, he ran his hands through his hair. His memories were like rusty machinery—too corroded with disuse to move freely. But that was the way it was supposed to be, wasn't it? When people you loved died, you were supposed to get over them. Adjust and go on with your life.

Memories only fed the ravenous monster of grief, until it devoured you. Memories kept the pain circulating, churning, by dredging up little shards of agony that punctured your heart over and over again.

He couldn't live like that. That's why he'd come here. That's why he'd taken over his grandmother's house and started fresh, turned his life 180 degrees from what it had been.

He didn't want to remember. But Sara and Jeremy were forcing him to search for those fragments of the past. That's why he couldn't let them stay.

He'd tell her now, before the slivers of memory had a chance to puncture his heart again. Quickly he entered the house, heading toward the back. He stepped into the kitchen and froze.

Sara was at the sink, her hands immersed in sudsy water. He watched as she wiped a bowl, rinsed it and set it aside to drain. She was humming softly as she worked, and his gut twisted into a cold, aching knot.

The homey picture acted like a demonic triggering device, calling up memories that only moments ago had eluded him. Sights, sounds and images exploded in his mind like a star-burst firecracker, falling in hot sparks upon his senses.

A smile, the touch of a hand, an echo of laughter, the warmth of an embrace, the fragment of a song—too many things, too fast to catch and examine.

Then the images slowly dissipated, fading back into the darkness, leaving him desolate and hollow inside.

Gritting his teeth, he focused his attention on Sara again. He was a fool to allow her and Jeremy to stay here. He had to get them out of his house.

"I'll do that," he said, walking briskly to the sink. Sara's fragrance curled around him seductively as he approached, slowing his steps. He willed himself to ignore it.

"I'm almost done." She set a plate in the drainer and blew a little trail of air upward, lifting her hair off her damp forehead and wreaking havoc on Cable's insides.

"Leave it!"

He immediately regretted his harsh tone, but he hadn't expected her simple gesture to impact upon his senses. Hadn't expected to feel the thundering desire to touch the silky cap of her hair.

Sara stiffened and tossed the wet rag into the water, sending little clouds of soap bubbles shooting up into the air and onto the counter. "Fine. I was just trying to help." She walked stiff backed across the kitchen and picked up her phone.

Cable's conscience stung. He shouldn't have taken his discomfort out on her. She knew nothing about him, about what she was doing to him by having her son here, by being here herself. "I didn't mean to shout. I'm used to living alone," he rasped.

"It's none of my business how you choose to live your life," she replied.

"It was the only choice I could make." Inwardly Cable flinched. He hadn't intended to say that. It had poured from his lips unbidden. He stole a quick look at Sara, hoping she hadn't heard him, but he could see from her expression that she had.

Her blue eyes reflected curiosity and puzzlement. He wanted to look away, but her gaze held him, tentatively probing deeper, poking his edges as if seeking life, almost puncturing his emotional barriers.

It took all his willpower to finally turn away. "Where's Jeremy?"

"On the back porch. With the cat."

The displeasure in her voice was obvious. He hadn't stopped to consider how Sara would feel about her son having a kitten. "Yeah, well, it took a shine to him."

"Unfortunately, the feeling is mutual."

Shoving his hands into his pockets, he faced her again. "I'll take it back."

Sara sighed in exasperation. "It's too late for that now. He's in love with the thing."

"It's just a cat."

"With fleas and vet bills," she retorted.

She was looking at him again, that probing, investigative scrutiny, trying to see behind his facade, trying to expose him. He glanced back at the sink. "I'll finish the dishes. Go be with your son."

His offer brought a look of surprise into her eyes, though he couldn't imagine why.

"Thanks. I think I will."

Cable watched as she moved briskly to the screen door and walked out. It banged loudly, bounced once, then stopped. For some reason he felt lonelier than he had in his whole life.


Sara found Jeremy sitting on the back steps with the stupid cat. She glanced once at his happy smile, and love washed away all other emotions. "Come on, sweetie, it's time for your bath," she said, gently stroking his silky hair. "Put the cat down. You can play with him again in the morning."

"No, mine."

"Jeremy, your little friend would be happier outside."

The little boy hugged the animal closer, twisting away from her. "Doggie wants to stay with me."

"Sweetie, it's not a dog, it's a cat," Sara explained patiently.

"His name is Doggie," Jeremy announced firmly, draping the little creature across his chubby knees.

"Oh, no, honey, you can't call a cat Doggie. Let's think of a really good name for him, okay? How about Boots, or maybe Scruffy," she added, thinking of Cable.

"Doggie."

"Why can't he call it Doggie? It's as good a name as any."

Sara heard the screen door open behind her and the heavy tread of Cable's boots as he crossed the porch. She replied without looking at him, "Because it's not a dog, it's a cat. I don't want Jeremy getting confused."

Cable descended the steps and hunkered down in front of the boy. "What's your name?"

"Jermi."

Cable nodded wisely. "What's my name?"

"Cable."

"And your friend here, what's its name?" Cable scratched the cat behind the ear, eliciting a soft purr.

"Doggie!"

Exasperated, Sara tried again. "Jeremy, you wouldn't call your nose a finger or your chin an eye would you?"

Jeremy looked thoughtful a moment, then shook his head.

"Right, so you don't call a cat Doggie."

"Doggie." He frowned at his mother.

Sara wasn't sure in the faint porch light, but she thought she saw an amused, triumphant twinkle in Cable's eyes. "Seems Jeremy has made up his mind," he said, rising.

Sara pursed her lips. "If you want to call him Doggie, Jeremy, I guess you can. But I'm sure Cable doesn't want you to keep your little friend in the house." She looked pointedly at their landlord. "Do you?"

"Cat's got to sleep somewhere. Might as well be in a warm house." Turning on his heel, he walked across the lawn, disappearing into the night shadows and leaving Sara grinding her teeth in irritation.

"I'm not tired, Mommy," Jeremy whined.

*But I am,* Sara thought. She combed Jeremy's damp hair neatly to one side, smiling at the adorable picture he made. He smelled like baby shampoo and soap. His little body was warm and rosy from his bath, and she pulled him close, her heart bursting with love.

"It's time for bed. You had a big day and so did Mommy. I looked for a day care for you and talked to a lady about finding us another house."

Jeremy moved the legs on his favorite toy dinosaur. "I don't like day care."

Sara stopped buttoning his pajama top and studied her son quizzically. He'd always loved playing with the other children. What had happened to change his mind? "Why not?"

"I want to stay here."

That was not the response she'd expected. "You do?"

Jeremy nodded, his expression solemn. "I want you to stay here, too."

Sara ached with sympathy and sadness. She'd dearly love to spend more time with her son. To be able to work less, yet make the same salary was the wish of millions of single mothers. It just wasn't realistic. "You know Mommy has to work, Jeremy. That's why Mrs. Louis stayed with you when I was at the office or on a trip."

"Where's Mrs. Louis?"

"She's not feeling well. She had to go home for a rest." How did you tell a three-year-old that someone he loved had been diagnosed with cancer?

"Who'll take care of me now?"

That question was going to keep her up most of the night. "Maybe Miss Edith. Would you like that?"

Jeremy's eyes lit up. "And Cable, too?"

The name sent shock waves along her nerve endings. "Do you like Cable?"

Jeremy nodded his head rapidly. "He said I could keep Doggie."

As if recognizing his name, Doggie meowed and rubbed against Jeremy's leg, and he scooped the kitten up under his arm. "How come Doggie didn't get a bath?"

Visions of a battle with a screeching, sharp-clawed feline burst into her mind. "We'll let the vet do that."

"Okay." Jeremy skipped off to the sitting room, the kitten's back legs dangling and swaying with each movement.

Sara stood, clasping her hands under her chin, her mind consumed with the question of Jeremy's rapid and unexplainable attachment to Cable. Her mom always claimed that children were good judges of a person's character. Was she right?

Probably not. Her mother was also the one who swore true love could conquer all, and Sara was living proof of the fallacy in that old adage.

Folding a thick blanket, she placed it on the Victorian sofa, then covered it with a clean sheet. What did Jeremy see that she couldn't? And what would happen when the time came to leave this place and go home?

Jeremy was young and formed bonds with people quickly. He'd made new friends today—Edith and Cable. But they would be part of his life for only a few short weeks.

She didn't want him getting attached to Cable. Jeremy didn't understand that relationships couldn't be counted on. That people you loved could stop loving you when doing so became inconvenient for them. She had to protect him from the emotional scars that could result if he became too close to Cable.

It was only natural that her son should be drawn to Edith, a warm, grandmotherly type. It was his fascination for Cable that puzzled her. Part of it was simply the fact that he was a man, a potential role model. Jeremy had few of those in his life. His father never came to see him, her brothers and their children were scattered across the country and Jeremy's grandparents were in Florida.

She wasn't sure Cable was the kind of man she wanted her son to look up to, since he was a gruff, disagreeable, eccentric old crab. Well, not old. Sexy, yes, virile, yes, but always keeping the world ten feet away with his piercing scowl and his chilly aloofness.

And yet, since her return from Nashville, those labels didn't fit as securely as before. She'd been seeing glimpses of another Cable, one that bore little resemblance to the irascible hermit crab.

Like tonight, when Jeremy had been determined to call that kitten Doggie. Cable had stooped down in front of him, eye-to-eye, and calmly discussed the matter. It had been a very sweet, uncrablike thing to do. There had been a softness about Cable, a compassion that beckoned her to look deeper.

Sara viciously tugged on the blanket, tucking in the edges. What an absurd idea. It was nothing more than the porch light reflecting in his eyes. Softness and Cable didn't go together. He was all hard oak and tough leather. Nothing got under his skin.

*It was the only choice I could make.*

His words had glanced off the edges of her thoughts all day. What had he meant by that? What had caused the deep sadness and fear she'd seen in his eyes? What was he hiding from? These new pieces of Cable refused to fit together logically.

Sara plumped the pillow and laid it on the makeshift bed. A lot of things didn't fit with Cable. Like this old house. He didn't belong in a Victorian house with stained-glass windows, prism-bedecked chandeliers and antique furniture.

No, she saw him as more of the outdoor type, living high in the Colorado mountains in an isolated cabin. Or riding across the southwestern desert on a sturdy horse, a six-gun strapped around his hips.

With quick movements, she smoothed back the blanket, silently scolding herself for wasting one second trying to figure him out. Her assessment of a man's character was about as reliable as a gambler's luck. Fortunately, they'd be back home in a few weeks and the question of Cable's character would be immaterial.

She made a few more unnecessary adjustments to the covers. "Come on, sweetie," she called softly. "You get to sleep in this funny little bed tonight."

Jeremy climbed onto the sofa and snuggled down, nearly choking the kitten in the process.

"Let me have the cat. He'll have to sleep on the floor."

"No," the boy whined, holding the kitten away from Sara's grasp. "Doggie needs me."

Fatigue won out over better judgment. It was getting late and Sara still had to go over the housewares manifest and double-check the shelving totals for the toy department.

"All right, Jeremy. But don't think this kitten is going to sleep with you every night." She pulled the covers up close to his chin, her heart warming with love and pride as it always did when she looked at him.

He was a beautiful child, bright, curious and lovable. He was her most precious possession, and though she often worried over him, he was her constant source of happiness.

He was her heart. "Mommy loves you, little Jeremy," she cooed softly, kissing his silky cheek.

"I love you." He smiled back.

Pulling up a chair, she began to read from one of his favorite books. Before she'd turned to page three, he was asleep.

Sara watched him sleep for a few minutes, then rose and gathered up her stack of binders from the chair. Quietly, she left the room, grateful for the nearness of the expansive, if outdated, country kitchen.

The huge oak table was large enough to spread out papers and binders and still leave space for her laptop computer. It was also within earshot of her rooms. With the door open, she could easily hear Jeremy if he should waken and need her.

After fixing a glass of iced tea, she sat down and picked up a pen, only it wasn't work that came to the forefront of her mind.

Having Jeremy here with her was going to be more complicated than Sara had first thought. How would she manage their meals? What if Cable refused to let Edith watch him?

What about the inevitable overtime she herself would need to put in to get the store open by Memorial Day? She was way behind schedule, and if she wanted a shot at the director's job, she had to get the store opened on time, no matter what.

Problems were arriving by the truckload. There were so many more details to take care of with Jeremy here. Pulling out a notepad, she started a list to help her remember them all.

First thing tomorrow, she'd have to call home and have her utilities stopped for a month. She added the newspaper and the cable company to the list and made a special note to ask Edith to recommend a local pediatrician.

Tearing off that sheet, she started another list, of things she needed to buy tomorrow. As she drained her glass, a new thought surfaced and she started yet another for groceries.

She wrote down the name of Jeremy's favorite cereal and smiled. It was going to be wonderful having her baby with her. But what about him? How would this sudden disruption in his routine affect him? Children needed stability and consistency. Thrusting him into a whole new way of life could be emotionally traumatic.

"Jeremy asleep?" Cable's deep voice rumbled, bringing an abrupt halt to her introspection. He stood in front of the table, a glass in one hand, the other hand resting carelessly on his hip.

His blue plaid shirt was unbuttoned and the white T-shirt underneath was molded to his chest. Jeans rode low on trim hips and hugged his long legs. The fabric was so old and faded there were white spots in all the places that had known the most stress. The front pocket was frayed at the edge, as if he habitually slid his hand in and out of it. The knees were thin, and there was a white patch just to the left of the zipper that . . .

Damn! Sara looked away, breathless and flushed with embarrassment. She cursed herself for noticing such a thing. But now that she had, she couldn't get it out of her mind. Cable's earthy maleness had stirred something primal deep inside her, a need she'd denied for a very long time. Obviously, she was stressed to the limit of her endurance. What was it he had asked? Oh, yes, about Jeremy. "Yes, he is. And so is Doggie," she added pointedly.

"Every kid needs a pet." He turned, walked to the refrigerator and pulled out the tea pitcher, filling his glass again.

There were white patches on the seat of his jeans, too. . . . Sara yanked her mind back into line. "This move is going to be difficult enough for Jeremy. I've torn him away from home and school and people he loves."

Cable took a long drink from his glass. "Then it seems a pet would give him a little stability."

Sara shut the lid on her laptop computer and stacked it with her binders. He was absolutely right, but she didn't appreciate him pointing it out to her. Besides, he had an irritating way of making her sound like the villain.

"Sure, for now, but what about when we go home?" Picking up her glass, she carried it to the sink. "What do I tell him when he has to leave it behind?" Turning on the faucet, she soaped up the glass and ran hot water over the glass until she was satisfied it was clean. Then she dried it and set it back in its place on the shelf.

Picking up the dishrag, she started wiping off the counter, lifting boxes and pushing aside canisters to clean beneath and behind. There was a spot near the edge of the sink that just didn't want to come off. Maybe if she rubbed a little harder . . .

Without warning, Cable reached around her and clamped his hand on her wrist. "Don't rub the damn finish off."

All of Sara's senses kicked into high gear. She was surrounded with male strength and virility. She stared down at his hand, acutely aware of the power in his long, tapered fingers. There was gentleness there, too, and a disturbing warmth that was slowly spreading through her body.

The back of his hand was broad and darkly tanned. A smattering of black hair curled between the prominent tendons and thickened as it spread up his forearm, disappearing beneath the worn flannel sleeve.

His body heat encompassed her. Warm flannel brushed against her arm and she turned slightly, only to find herself

flush against him. She'd never realized how tall he was or
how broad through the shoulders. Her eyes were even with
the hollow of his neck and she could see the throbbing
movement as the blood coursed beneath the skin there. It
seemed to beat faster and faster as she stared.

He smelled clean, robust, of the outdoors, of sawdust and
a faint lingering of cinnamon. She watched his chest rise and
fall and fought a ridiculous urge to rest her hand over his
heart and feel it beating, strong and steady, under her palm.

Until this moment, she'd seen Cable McRay as an irascible landlord with an unpredictable streak of thoughtfulness. Now all she could think of was the blatant sexuality of
the man. It was potent, hot and deep, like steam rising from
the depths of a volcano.

It was disturbing to think that the cold crab might be
harboring banked fires.

Gathering her courage, she met his gaze and found herself drawn into his warm brown eyes. She could clearly see
the understanding and compassion in the dark depths now.
But there was something else there as well. Loneliness. A
loneliness she recognized and understood.

Was this what Jeremy saw? A kind, understanding but
lonely man? A man buried alive behind that cold, impreg-
nable scowl? Had she been totally wrong about him? "Cable, I was just trying to help...."

The warmth in his eyes vanished so quickly it left her
breathless. "I don't want or need your help." He released
her and moved away, shoving open the door and disappearing outside.

Sara flinched as the screen door banged shut. Struggling
to bring her scattered senses under control, she nervously
rubbed her wrist, inhaling softly when she realized it still

tingled from the imprint of his hand. In fact, all of her senses still vibrated.

And the lost look in his eyes still echoed softly in her heart.

## Chapter Three

Cable stopped at the bottom of the porch steps and looked back toward the door. Why had he taken his irritation out on Sara? He'd laid this emotional mine field, and he was the one who would have to negotiate it.

Through the screen door, he could see her as she picked up her notebooks and left the room. Tilting back his head, he closed his eyes and sighed. He shouldn't have agreed to let her stay here.

He hadn't realized how hard it would be to share his space, to keep his life separate from theirs. He'd been alone a long time and he'd foolishly believed he could coexist and remain isolated. He saw now that it was impossible. Even the smallest, most insignificant things forced him to interact and respond.

He'd made a few calls today that only confirmed his suspicions. There were no rooms, houses, apartments or any other living quarters available in Carswell. Sara had no choice but to stay with him. He'd never been able to say no to Ken and now he was trapped by his own weakness.

The ringing of the telephone summoned him back inside the house. Reluctantly, he answered it. When he hung up a few minutes later, he was seriously questioning his mental stability.

He had just agreed to let Edith watch Jeremy here in his home while Sara was at work. What was happening to him? He was losing control of his life. First he'd allowed himself to be coerced into sharing his home, then Sara had brought her son here and now he had agreed to have the boy around all day for four weeks. When had the word *no* been eliminated from his vocabulary?

God help him, how would he endure it?

He thought about that morning, about the sight of son and mother at the table, Jeremy holding up his dinosaur and showing him how he could make the legs move. He remembered the way the little boy had giggled at the kittens. An ache began deep in his gut, a gnawing sensation that left him hungry for things he could no longer have—a family one of them.

Did he possess some self-destructive streak he didn't know about? Why was he systematically allowing Sara and Jeremy into his life, when all he wanted was to get them out?

He took a deep breath, and his nostrils filled with her fragrance. Was it lingering in the air? Or was it just etched forever in his senses?

Every particle of his body still vibrated from touching her. It was as if she'd struck a tuning fork deep in his being, one that refused to stop reverberating.

She'd been so soft, so alive and vital beneath his hand. It had been a shock to plug into all her energy. Desire, swift and unexpected, had lanced through him.

What scared him, though, was the realization that he hadn't been able to let go. He'd been nailed to her, unable to pull free. The connection was more than physical. Sara had peeked over his wall and seen his loneliness and understood. He suspected she'd seen much more as well. Damn her pretty probing eyes. She had no right to look into his private rooms. Now, due to his inability to say no, she would be poking at him incessantly.

Running his hands along his scalp, Cable started to leave the room, stopping at the table when he caught sight of some papers shoved up near the junk bowl. He picked them up and shuffled through them. Lists.

Sara had one for everything—Grocery list, Don't Forget list, People To Call list. There was even a Things To Buy list. The first item she'd written down was a bed.

Bed. He hadn't thought about where the boy would sleep. If he remembered correctly, there was an old bed in the attic that should be about the right size. If he had time tomorrow he'd try and track it down.

Cable tossed the stack of papers back onto the table. One drifted to the floor, and he picked it up, glancing at the heading: Ask Cable About. A knot of fear twisted in his gut. Damn. He didn't want to be a part of their lives. Not even a name atop a list.

He'd been a fool to think he could have them here and not get involved. There had to be a way out of this. It was just a matter of taking the necessary precautions, of keeping as much distance between himself and them as possible.

He'd be wise to keep out of their way, keep from getting involved in their little daily problems.

He'd give Edith carte blanche with the child and the running of the house. He'd stay in the shop. He had more than enough orders to keep him working round the clock, if need be.

That was the most logical solution. Stay out of the house and stay out of their way. No problem.

Laying the last list with the others, Cable switched off the kitchen lights and headed for the safety of his room.

Sara retreated quickly and quietly to her rooms, setting her binders and computer on a chair. She turned back immediately, shutting and locking the door, then rested her forehead against the dark walnut finish.

Safe at last.

She lifted her head abruptly. Safe from what?

Cable? He was no threat to her. He was just a man. A man who scared her socks off.

What had just happened between them? Nothing. Everything.

From the moment Cable had touched her, everything had changed. He was no longer an irritation, something to be tolerated. Suddenly he'd become a danger to be avoided at all costs.

She'd made one horrible mistake in her life—marrying Drake. She'd believed in love once—in the till-death-do-us-part kind, the love-conquers-all kind, only to have her life shattered and her dreams destroyed.

She wasn't a starry-eyed romantic anymore. The mere fact that she found Cable attractive on some primitive level meant nothing. She'd learned the hard way that even when you thought you knew a person inside out you didn't really know him at all. He could change without warning, turn into someone you didn't recognize and do something so out of character that your faith in your own instincts was shattered.

She'd believed she had the perfect marriage, that she and Drake shared complete understanding. Until she'd told him she was pregnant, and he'd turned into a stranger before her very eyes. He'd rejected both her and the baby and walked away from eight years of life together.

How could she have been so blind? How could she have lived with Drake for eight years and not realized he was so afraid of responsibility? And how could she ever again trust her own observations about men?

Not that she needed or even wanted a man in her life. She and Jeremy were doing just fine on their own. If she ever took the plunge again, and she seriously doubted she would, the man she married would have to be one spectacular human being. One part Ward Cleaver, one part Mel Gibson and one part Mr. Mom.

Even a diehard romantic knew that such a combination didn't exist.

Walking into the sitting room, she checked on Jeremy. He was sleeping soundly, with Doggie curled up at the foot of the sofa. The kitten raised its head and blinked at her.

Sara grimaced. "Don't get used to this, cat."

Reaching out a hand, she gently smoothed her son's silky hair. What had she ever done to deserve such a beautiful, perfect child? The Lord had truly blessed her.

Curling up on the window seat, she stared at the sleeping boy. Sometimes, like tonight, she wondered if she was strong enough to raise him alone.

He should have a father, someone patient and kind who would speak lovingly and softly to him—the way Cable had spoken to him tonight. But was that really gentleness she'd seen or a chance to irritate an unwelcome guest?

Suddenly too tired to think, Sara rose and prepared for bed, but even the mindless routine couldn't stop her burdensome thoughts. The encounter with Cable had stirred parts of her she didn't want stirred. He'd looked at her with appreciation, the way a man does when he finds a woman attractive and desirable. And his intense, dark eyes had made her feel exactly that way. She'd nearly forgotten how thrilling that could be.

Sara put on her favorite cotton nightgown, then walked toward the bed. It looked huge and cold and empty. Loneliness blasted into the hollow in her heart, choking her. Tears stung the corners of her eyes.

How long had it been since she'd known a man's touch? How long since she'd been cradled in strong arms and had comforting endearments whispered in her ear?

Empty words, whispered with emptier emotions. Hadn't she learned that she couldn't rely on anyone but herself? The only thing she should be counting on was getting that promotion. Then she could begin the life she wanted, one with stability and permanence and plenty of time with her son.

She climbed into bed and stared at the ceiling.

If she didn't travel so much, maybe she could meet a nice guy. Landing that director's job was the answer. But if she didn't get this store open on time she'd never be promoted. Time was running out.

With a soft groan, she rolled onto her side and closed her eyes. The darkness was immediately filled with visions of Cable, hunkered down in front of Jeremy, his eyes filled with kindness as he asked about Doggie's name.

Cable, looming at her side, all broad shoulders and strong hands. He was the first man she'd been attracted to in a long time. But he was, unquestionably, the last person she'd become involved with.

Cable, his dark eyes filled with tenderness and a hint of desire.

Her last thought, thin and delicate like a thread of spider silk, barely imprinted itself on her conscious mind before she fell asleep: what would it be like to experience all that tenderness firsthand?

* * *

"I can't believe it. You mean he actually agreed to let you watch Jeremy here, in his house?" Sara carried a glass of juice to the table, frowning when she saw her son pushing cereal flakes around in the bowl with his fingers. "Jeremy, stop playing with your food.... What did you do, hold a gun to his head?"

"Of course not," Edith replied. "Why would you think I'd have to?"

"Because," she explained, moving to the coffeepot and refilling her cup. "he's got a big sign in front of him that says Keep Away, Trespassers Will Be Freeze-dried."

"Mommy, can I give some cereal to Doggie?"

"No. It'll give her worms."

"Why?"

"Too much milk isn't good for cats."

"Why?"

"Because it makes them sick."

Edith wiped her hands on the dishcloth. "There are reasons for Cable's attitude. Personally, I think having you and Jeremy in the house might force him out of the isolation he's lived in since he came here."

Sara lowered her cup and looked at the woman, consumed with curiosity. "You mean he's not from here?"

"No. He grew up in San Antonio, but he lived with his grandmother while he was attending J.B. Woods University here in town."

"Why doesn't milk make me sick?" Jeremy asked.

"Because you're a little boy, not a cat," Sara responded absently. So Cable had a previous life...

"Why?"

"Because God made you that way."

"Why?" Jeremy persisted.

"Because He wanted you to grow up to be a big, tall, strong man."

"Like Cable?"

Sara stared down at her son a moment, then looked at Edith. "What is this sudden fascination with Cable? He hardly knows the man. Finish your cereal, Jeremy."

"Children see with clearer eyes than grown-ups," the housekeeper said in a wise tone.

Sara raised a doubtful eyebrow.

"Cable has a good heart, Sara. He's just a man of few words."

"That's the understatement of the year. But I don't care if he's as mute as the Great Stone Face, I'm just grateful he's letting you keep Jeremy here. Well," she said, placing her empty coffee cup on the counter, "now that you've broken the ice, I guess I'd better go hammer out the details. Do you know where he is?"

"Out back."

Despite her brave statement to Edith, the thought of confronting Cable stirred the butterflies in her stomach again. After last night, she wasn't sure how to approach him. She glanced down at her wrist as she headed outside. Even now her skin tingled with the memory of his gentle touch.

Gentle touch, maybe. But his words and attitude were anything but. Last night he'd made it clear he didn't want her help or her interference in his life. But this morning he'd agreed to let Edith watch Jeremy in his house.

Maybe he'd had a change of heart. Maybe Edith was right, and he was kind and thoughtful once you got to know him. She had sensed a more compassionate side to him. Buoyed by the thought, she started across the sidewalk.

She stopped at the garage, but saw no signs of life. There were, however, sounds of activity coming from the old barn that stood behind the garage.

She could hear the high-pitched squeal of a saw as she approached the entrance. The doors stood open, so she stepped inside, scanning the vast area. When she finally located the source of the noise, she also found Cable.

He was bent over a workbench. Even beneath the flannel shirt, she could see the muscles across his broad back ripple as he manipulated a small piece of machinery. Curious, she moved farther into the large shop, inhaling the mingled smells of varnish, oil and sawdust. Wresting her attention from Cable, she surveyed her surroundings.

Workbenches and several massive pieces of machinery crowded one side of the room. Large glass windows partitioned off the other side, and through them, she could see a computer and three pieces of furniture in various stages of completion. Is this what Cable did for a living? He built furniture?

Astonished by the discovery, she looked back at Cable, watching him more closely this time. He'd attached a long slender block of wood to one of the machines and had set it to turning.

He pressed a small tool against the spinning wood, and before her eyes, the square block became an intricately turned spindle. Turning off the motor, he released the piece of wood, holding it gently in his hands, giving it a thorough inspection.

Mesmerized, Sara watched as he carried it to a nearby table and continued to work on it. She couldn't see exactly what he was doing and probably wouldn't have understood if she had. What she did understand, however, was the extraordinary care with which Cable worked.

There could be no doubt that he loved his craft. He held the spindle like a precious, fragile object, giving it all his attention. His fingers caressed the virgin wood with infinite tenderness and steadfast strength.

Sara found herself wondering how those strong, capable hands would caress a lover. Would he be as gentle? As sensitive? Would he use the same care and devotion with a woman as he did with this delicate wood creation?

She'd never thought of Cable as a creative person. She'd labeled him a hermit, someone who shut off all expression, closed his heart, mind and soul to the world.

That image didn't coincide with what she saw in front of her now. Cable had channeled his emotions into perfecting the most basic of skills, woodworking. Finally she had an explanation for where he disappeared to all the time.

He was completely at home in this haven of wood and machinery. He belonged here. The house revealed none of Cable's imprint, but out here, if she wanted, she could learn everything about Cable McRay. It was an intriguing thought. One she was inclined to pursue. "I always suspected you had a hideout."

Cable looked up sharply, met her gaze, then went back to fiddling with the small machine he'd picked up. "Did you want to see me about something?"

His tone was distant, and she realized he was uneasy with her presence. If he didn't like having her in the house, he'd hate her being here in his inner sanctum. "Yes. First to thank you for letting Edith watch Jeremy here."

"There weren't many options."

"No, I suppose not," she agreed, trying to put as much understanding in her tone as possible. "I know this will be an imposition, so I thought it might make it easier if we worked out some of the details."

Cable sighed. "Such as?"

Sara found her bravery wavering. He didn't seem any more congenial than he had before. "Well, kitchen privileges, for one. I'll be making breakfast and supper for Jeremy and myself. If you'll let me know what time you usually eat, I'll try and work around it. We could set up a schedule—"

"I don't like schedules." Cable stared at her a moment, then went back to work.

Silently she cursed herself for her foolishness. How could she have seen anything gentle and sensitive in this crusty crab? Obviously she'd misjudged his reactions. When would she ever learn not to put any credence in her impressions of men? She was always seeing qualities in them that weren't there. "Edith said she'd try and keep Jeremy out from under foot as much as possible during the day."

"That doesn't concern me."

His indifference turned up the heat under her anger. Served her right for trying to give him the benefit of the doubt. "So, I can assume that if you have any complaints about anything Jeremy or I do, you'll let me know?"

Cable set the tool down on the workbench with a loud thud. "You can count on it."

That did it. Her anger was nearing the boiling point. So much for Cable's change of heart; he had to *have* a heart before he could change it. He was being as cantankerous as ever—that much of her judgment was on the mark. Small comfort.

Crossing her arms over her chest, she assumed her management mode. "The temperature was in the upper eighties today and the windows on my side of the house won't open. Would you please turn on the air-conditioning?"

"The house doesn't have central air."

Sara rolled her eyes. Great. She'd forgotten Cable lived in the Stone Age. "Then please fix the windows so I can open them. Unless there's a reason they're sealed shut?"

"My grandmother lived alone. She wanted it that way."

"Okay. What about the ceiling fan? I can't find the switch."

"It's not electric. It's spring driven."

She waited for instructions, but Cable ignored her. "So how do I get it to work?" she finally prodded. "Is there a squirrel and a treadmill in the ceiling?"

"I'll have to show you. Sometime."

Taking a deep breath, she planted her hands on her hips. "You're not making this situation any easier. I'm just trying to ease any potential problems that might arise."

"No," Cable said, scowling at her. "You're trying to complicate an already difficult situation with details. I agreed to having the boy here. Let it go at that. You stay out of my way, I'll stay out of yours."

Sara gritted her teeth. "That suits me just fine. In fact, I'll start right now." Turning on her heel, she marched out of the workshop.

Cable watched Sara until she disappeared out the door, then he loosened his death grip on the router handle. Her presence in his shop left him unnerved and agitated. She'd been poking at him again, nudging him toward a friendship, probing for a foundation on which to establish some form of relationship. He couldn't permit it.

She'd come too close, stepped over some invisible barrier that he hadn't even been aware of until that moment.

Hideout. He'd never thought of his workshop in that way. He'd always viewed it as more of a sanctuary, the one place he truly belonged.

Moving away from the workbench, he rubbed the back of his neck. Physically, Sara hadn't come within three feet of him, but somehow she'd reached over his wall, seeking out that part of him he'd sealed up, threatening to draw him out. He'd tried to concentrate on her words, but she'd been talking about schedules and arrangements and Jeremy being underfoot.

He'd recoiled, retreated deeper, pushing her away. And it had worked. But for some reason, he didn't feel relieved. The impact of his agreement with Edith threatened to smother him. He'd have to deal with Sara and the boy daily, and whether he ran into them or not, he'd feel their presence.

She'd be coming to him as she had now, asking him to fix something or seeking his permission to do something, needing his help to carry or put things together. Well, he'd refuse. He'd stay here in the shop, round the clock if need be, but he'd be damned if he'd get drawn into the lives of Sara and her child.

Cable stood back and made a final examination of the small bed. The old mahogany frame fit perfectly in the bay-window alcove. He pressed down on the mattress, testing its firmness. It should be sturdy enough for the boy to sleep on. The bed hadn't been difficult to locate, though Cable still couldn't explain why the hell he'd gone in search of the thing in the first place.

He wasn't going to get involved. But the boy needed a place to sleep. Setting up a bed wasn't exactly getting involved, it was more a matter of self-defense. One less reason for Sara to seek him out.

Cable glanced over at the two boxes he'd also brought down from the attic. The bed had been stored behind them, so he'd had to move them to get to it. But that didn't explain why he'd carted them downstairs. Was it to keep the boy occupied and out of his way?

Compelled by some force he didn't understand, Cable walked over to the box and hunkered down, lifting out the toys one by one. There were two bright red metal trucks, a green tractor, a box of farm animals, a checkerboard and a stack of books tied with string.

None of them looked familiar. How old were these things? Had he played with them as a child? Or were they toys Grandma had kept for Todd? He rubbed his head, trying to remember the last time he, Amanda and Todd had all been here as a family. Nothing came to mind. He couldn't conjure up any memories of his life before coming here to live five years ago.

He knew they'd spent several Thanksgivings here, but locating specific incidents seemed futile.

Reaching again into the box, he pulled out a teddy bear and a battered cowboy hat. Had Todd played with these? Closing his eyes, Cable tried to summon a vision from the past, a tiny scrap of a memory to reconnect him with his son. Nothing came. Why couldn't he remember?

He swallowed, forcing down the lump in his throat. What difference did it make? He didn't need to remember. Didn't want to remember.

Frustrated, he tossed the toys back in the box, giving it a shove with the toe of his boot.

He used to pray fervently that his memories of Amanda and Todd would go away, so the pain of remembering would cease. He'd assumed that banishing the memories would give him peace, that severing the past neatly and cleanly was the best way to heal.

For five years he'd believed the operation successful. But now, when he searched for memories and found nothing, it left him with a sick, fearful sensation deep inside, like waking up and not knowing who he was.

He'd always believed his memories were neatly locked away and someday, when he was ready, he'd turn the key and draw them out. To his horror, when he'd opened the vault he'd found it empty.

Dear Lord, he'd never wanted the memories obliterated, just hidden away so they wouldn't hurt him anymore. Where had they gone? How could he get them back? How was he supposed to unearth his past with Sara and Jeremy around to muddle his present?

Maybe he should go away until Sara was finished opening the store. He could visit his sister in Savannah, Georgia, or his cousin in Gahanna, Ohio.

Yeah, that was a perfectly cowardly thing to do. It was far nobler to hide out in his shop. Hideout? Sara had called it that. Was he hiding? No. The shop was his business, nothing more. Sara just didn't understand that.

With a curse directed at no one in particular, Cable gathered up his tools and walked away from Sara's room.

Sara hurried down the hallway behind an excited Jeremy. She'd come home early to spend some time with her son, and he had met her at the door bursting with news. "And there's trucks and little animals and a big bed, too! See?"

She stared in mute amazement at the little wooden spool bed nestled into the alcove between her room and the sitting room. It fit as if it had been designed for that spot and for someone Jeremy's size. "Where did it come from?"

"Cable got it," Jeremy answered with a big smile.

Sara hadn't realized she'd spoken aloud. "Cable?" Damn. There he went again, one minute hot and the next cold. He was as unpredictable as the weather. Why would he do such a thing? He'd made his position clear enough this morning. What had prompted this about-face?

"Mommy, come here," Jeremy whined impatiently.

Sara saw him motioning her toward a big box. "What else did you get?"

"See?" He pointed into the box. "Blocks and little cars and a hat."

Sara reached down and lifted out a bundle of books, smiling when she recognized the titles. They'd been her fa-vorites as a child. "This was very nice of Cable, wasn't it?"

"Uh-huh."

Jeremy plopped down on the rug and started pulling out the little cars. Sara untied the books, opening the cover on the first one. *Scuffy the Tugboat.* There was an inscription inside: To Todd from Grandma. Who was Todd?

Walking back toward the old bed, she laid the books on the mattress, running her hand along the headboard appre-ciatively. It was a lovely antique. What had possessed him to do this?

One minute Cable growled and told her to stay out of his way, then the next he went to the trouble of getting Jeremy a bed and toys. His mixed messages were driving her crazy.

*He's really a very kind and thoughtful man.*

Could there truly be a soft spot under all that granite? Or was she reading too much into it? For all she knew, setting up the bed may have been Edith's idea, and Cable had merely carried out her instructions.

"I knew nothing about it," Edith declared a few minutes later, when Sara questioned her. "Jeremy and I walked to the park, and it was all done when we got back."

"Edith, I don't understand him at all. Last night I ex-pected him to draw a red line down the middle of the house to mark off our territory, and today he pulls out a bed and toys to give to Jeremy." Sara shoved her hands into the pockets of her navy slacks and shrugged ruefully. "He's so temperamental."

"I don't know if *temperamental* is the right word. He's just trying to protect himself."

"From what? As far as I can see he's got more protection than anyone needs. He's shut himself up in that shop. He doesn't see anyone, doesn't go anywhere. He's a human hermit crab. In fact, I don't know why he bothers to have this house at all. That impenetrable shell he carries with him is all he needs."

Edith smiled tolerantly. "Ever ask yourself why he's that way?"

She had. Thousands of times, from the moment he'd opened the door that first day. She wasn't about to admit it to anyone though. "He hates the world?" she suggested sarcastically. "If that's how he chooses to live his life, it's fine with me."

"We all make wrong choices at some time in our lives."

Sara recalled Edith's words later that afternoon as she brought her empty tea glass back into the kitchen and rinsed it. She had certainly chosen the wrong man to marry. Drake had destroyed her faith in herself and in others.

But what wrong choice had Cable made? What had he meant when he'd said, "There was no other choice I could make"?

Whatever it was, it was none of her concern. Cable was impossible to understand. One minute he was a lion, the next a lamb. She liked order and predictability in life and in people. She'd had enough surprises during the past four years to last her for decades.

Outside, the roar of the lawn mower engine grew louder. Sara looked out the screen door and saw Cable cutting the grass. Was staying here a good or a bad choice? If she couldn't find some reasonable arrangement with Mr. Crab, it was going to be a very long assignment.

She didn't handle change as well as she used to, thanks to Drake. She liked to know where she stood in a relationship. Even one as temporary and superficial as hers with Cable.

She had enough to deal with at the moment without having to walk on eggshells, wondering if Cable was going to be cooperative or recalcitrant. All she wanted was some kind of working rapport, an agreeable pattern to follow.

The squeaking of the screen door drew her attention, and Cable ambled into the kitchen. She turned to face him and her mouth went dry. He was naked from the waist up, his shirt draped carelessly over one shoulder. His hair clung in dark waves to his skull. Rivulets of sweat trickled down his throat onto his chest and disappeared into the waist of his painted-on jeans.

When she finally lifted her eyes from their tantalizing journey along Cable's form to his face, she was overcome with embarrassment. It was obvious from his icy glare that he didn't appreciate her staring.

"You're home early."

"What? Oh, yes. I'd accomplished all I could at the store for now so I thought I'd spend some time with Jeremy."

Cable strolled languidly over to the cupboard, grabbed a glass and proceeded to fix a drink. Sara couldn't tear her gaze away from the muscles in his back. Each tiny movement undulated through him in the most fascinating and evocative way.

He turned abruptly and tilted back his head, taking a long swallow. She stared in fascination as the tendons in his neck convulsed and the muscles in his chest moved under the firm, tanned skin. She forced herself to look away, and the first thing she saw was the small book she still clutched like a life preserver.

"Thank you for the bed and the toys. That was very thoughtful of you."

"The boy needs a place to sleep," he replied. Lifting the glass, he placed its chilled surface against his damp forehead.

Sara swallowed and moved a few steps toward the hallway. One minute hot and steamy, the next cool as ice. The images sparked desire from someplace deep inside, and she was forced to pull her gaze away from Cable's torso yet again. She wished he'd put his shirt on. His half-naked state made her extremely uncomfortable.

The sight of the lean, hard muscles undulating across his chest and abdomen played havoc with her senses. It was hard to remember that Cable was cold and unapproachable when the man in front of her was all hot and virile and throbbing with life. She had to get control of herself. Her reactions were perfectly normal. Whatever else Cable might be, he was a superb specimen of male strength and virility.

All she had to do was keep the conversation going, talk about trivial things until she could retreat.

Taking a deep breath, she blurted out the first thing she thought of. "Where did you find all those things? The bed is very old, isn't it?"

"In the attic. My grandmother never threw anything away."

He took another drink, and Sara swallowed convulsively. "I appreciate the books. Jeremy loves it when I read to him." Cable remained silent. Nervously she toyed with the book, remembering something she'd seen inside. "Do you know who Todd is?"

Cable went rigid, his eyes turning hard and cold as a glacier. The muscles in his jaw flexed violently. Sara held her breath, wondering what she had said to upset him.

"Where did you hear that name?"

"It's written in this book—'To Todd from Grandma.'"

All the color drained from Cable's face. His fingers tightened around the glass, gripping it so hard she feared he would crush it.

"My son," he said at last. Turning his back, he picked up his shirt and jerked it on, but Sara could see he was pulling his hard shell around himself as well. He was crawling back into his protective cover. She knew she should allow him his privacy, but she couldn't stop herself from pressing on. Her curiosity was too strong to ignore.

She'd be willing to bet Cable was a divorced man who had little time with his child. "I didn't realize you were married. Is he with his mother?"

"Yes."

"Do you get to see him often?"

Cable turned and faced her, his eyes as black and empty as the vast nothingness of a starless night. Sara's heart pounded violently with apprehension. Afraid to move or even breath, she realized that she'd gone too far this time. Bracing herself, she waited for whatever fury he was going to unleash.

"My wife and son are dead."

## Chapter Four

Sara stood in the kitchen for a long moment after Cable had left the room, his words washing over her repeatedly in chilling waves.

Oh, dear God. She'd had no idea. No hint that he was a widower. It had never entered her mind. Why hadn't Ken warned her? If she'd known about Cable's situation, she never would have stayed here. At the very least, she would have handled things differently.

It must have been awful for him, finding a little boy in his home with no warning, no time to prepare. She remembered the fear and sadness in his eyes. Now she understood the icy reception in the kitchen that first night and the way he would brace himself each time Jeremy approached.

It was bad enough that she'd barged into his life, but bringing Jeremy along had only increased his torment. She closed her eyes, her heart overflowing with sorrow at the magnitude of his loss. His wife and his son. The poor man.

She couldn't imagine losing a child. Just the thought of losing Jeremy turned her blood cold. It would be easier to die herself.

No wonder Cable hid away in the shop. Seeing her and Jeremy laughing, sharing time together, would only magnify his grief.

It explained so much about his attitude, about his fierce need to shut himself off from the world. She'd seen her brother react that way after his wife had died. He'd been angry at the world for months. The family doctor had assured all of them that his attitude was perfectly normal, just one stage of the long grieving process.

Now she had a reason for Cable's hard shell, but she also had a truckload of new questions. She couldn't help but wonder about the circumstances surrounding his family's death and when it had happened. Given his reclusive habits, she'd be willing to guess his loss was fairly recent.

Edith had said he wasn't from Carswell. Perhaps he'd returned to this small town to be alone and work through his grief. In which case she didn't need to be here complicating his recovery. Their presence would only hurt him further, and she didn't want that. Better for them all if they left and found another place to stay.

Overcome with sympathy for Cable and his situation, Sara turned her irritation toward the person responsible for her being here in the first place—Ken.

Why in the world had he arranged for her to stay, knowing his cousin's situation? She'd never known Ken to be cruel, but surely sending a woman and child to live with a grieving man was completely heartless.

Sara picked up the phone and dialed the home office. When Ken answered, she wasted no time in expressing her displeasure. "I want to know why you didn't warn me about your cousin."

"If I'd told you what a bear he was you wouldn't have agreed to stay there," he responded lightly.

Something in Ken's tone made her suspicious, then angry. "Why exactly did you arrange for me to stay with Cable?"

"You know why. It was either stay with him or drive two hours back and forth every day. You're on a tight schedule. Wasting four hours on the road every day wouldn't be smart."

"No, that's the business reason. I understand that. I'm talking about your personal reasons."

"I don't know what you're getting at."

She was all too familiar with that innocent, noncommittal tone. "Don't play dumb with me, Ken," Sara said firmly. "I know you had some ulterior motives and I suspect I know what they are."

"What possible motives could I have?"

"Funny how you're constantly reminding me that Jeremy needs a father, that I need a husband. Any of this ringing any bells?"

"I'm just looking out for you."

"Well, don't. And if you're trying to play matchmaker, you picked the wrong candidate."

"Hey, I was just trying to find you a safe place to stay, and Cable is as safe as they get. He doesn't let anyone get close to him."

"With good reason. Why didn't you tell me about his family?"

There was a long silence on the other end. "He told you about that?"

"Yes. After I stuck my foot down my throat by asking him who Todd was."

"How did you find out about Todd?"

"His name was written in some books that Cable gave Jeremy. Why?" Sara didn't like the sense of dread that was beginning to form in the center of her chest.

"He gave Jeremy some of Todd's toys?"

The note of amazement in Ken's tone heightened her apprehension. "Yes. Some toys and a few books. Why? What's wrong with that?"

"Nothing, nothing at all. Sara, I'm going to ask you for a big favor. A really big favor."

She'd heard that tone before, and it always preceded something unpleasant. "Ken, whatever it is, I don't have time, and if it involves Cable, the answer is no. I've hurt the poor man enough as it is by being here. Besides, if I'm going to get this store open on time, I'll—"

"This is more important than the store, Sara."

Sara tensed at his words. Ken was a driven, obsessive taskmaster when it came to setting up new stores. She couldn't imagine anything that would take precedence over that. "Nothing is more important to you than opening another store."

"This is, Sara. This is personal, something I promised never to interfere in, but it's gone on too long and you're the first person who's been able to reach him even remotely since the accident."

She had a feeling she already knew what Ken wanted. "Go on," she said, holding her breath.

"When Amanda and Todd were killed, Cable totally withdrew from the world. He left San Antonio and buried himself in Mississippi, cutting himself off from practically everyone. He only keeps in touch with me because I refuse to let him ignore me.

"It's like he erased the past. He never talks about Amanda and Todd or anything that happened before the accident. If he's told you about them, of his own free will, then maybe he's ready to start rejoining the world.''

Sara understood Ken's concern, but it wasn't her responsibility and she didn't appreciate being manipulated. ''Is that why you sent me here—to get through to Cable?''

''No. Well, I'll admit the idea did cross my mind. But it worked, and now I'd like you to try and help him.''

''You're not serious. I can't help him. He's got a shell around him thicker than an armadillo. I'm no therapist and I don't have time to play shrink to a crab.''

''You don't have to. Just get him talking, draw him out, ask questions about Amanda and Todd.''

''Oh, right, and lose my head in the process. I won't be much good to you in the future without a head, Ken.''

''Sara, you don't have to make this a crusade or anything, just be friendly and curious and concerned. The way you are with everyone else. You know you have a way with people. They love to confide in you.''

She hated to admit it but that was true. It wasn't something she did intentionally. In fact, sometimes it was a real nuisance. She often wondered if there was a sign plastered on her forehead that read Dump Your Troubles on Me. People loved to unload on her. Probably because she'd never learned to say, ''No, thank you, I don't really want to hear this.''

''Ken, you're giving me too much credit. He doesn't even like me.''

''Who says? How could he not like you? Everyone likes you, Sara.''

''He resents me being here. He's positively grim about Jeremy being added to the equation. Shoving a microphone under his nose and playing reporter isn't going to go over well. He'll never sit still for questioning, let alone agree to spill his guts to me. Besides, give me one good reason why I should get involved.''

''Because you have a heart as big as the great outdoors.''

Sara sighed with irritation. She had a big heart, all right. A heart she had to keep a tight rein on or it would soften and melt with little provocation, and the next thing she knew she'd be starting to care for someone, someone completely untrustworthy and wrong.

Her big heart was given to careless acts of affection if she didn't keep her practical mind in control. Getting involved with a sad-eyed, handsome man was playing with fire.

''Please, Sara. All I'm asking is that you do for Cable what I tried to do for you.''

Great. The one thing she couldn't refuse—the old Golden Rule thing. Ken had been a rock after Drake left, and during her pregnancy, he and his wife, Linda, had been like family. Without their help, she might have caved in under the stress.

''Ken, I'll try. But I honestly don't know what I can do. I rarely see him. He hides away in his shop all day, and whenever he meets me he scowls like he's going to attack if I look at him crooked. When I talk to him he just snaps back at me.''

''That's great! Usually he doesn't even reply. You've made serious inroads, kid.''

Sara wanted to help, but if she started poking sticks at Cable she could end up shredded and spread on the lawn as fertilizer. ''I just don't think it'll work,'' she murmured.

''Please, Sara.''

Her reluctance battled with her sense of gratitude and obligation. She owed Ken personally and professionally. After all, he was the one pushing the higher-ups to give her the promotion. ''Okay, but I'm not promising anything. If I find an opportunity to talk to him, I will.''

"Thanks. This means a lot to me. It'll mean a lot to Cable, too."

Sara sincerely doubted that. "All right, but can't you tell me a little more about him so I don't stick my foot in things again?"

"No. I think it's better if he tells you himself when he's ready. He needs someone to help him find his way back. All I'm asking is that you make yourself available to him in case he wants to talk. He's closer than a brother to me, Sara, but I've done all I can. It's up to you now."

"Thank you, Ken," she said sarcastically. "You've made it impossible for me to refuse, haven't you?"

"Help him, Sara. For me. Just remember, losing his family nearly destroyed Cable. He turned his back and walked away from everything."

Sara hung up the phone, her boss's final words echoing in her mind. *He turned his back and walked away from everything.* Those words could apply to her own situation with Drake. How could some people do that—turn off their feelings, cut the emotional cord and behave as if people and relationships had never existed?

Drake had had little difficulty in walking away from his pregnant wife. Other than a brief meeting during the divorce settlement, she'd never seen him again. He never called, never inquired about the baby. She'd sent him a letter after Jeremy was born, feeling in her heart it was the right thing to do and hoping he would at least acknowledge his own son.

But after the weeks turned into months, she'd had to face the truth. Drake Nelson wanted no part of his child. As far as he was concerned, the baby and his ex-wife didn't exist.

And according to Ken, Cable had done much the same thing. After his family was killed, he'd shut down that part of his life and gone on as if they had never existed.

She didn't understand it. And Ken was asking her to try and draw Cable out, to get him to talk. He'd obviously made his choice and was content with his life.

Part of her saw an opportunity to get some questions answered. Perhaps Cable could explain to her how love could be turned off. How years of sharing and caring could be shut down with as much carelessness as shutting down a computer.

But another part of her didn't want to know the answers. She was afraid the truth would hurt too much. Because if both Drake and Cable could dismiss love so easily, then they had probably never cared in the first place.

Sara walked to the window, brushing aside the lace curtains. As she looked out toward the sunset, she admitted she was being unfair to Cable in comparing him to Drake.

The situations were different. Cable had no control over his separation from his family. But the fact that he could turn his back, choose to deny his grief and walk away from his past, troubled her considerably. It warned her not to let her soft heart lead her into another mess. The trouble was, her brain wasn't talking as loudly as her heart right now.

What was she doing? She shouldn't even be thinking about Cable and his problems. At least not on an emotional level. She had to look at this from a purely objective point of view.

She was genuinely sorry for Cable, but the way he dealt with his grief was no concern of hers. Besides, there was only so much she could do, and if her impression of him was right, he wasn't about to confide in her, no matter what Ken might think. All Cable had done was tell her his wife and son were dead. It hadn't exactly been a plea for help.

Ken believed that his cousin needed someone to bring him back to life. Maybe he did, but that someone wasn't her. She had only one purpose here—open the Dixie Mart on time and get the promotion.

Learning about Cable's past had shifted her assessment of him a bit. But Ken's comment still lingered in the back of her mind. *He'd walked away!*

Well, she'd agreed to try and she'd make a few stabs at it if the opportunity arose, but she wasn't getting involved.

Cable hosed down the mower, taking an inordinate amount of time to do a task that normally took only a few moments. He knew he was delaying the inevitable self-confrontation. Easing up on the sprayer handle, he let his arms hang at his sides, as he stared out at the fields behind the house.

Why had he told Sara about Amanda and Todd? Yes, she had asked point-blank, but he could have denied knowing anyone named Todd. He could have said nothing; that was his usual response. A direct, unwavering stare could accomplish much, he'd discovered.

But Sara had asked and he'd given her the truth, blunt and unvarnished. He wasn't sure why, except that she'd caught him off guard again. She possessed some kind of mystical ability to touch upon his vulnerabilities and lure him into the open.

Sara was the first person in a long time who had dared to challenge him. Most left him alone. But she was unaffected by his gruff demeanor. If anything, it made her more curious. Each time she looked at him, he felt her probing, inspecting, trying to see who he really was.

He couldn't decide if he admired her pluck or resented her intrusiveness.

Mostly he was curious himself. What did she see when she gazed into his eyes? What would she do if he let her see beyond the wall? Would she climb over for a better look or run and hide? What would she think of the real Cable McRay?

If things were different—if he were different—he could become very interested in Sara. He couldn't deny that his attraction grew each time he was around her, a fact that was beginning to concern him. He'd never responded to a woman the way he had to Sara.

But he couldn't allow himself to become infatuated. He hadn't forgotten what it was like to have his soul ripped out, his heart shredded. No. No one would ever get that deep into his heart again.

It would be best if he avoided Sara and Jeremy as much as possible. Too much exposure to them would be dangerous. In a few weeks they'd be gone, leaving him alone again, and he liked being alone. Didn't he?

Unwilling to delve into that question more deeply, Cable turned off the water and rolled the mower into its place in the garage. If he was going to avoid Sara, he'd better start by taking care of the windows in her rooms. Then she would have no further reason to seek him out. At the first opportunity, he'd fix them and be done with it.

His chance arrived the next afternoon, when he noticed Sara's car gone from the drive. She was probably at the store, which meant he had the house to himself. He could get into her section of the house, fix the damn windows and be done with it.

The moment he stepped into Sara's rooms, he experienced that same sense of vulnerability he always felt in her presence. Even when she wasn't around, she could reach out and touch him. The room smelled like Sara, that heady, sassy scent that lingered in her hair and everything she touched.

Irritation swamped him. He wasn't here to remember her scent. He was here to make sure his life didn't collide with hers any more than necessary.

It had been a long time since a woman had captured even his briefest attention. His mind had been focused upon survival, on starting a new life. His vision was tunneled toward that one goal. It was best that way. If he wasn't careful, Sara could widen his scope to include herself and the rest of the world. The prospect was unsettling.

With brisk movements, Cable pulled aside the furniture and spread out his tools, studying the silicone seal that had been applied to the window frames. It would be a bear to remove. He'd have to go slowly so as not to damage the old cypress wood or break the original glass panes. He wanted the job done quickly so he could keep himself from reminders of Sara.

Pulling out a small chisel, he started at the top of the far window.

"Cable?"

Intent on his task, he wasn't prepared to hear his name being called. He jerked around and froze, stunned by the sight that greeted his eyes.

Sara was poised in the archway, wrapped in only a towel. Her damp hair hugged her head, framing her blue eyes, which were wide with surprise and embarrassment.

Slowly he stood, facing her, his mind and body waging a fierce battle. His mind told him to do the gentlemanly thing and leave. His body had other ideas. He felt a sudden heaviness in his loins and a building heat in his blood.

His eyes moved from Sara's creamy shoulders to her slender calves, and back up to her softly parted lips. All he could think about was unwrapping the towel and wrapping himself around her instead.

He cleared his throat and focused his eyes on the chisel as he laid it in the toolbox, struggling to contain his wild, erotic thoughts. But when he looked back at her, he knew the battle was lost. "I thought you were gone. I didn't see your car."

As if reading his mind, Sara wrapped the towel more closely around her, her eyes locked with his. "I let Edith out. I parked on the street."

He hadn't thought to look beyond the drive. Halfheartedly, he searched for a gentlemanly way to exit from the situation. But the gentleman in him apparently had been subdued by a more powerful side of his nature. Until he remembered the third person living in the house. "Jeremy?"

"He's with Edith."

They were alone in the house. The realization acted like an aphrodisiac upon his already stimulated senses. Cable willed himself to ignore the fact that they were a man and a woman, keenly aware of one another, all alone in a huge old house. He failed.

Looking at Sara, her warm flesh moist and pink from her bath, those blue eyes huge in her face, all he could do was stare and ache.

He wanted to touch her, to know for himself the softness of her skin. He wanted to kiss the lingering drops of scented water from her shoulder. He wanted to run his fingers through her damp hair, to feel its coolness against his hot hands. Arousal shot through him with alarming force.

"What are you doing?"

His befuddled brain was slow to respond. He gestured weakly toward the window. "I was, uh, trying to open you up."

His words were like a switch in Sara's mind. She knew he referred to the window, but he might as well have been speaking about her. Her whole body was opening up to him of its own volition. She gripped the towel more tightly, afraid of what she might do if she didn't hold on.

She thought of his hands, so skilled, so gentle when he worked with wood. She saw the tenderness in his eyes when he looked at Jeremy. She heard the caring in his deep voice when he spoke.

More than anything she wanted him to touch her. She wanted to be held. But she knew if he so much as reached toward her, she would run like a scared deer.

Cable stood transfixed. He should run like hell as far and fast as his legs would carry him. He shouldn't be memorizing her every curve, shouldn't be drinking in the sight of her, fresh and vulnerable, so he could store it in his mind.

This was a dangerous situation. He was fanning a brush fire. He couldn't afford to notice Sara, to want her the way he did at this moment. It would be emotional suicide.

But it had been a long time since anyone had stirred these feelings of protectiveness, of tenderness in his heart. They were strangely welcome, yet he feared the consequences if he should indulge in them.

He started toward the door, but his feet carried him toward Sara instead. She was so tempting, so warm and soft, so exciting and full of life. He hadn't noticed life much these last years. But Sara was life at its most vital. He wanted to hold her, to feel that energy flowing into him. He wanted to capture it and marvel at its power.

Slowly he walked toward her. Her scent enfolded him again, and he filled his senses with it. She didn't move, didn't ask him to leave.

He reached out a hand and touched her cheek. It was soft, like the petal of a camellia. He looked into her eyes and saw her confusion, but he also saw her desire. She was feeling the pull, too. The need was in both of them, strong, fierce, swirling like the birth of a tropical storm. If they weren't careful, it would gather speed and become a full-fledged hurricane.

His eyes feasted upon her sensuous mouth, lips slightly parted, and he knew he needed to taste them just for a moment, to see if they were as sweet as he imagined.

If he did, if he touched her, he'd be doomed. He started to say her name, but sensed that even that would be dangerous.

"You'd better lock your door," he murmured as he stepped away and turned to go. "I'll finish later."

Sara inhaled a ragged breath and closed her eyes. She touched her cheek where Cable had caressed it. His warmth lingered on her flesh as curiosity curled through her. She wanted more. Wanted to feel his touch on her everywhere.

She wanted to rest her head on his strong shoulders, to let go of the burdens for just a moment and be free. She wanted to unload the guilt, to be a woman again—not just a mother and a manager. She wanted to feel cherished, to know that someone understood, that someone would help so that she didn't have to do it all alone anymore.

Lifting her chin, she picked up her robe and started to undrape the towel. Unable to stop herself, she looked back at the door. Cable was gone. She was alone. But she was alone because she had a bad habit of picking the wrong men, of letting her heart make decisions better left to her head.

Did that explain why she hadn't ordered him out of the room? Or why she hadn't screamed? Her heart had allowed her to stand here draped in a towel, while thoughts of them entwined in the old mahogany bed had swirled in her mind.

She was a fool! She wasn't going to let some brief, idle fascination lead her into doing something stupid again.

They were both lonely and needing to reconnect with another human being. They were alone, physically and emo-

tionally, and caught in a sexually charged situation. There
was nothing at all behind this brief encounter but simple
chemistry.

The best way to deal with it was to pretend it had never
happened. No problem.

## Chapter Five

"Look, Mommy."

Sara glanced down at her son. He was holding one arm out at a right angle, fist clenched. "See? I got big muscles. Cable said."

Oh, great. Sara sighed inwardly. From now on, "Cable said" was going to be tagged on to Jeremy's every sentence. "He did?"

"Uh-huh. That's 'cause I can lift Doggie with just one arm, like this." Jeremy screwed his little face into a mean grimace and hoisted the kitten. "See?"

Sara stifled the grin that played around her mouth. Doggie weighed next to nothing, but she wouldn't dream of pointing that out to him. "I didn't realize how big and strong you've gotten. You'll have to start helping me carry my briefcase to the car."

Jeremy beamed. "Okay." He climbed up onto the bed. "Mommy, can we stay here for always?"

Sara stopped midmotion in pulling up the covers. Her heart sank like a stone in her chest. She didn't want Jeremy to get comfortable here. It would only make it harder when they left. "Would you like to stay here?"

Jeremy nodded and reached for the cat, which had jumped up onto the bed. Sara started to lay down the law about the ongoing sleeping arrangements, but she was too tired to work up the necessary indignation. It was easier to let Jeremy sleep with the dumb cat.

"We'll stay for a while," she answered, kissing him tenderly. "Then we'll go home to our house and all your toys, and you can sleep in your own little bed. Won't that be nice?"

"I like this bed."

"It's a real special bed, but wouldn't you rather be in your own comfy bed?"

Jeremy shrugged. "What about Doggie? Will she come home with us?"

"I don't think so. She'll be happier here with Cable and her brothers and sisters."

"Can we come visit Cable again?"

"We'll see. You better get to sleep. Do you want me to read to you?"

"No. I want my songs."

Sara gave him the small, sturdy tape player and inserted his favorite cassette. Then she went into the sitting area, where the sheer curtains fluttering in the breeze captured her attention. Sometime during the last two days, Cable had finished unsealing the windows.

Cable. No matter where she looked or what she was doing, he seemed to intrude more and more into her thoughts. Even before Ken had asked her to help Cable she'd found herself wondering why he'd come to this old house and why he was so gruff and defensive.

She knew part of the reason now, but she sensed there was much more to it. There was something else driving him, something deep inside....

There, she was doing it again. Thinking about Cable when what she should be thinking about was getting this store open. Time was slipping through her fingers like water. She couldn't afford to be diverted with pointless speculation about her reclusive host.

Besides, Ken's request would be impossible to fulfill. Cable wasn't about to tell her anything, and she had no special gifts for drawing people out, no matter what her boss thought.

What she couldn't understand was Jeremy's growing attachment to Cable. He spent his days with Edith, and as far as she knew, Cable was holed up in his shop. But it wasn't Edith Jeremy talked about incessantly—it was Cable. Jeremy seemed oblivious to his surly attitude and cool demeanor.

Having a man to look up to was a good thing. Sara wanted Jeremy to have a male influence in his life, especially since he was missing so much by not having a father. But what would happen when they left Carswell behind? She didn't want Jeremy to go through what she had—having someone you loved turn his back on you.

Of course, this was a totally different situation. There was no commitment between her and Cable. Theirs was a business agreement with definite boundaries and devoid of any emotional complications.

But Jeremy was a little boy who didn't understand the facts of a relationship. Once they left here, he would never see Cable again, and it would fall to her to explain to her young son why yet another person had been removed from his life. It was her duty as his mother to see that he didn't become too attached.

Sara turned out the light and stared out the window. The hollow beneath her heart ached more than usual tonight. Closing her eyes, she sighed.

It wasn't supposed to be like this—a mother and her child alone, struggling to do it all. There was supposed to be a partner. A father. Like Drake. Only Drake couldn't be bothered. Drake didn't want kids. And now Jeremy was missing out on something wonderful—a real family with brothers and sisters, and most importantly, a daddy.

She'd had so many hopes and dreams for her life. Everything had been perfect until she'd become pregnant. How could she have been so wrong about Drake? So wrong about a person she thought she knew, a person she loved and trusted?

Whatever it took, whatever sacrifice was necessary, she would protect her son from that kind of cruel rejection. It was hard enough talking about Drake to Jeremy, even though he rarely asked about his dad. Someday she'd have to explain why his father never came to see him, why he had walked away from them.

If only she could find someone steady, someone who wanted what she wanted. An ordinary family man. A man with a gentle hand and a strong heart, who would be there in good times and bad, whose world would only be complete with his wife and children at his side. She wanted a man whose favorite pastime was sitting on the sofa with his wife, watching their children play.

An image of Cable filled her mind, and she recalled the faint smile in his eyes as he'd talked to Jeremy.

But it was a different look in his eyes that pushed its way to the forefront of her thoughts now—a look of hunger, of need, of desire. She recalled the gentle, delicate touch of his hand against her cheek. She was once again wrapped in a damp towel, her every nerve tingling and alive as it recognized and responded to the pure masculine energy and strength of the man who stood in front of her.

Suddenly the room seemed stuffy and confining. She needed air and space to move. Quietly she slipped out the side door and crossed the porch to the swing. Since childhood, a swing had always been her favorite place to go and sort out her problems. There was something comforting about the slow, steady movement, something that made her feel safe and secure.

For reasons that weren't quite clear to her, she needed that comfort now. She also needed energy to get this store open. She needed strength to raise her son alone and she needed...

Sara stopped beside the swing when she saw the solitary figure leaning against the post at the edge of the front porch.

Cable.

Dusky twilight outlined his distinctive silhouette, from his broad shoulders down to his long, muscular legs. His hips were cocked at a seductive angle as he leaned on the railing.

There was something different about him tonight. He didn't seem defensive, but rather thoughtful and contemplative as he stared out into the distance. It took her a moment to realize that this was the first time she'd seen him out of his shell and vulnerable.

Reluctant to disturb his privacy, Sara quietly turned away. "Don't."

Caught in midmotion, she cringed, anticipating Cable's angry dismissal. She'd been caught. He would be furious. "I'm sorry. I didn't mean to intrude," she said hastily. "I was just going to sit on the swing for a while. I'll leave you alone."

"No reason to."

There was a tone in his voice, a wistful, lonely quality that wrapped itself around her heart. Slowly she turned back to face him. He was still staring off into the dusk, but now she could see a heavy sadness revealed in his posture.

Was Ken right? Did Cable need to rejoin the world? Did he need help doing that? Maybe he'd been gone so long, had hidden so well that he was finding it hard to make his way back.

Ken was crazy! She didn't have a clue how to help him and wasn't at all sure she wanted to try. Prying open Cable's shell would take more strength than she possessed.

Her kind but misguided boss was just trying to play matchmaker, and he was doing a horrible job. He didn't know what it would cost her to open herself up and offer a helping hand. To do that and be successful, she would have to allow her heart to get involved, and she wasn't about to risk letting her soft, emotional side control her head.

Cable was the last man she wanted to feel anything for. She would never trust her heart to another man, especially a crusty hermit who snapped at anyone who came close.

She looked at him again and her attitude softened in spite of herself. He didn't look crusty now. Just sad and alone. Uncertain of what to say to him, Sara searched for something impersonal. "Thank you for opening the windows. It helped a lot."

Too late she realized her mistake. She saw the flash of memory light Cable's eyes; even the shaded twilight couldn't hide it. He was remembering the other day, when he'd found her wrapped in a towel, and the strange physical pull that had spiraled unexpectedly between them. Her mind filled with images of how that encounter might have ended, and a warm flush stained her throat when she realized she wished it had.

She took one look at Cable and knew he was thinking the same thing. Sara held her breath as their awareness of one another grew yet again. She could sense his eyes skimming over her and knew his breath came as quickly as her own.

They were two hearts beating in tune with the world around them. Man and woman calling to each other.

Frightened and embarrassed, she searched for a way to break the moment. What did you say to a man who had seen you in nothing but a towel?

Cable saved her the trouble. "Your fan is broken."

"What?" The incongruity of his words left her dazed.

"In your room. The mechanism has deteriorated from disuse."

"Oh, well, it's okay." Had she missed something? Had the energy and physical awareness been only on her part?

Perhaps it had. Her heart always did have a mind of its own. Sara moved to the swing and sat down. "With the windows open I don't really need a fan."

Cable pushed away from the post and started toward her, causing her heart to pound rapidly in her chest again. She wasn't sure if it was from excitement or apprehension.

For a moment she thought he was going to join her on the swing, but instead he perched one hip on the rail and stared down at her. It took only one glance to see that Cable had his shell in place again. The tension between them, at least on her part, remained.

"So," she said, striving for a casual tone of voice, "you build furniture for a living? Have you been doing it all your life?"

"No."

So much for idle conversation. "You do lovely work." She wasn't about to give up so soon.

"Is that your expert opinion?" he asked bluntly.

Couldn't the man accept a simple compliment? "No," she replied, "just an observation based on what I saw in the shop the other day."

"What else did you observe?"

Sara tilted her chin up defensively. He really was too sensitive about his work. "That you love what you do."

Cable shifted on the railing, staring off into the night sky. Had she hit a nerve or was he truly uncomfortable with a compliment?

"It's rewarding work," he finally replied.

"I'm not very good with my hands," she confessed, hoping her candor would encourage him to reveal more. "I can't sew or play the piano or draw. I've always envied those who can."

"I'm sure you're good at something."

"I'm a good organizer. A valuable talent, I suppose, but not very creative."

"You're a good mother."

His statement caught her by surprise. What had prompted the comment? She looked at him for some explanation, but his eyes were averted, as if he was afraid of what she might read in their brown depths.

Was he merely making small talk or was he sincere? Somehow she doubted if Cable said anything unless he meant it.

If he thought she was a good mother, then he must have been observing her in action. But why would he do that? He was a difficult man to understand.

Still, his observation pleased her greatly. "I'd like to believe I am a good parent, but I'm not sure." She started the swing moving slowly. "Lately it seems like the only time I see Jeremy is when he's waking up or going to bed. I wish I could be with him more."

"Why can't you?"

"I'm trying. If I can get this store open on time, I've got a chance at a promotion, and then I can stay in one place and give Jeremy the kind of security and consistency he needs."

"And if you don't get the promotion?"

Sara didn't even want to think about that possibility. "I don't know. I just know I can't keep this up anymore. I'm gone too much. I should never have taken this job in the first place."

"Why did you?"

"Because your cousin assured me it would be a great opportunity, and at first it was. I was only supposed to be away from home one week every couple of months, and the salary and benefits were outstanding. I hadn't expected the company to grow so fast, and when it did, my job had to change to keep pace. The next thing I knew, I was on the road more and more." Sara sighed. "This assignment is the longest so far."

"Couldn't you have turned it down?"

"Sure, but this store is a prototype of the next wave in discount retailing. We're trying out new set-up methods, and it's my responsibility to prove the system works. It's a once-in-a-lifetime opportunity that I can't afford to ignore, because who knows what tomorrow will bring?"

Cable looked off into the distance. "Tomorrow everything could change."

Instinctively Sara knew he wasn't talking about her job anymore. He was thinking about the family he'd lost. A huge wave of guilt crashed over her.

Here she was whining about not having enough time with Jeremy, when Cable's opportunities for time with his son were lost forever.

She understood how he felt. She'd lost, too. Not by death, but the separation was equally as permanent.

Cable looked so sad, so defeated that she ached to say something comforting to him. "I'm sorry about your family."

He braced and withdrew further into himself. She'd known it was the wrong thing to say before she'd completed the sentence, but it had been too late to call back the words.

"That's in the past."

"How did it happen?" she asked softly.

"A drunk teenager in a pickup."

Sara's conscience stung. From the roughness in his tone, she knew he regretted telling her about his loss. Ken was wrong; Cable wasn't ready to talk. It was probably too soon after the accident. His pain was still too raw to share with anyone. Especially a woman he hardly knew.

Still, she had promised Ken she would try. After her sister-in-law died, her brother had found it very therapeutic to talk.

Taking a deep breath, she decided to risk it. "How old was your son?"

"Ten."

Sara's mind telescoped into the future, trying to imagine Jeremy at that age. He would be gawky and awkward and full of energy and curiosity. He'd be starting to test the limits of his world, full of his own importance. "That must have been a wonderful age. Was he into sports?"

"I guess so. I, uh . . ." Cable moved away a few steps.

Sara could see how it hurt him to even think about it. His shell was hardening and thickening before her eyes. Didn't he realize that keeping all the pain and sorrow inside wasn't healthy? It was the worst thing he could do.

"You know, talking about loved ones we've lost makes the burden easier to bear."

"No!" He whirled around, his dark, angry eyes boring into her. "What makes it easier to bear is not talking about them, not thinking about them and not being reminded."

"You're wrong!" Sara's heart ached for him. She hoped to God he didn't really believe what he'd just said. "I know it seems like that at times, but locking all that away will only make things worse. It could end up destroying you. You need to talk to someone and get it all out...."

"Who made you my guardian?" he growled, glaring at her.

Sara exhaled in irritation. "Cable, I just want you to know I understand."

"What do you understand?" he demanded, advancing on her. "Huh? What?"

She stood her ground in the face of his intimidating scowl. "I understand the need for privacy, to shut out the world because the pain is so personal, so unbearably fierce. And I understand the need to be alone with your memories."

Cable's eyes narrowed, his fist raised in front of her face. "I don't have . . . want to remember!"

Sara wanted to punch him, to knock some sense into his thick skull. He had to be the most obstinate, pigheaded man she'd ever known. It was a struggle to contain her irritation and keep her tone calm and even. "I know it hurts to think about them and I know it must be hard for you with Jeremy and me here, but if you'll only—"

"Dammit, I didn't ask for your advice or your understanding or your infernal meddling!"

All attempts to remain calm vanished. "Fine. Forget it. I was just trying to help. I'm so sorry we intruded into your inner sanctum. If you have any suggestions for a solution to our living arrangements, I'd be more than happy to hear them."

Cable looked away. "You know there isn't one."

"No," she agreed grimly, "there isn't. But don't worry, we'll be gone in a few weeks and then you can have your precious solitude back. In fact, you can crawl into your shell and stay there until the next millennium, for all I care. All I'm interested in is getting this store opened on time so I can get out of here."

"Then we both want the same thing."

Sara gasped softly. His comment hurt more than it should have. She crossed her arms over her chest protectively, watching as Cable strode off the porch and disappeared around the side of the house.

Ken's request was impossible; she was more convinced of that than ever. Cable refused to talk about his family. He didn't see that keeping all his pain and sorrow locked up inside was dangerous and unhealthy.

But it was his life and his choice, and there was not a thing she could do to change it. She was only concerned because Ken had asked her to try and help. Well, she'd tried, but Cable had posted a Trespassers Will Be Shot sign, and she'd learned to read a long time ago.

Cable entered the shop and went directly to the table saw. He slipped on his protective goggles, reached for the stack of scrap wood and began slicing it up into various small-sized blocks for Jeremy to play with. The whine of the blade made it hard to think. But not impossible.

He was losing control, forgetting how to survive. Twice now, without intending to, he'd confided personal, private things to Sara. Tonight he'd come close to telling her he didn't remember anything. For one fleeting second, he'd wanted to tell her, wanted to reach out and ask her to help him dig up his lost memories.

But he couldn't. What was it about Sara that made him want to reconnect with the things he'd lost?

Maybe it was those wide blue eyes that reflected sympathy and understanding. Or maybe it was the way she refused to let him stay in his shell too long. He found an odd sort of amusement in that. Each time he tried to withdraw, Sara would find some way to coax him back to face reality.

And then there was the way his body seemed to gain a mind of its own whenever he was near her. Just hearing her voice sent a low-voltage current into his loins.

Sara was a damned walking contradiction. One minute she was fueling his passion and the next she would probe and poke into his psyche and fuel his anger.

Fortunately, tonight he'd come to his senses in time to prevent a horrible mistake. He knew she was only trying to help. But Sara didn't understand how deep his memory loss was. How could he explain it to her when he couldn't grasp it himself?

Sara was barely dressed the next morning when the phone rang. She answered as she continued to gather up her work. The agitated voice of her assistant manager, Bud, met her ears. "Guess who's on her way into town for a visit to store number twenty-one?"

Sara's heart plummeted to the pit of her stomach. "Nora Baker."

"None other, and she's expecting you to be here when she pulls into the parking lot. I've already lit a fire under everyone. We'll try and make it look better than it is."

"Thanks, Bud. I'm on my way."

Just what she didn't need. If Baker had come a few days later, they would have been caught up. The situation now would look ten times worse than it actually was. Nora Baker wasn't the most understanding of women, but Sara's regional manager was notorious for making surprise visits to her locations.

She wouldn't understand about the delays caused by Jeremy's arrival, that's for sure. Jeremy! What was she going to do with him? She had to be at the store immediately if she wanted to salvage her reputation. But Edith wasn't due for an hour yet. Maybe she could come early.

Quickly she dialed Edith's number, but the line was busy. There was no time to make other arrangements. She'd have to take Jeremy with her to the store and have Edith pick him up there.

"Jeremy, come on, honey, wake up. You'll have to come to work with Mommy for a little while." She grabbed up his clothes. She'd dress him at the store.

Jeremy sat up, rubbing his eyes, one arm around Clifford. "Can Doggie come, too?"

"No, sweetie. He's not allowed, but I'll show you Mommy's new store and you can play in my office. After we're done, we'll stop and get lunch, okay?"

"I don't wanna."

Sara shoved his shoes on his feet and stood him on the floor. "Jeremy, please. I don't have time to argue."

"I don't wanna!" He stamped one foot.

She didn't need an obstinate child now, either. Sara took firm hold of his hand. "Jeremy, I'm sorry, but you'll have to come with me."

"No." He went suddenly limp and sagged to the floor.

Sara picked him up and hauled him into the sitting room, grabbed her purse and headed for the back door, Jeremy crying all the way.

"I don't want to go!" He kicked his legs and arched his back.

Sara grabbed his arm to keep him from propelling himself out of her grasp and forced him to look at her. "Jeremy, I don't like it when you behave this way. It makes me angry. I'm sorry you don't want to go, but you have no choice. Now, you can either come and cry, or come and not cry. But you are coming."

"What's wrong?" Cable met her at the edge of the porch.

Sara stopped, suddenly staring down into Cable's dark, intense eyes. "There's a problem at work. Edith won't be here for another hour and he doesn't want to come with me." It flashed through her mind to ask Cable to watch him, but she wavered. It would be easier all around if she could go to the store, deal with Baker and not have to worry about Jeremy.

But she wasn't sure entrusting him to Cable was a good idea. Could she leave her son safely in his hands? What if Cable became preoccupied with his furniture building and forgot about him? No, she'd better take Jeremy with her.

"I wanna stay with Cable."

Sara couldn't tell who was more stunned by her son's request, herself or Cable, but judging by the fear in the man's eyes, he was the most affected.

Jeremy squirmed in her arms, and Sara was forced to set him down. He went immediately to Cable's side, smiled up into his scowling face and reached for his hand.

"No, Jeremy, I don't think that's a good idea," she said firmly.

Jeremy nodded, his mouth slanting into a big pout. "I want Cable."

Sara checked her watch. She didn't have time to get into a battle of wills with her son. Time was running out and she really needed to leave.

"Go," Cable said.

She met his gaze, looking for some explanation, some reassurance that his offer was sincere. She couldn't read anything in the dark eyes now. Not even fear.

"Go," he said again. "He'll be all right."

Sara hesitated another moment, questioning her own judgment. "Well, it's only for a little while. Jeremy, you be a good boy."

"Okay." He nodded again, a big smile on his face.

Reluctantly, Sara moved toward the car. She really had little choice in the matter. She reassured herself with the knowledge that Edith would arrive soon to take charge. What could happen in that short span of time?

Cable didn't realize the full impact of his actions until Sara's car disappeared from view. He was alone with Jeremy. Only for a short while, but the realization rocked him nonetheless.

What had come over him? Why had he agreed to do this? He must have lost his mind. He'd looked at Sara—so upset, trying to do the right thing, pulled in two directions—and he'd wanted to help.

When Jeremy had reached up to grasp his hand, something had cracked deep inside him, something hard and cold. He'd looked into the child's eyes, the happy brightness of his smile, and somewhere in the back of his mind he'd recognized this moment. For a brief second it was Todd's small hand he held, Todd wanting to stay with Daddy, and then he heard himself telling Sara to go on.

Now he was committed and completely out of his element.

Turning, he searched the yard for Jeremy. He found him squatting in front of the flower bed, staring intently at something near the edge. Curious, Cable strolled toward him.

"Look! A din'saur," Jeremy exclaimed.

Cable looked down at the small green lizard perched on the brick.

"What kind is it?" Jeremy asked studiously.

"A chameleon."

"Is he a baby?"

"I don't know."

"Will he bite me?"

"No."

Jeremy smiled with delight and reached for the reptile, only to have it scurry away.

Cable watched the scene play out with a strange detachment as Jeremy and Doggie chased the hapless little chameleon along the brick border. A current of chilling sadness jolted through him, and he closed his eyes against the pain.

This was a mistake. He'd let down his defenses only a fraction, and now he was paying dearly for the error. Sara had needed help, and he'd responded instinctively.

Now he could see that too much exposure to Jeremy might not be the best thing for his emotional health. The scant contact he'd had with the child so far had been hard enough. A steady dose would be disastrous. Thank God Edith would be here soon.

Cable looked around for Jeremy again. He'd given up on the lizard and was playing happily on the back steps. Cable cursed himself for being a coward. No reason he couldn't keep an eye on the boy for an hour or so. All he had to remember was not to get too close, too involved.

"I'm hungry," Jeremy announced, staring up at him expectantly.

Cable gazed back uncomfortably. Eat? Well, maybe a nice complicated task was just what he needed to pass the time. It would allow him to focus on something other than the pain building inside him. "Do you like pancakes?"

The little boy nodded again.

Once inside, Cable instructed Jeremy to sit at the table and began collecting the food and cookware he needed. The activity boosted his confidence and allowed him to adopt a more practical attitude toward the situation.

After all, this was no big deal. Edith would be here before they finished eating.

"Can I dress myself?" Jeremy asked.

Cable looked down at the pajamas he was wearing. Had Sara planned on letting him run around the store like that? Well, he couldn't play outside in those. Unfortunately, Cable didn't have a clue where Sara kept her son's clothes. Better take the easy way out. "Sure. Do you need help?"

"I can do it myself. I'm three and a half!" He was off like a shot, the cat at his heels.

The first pancake was barely off the skillet when Jeremy returned. "See? I dressed all by myself."

Cable's eyes widened at his choice of clothing. He wore a bright blue shirt with yellow stripes and red-and-green-plaid shorts that looked a couple of sizes too large. Cable doubted if Sara would have approved of her son's fashion statement, but there was no doubt Jeremy was all boy.

The look on the child's face was pure pride. He made such a comical sight that Cable couldn't help but smile. His stiff facial muscles rebelled at the unaccustomed action, and the smile was fleeting.

He realized that it had been a long time since anything had made him want to smile. That discovery should probably mean something, but he wasn't sure what.

They ate in silence for a minute. Cable didn't have the faintest idea what to say to a three-year-old.

"Do you like din'saurs?" Jeremy asked.

Cable swallowed and considered the question. Did the child want a truthful answer or an agreeable one? "Uh, well, I don't dislike them."

Jeremy took another mouthful of gooey pancake, shoving it into his mouth with his fingers. Then he reached up and brushed his hair out of his eyes.

Cable frowned, wondering how he was going to get the syrup off.

"Din'saurs don't eat people," Jeremy informed him seriously. "No. They like trees and grass and things. Do you like to eat little green trees?"

He didn't have the vaguest idea what the child was talking about. He was also at a loss to explain the child's fascination with dinosaurs. When Jeremy wasn't squeezing the purple Clifford under his arm, he was playing with the little pink plastic dino. Were dinosaurs the latest fad in toys?

Suddenly, Cable felt like a dinosaur himself, out of sync with the world around him.

Jeremy was still staring at him with wide, patient brown eyes. Cable searched frantically for a reply. What was this about little green trees? He was saved from answering by the phone. Quickly he moved to the counter. "Hello?"

"Cable, it's Edith. I hate to have to do this, but I'm afraid I have to leave town. My daughter has gone into premature labor. There're some complications and I really need to be there with her. I'm leaving on the eight o'clock bus to Baton Rouge. Please explain to Sara and tell her how sorry I am. She was counting on me and I hate to let her down. I tried to contact a few friends of mine to see if they could fill in, but they're all busy. I hope she can find someone. I'll call her as soon as things settle down."

Dazed, Cable hung up the phone, a cold knot twisting in his gut. Edith wasn't coming today. He was left to watch Jeremy, not for a few minutes but for the entire day.

Panic invaded his mind when another realization formed. Edith wasn't coming back at all. With her gone, who would watch the little boy? She'd said she didn't know of anyone else, and Geri's place was full. The obvious solution was to keep the boy himself, but that was out of the question. He wasn't up to it. He couldn't deal with the parent role again.

Well, it wasn't his concern. Sara would just have to find her own solutions. He'd agreed to keep Jeremy for a half hour. Now it had become all day. That was more than he was obligated to do.

The moment Sara got home, he'd explain the change in plans. It would be rough, but he was going beyond the call of duty as it was. Nothing on earth could get him to do more.

He looked at Jeremy, intent on his pancakes. He was covered with syrup from ear-to-ear and crown-to-chin. It was going to be a very, very long day.

## Chapter Six

It was after nine when Sara trudged up the porch and pulled open the door to the kitchen. Something smelled tantalizingly delicious, but she was too tired to investigate. She was exhausted. Her mind had shut down hours ago, and she was moving on instinct alone. She'd planned on getting out of the store by no later than six, but Baker had gone over every detail with a vengeance.

There hadn't even been a spare moment to call Edith and tell her she would be late. Thankfully, Edith was more than understanding about her erratic work hours.

Sara had wanted to get home at least in time to see Jeremy, but at this hour he was probably asleep, which meant she'd missed another night with him. If she could just get through this assignment, she'd take two weeks off and spend every second with him.

Walking down the hall, she realized how quiet the house

was. Edith was usually very visible and vocal. Come to think of it, she didn't remember seeing Edith's car in the drive.

"Edith, is everything all right? Oh!"

Cable loomed in the doorway to her rooms, a scowl creasing his forehead even more than usual. "It's late."

She wasn't in any mood to deal with a cantankerous crab tonight. "Yes, it is. Where's Edith?"

Cable slipped his hands into the pockets of his jeans. "Gone."

Well, that explained his cheery attitude. He was probably irritated at having to watch Jeremy twice in one day. She made a mental note to thank him. But first, she needed to see her son. "Jeremy asleep?"

Cable nodded as she brushed past him and headed toward the alcove. She stopped at the edge of Jeremy's bed, her heart warming at the sight of him, so sweet and innocent. He was an angel come to life. A gift from heaven so dear and precious she sometimes stood in awe at the wonder of him.

Sara bent down and placed a gentle kiss on his delicate cheek, then straightened the covers and touched the small hand that held his stuffed dinosaur lovingly.

She ached to hold him close to her heart and wrap him in all the love that she possessed, but she didn't want to wake him. Tears stung the backs of her eyes when she thought of how she was losing entire chunks of her son's life and there was nothing she could do about it right now.

He deserved every advantage, every opportunity she could give him. To do that she had to make sacrifices, and the biggest one was time. Time together, time to share. Time to enjoy him. Not only did she not have time for her son but there was no time for her own dreams, either.

With a heavy sigh, she wrapped her arms around her waist, aching for the things she was missing, and especially for what she wanted more than all else to give her son—a father. Taking a deep breath, she reminded herself there was no sense whining about something she couldn't have.

Wiping her eyes, she sniffed and turned around. Cable still stood inside the door. She'd thought he'd left. Under other circumstances she would have been humiliated to let him see her cry, but at the moment she didn't really care. She just wanted to be left alone.

"What do you want?"

"I saved you some supper."

"I'm not hungry," she replied brusquely, knowing the crab would snap back, but not really caring about that, either. When he didn't comment, she looked over at him, surprised to find genuine concern in his eyes.

"You really need to eat," he said softly.

Sara sighed, regretting her snippy attitude. His unexpected kindness was throwing her off-balance again. She wished he'd make up his mind whether he wanted them here or not. It would simplify everything if she knew where she stood.

Well, for now she would take his offer at face value. The thought of food was suddenly very appealing. He was right; she did need to eat. "Thank you."

They ate in silence. The meal was simple, a hearty stew and crisp, flaky rolls, which she gobbled down hungrily. Slowly her tense muscles began to relax and her strength returned. Though she was still tired, the dizzy, strung-out sensation that had hung over her all afternoon was fading.

She took another bite of roll and glanced at Cable, to find him watching her intently. She realized she must have gulped her food like a starving refugee. Self-conscious under his stare, she smiled sheepishly and shrugged. "Thank you. I guess I was hungry."

He took another sip of his coffee and met her gaze. "I could tell."

Sara wasn't sure if she heard amusement or disapproval in his tone. "Did Edith make this before she left?"

Cable shoved his cup aside and rested his forearm on the table. "No." He held her gaze a long moment before adding, "I do all my own cooking. My mother insisted all her sons know how to cook, clean and sew on a button."

So he had brothers. Another crumb of information to add to the scant pile. A small personal tidbit about the Crab.

Ken's request was never far from her thoughts. She owed her boss so much; he had helped her and she wanted to help Cable, for Ken's sake.

The big difference between the respective situations was that she had actively sought help in her grief. She wasn't sure Cable had. Though he did seem mellow and partially out of his shell tonight.

They were both relaxed and comfortable, and he had shared his meal with her. Perhaps this signaled a new phase in their relationship. Maybe all Cable lacked was the opportunity to talk with someone.

She could at least try to draw him out. If he confided in her, so much the better. If not, well, she'd fulfilled her obligation and her conscience would be clear. But what kind of verbal pliers could she use to crack a crab's shell? Closing her eyes, she rubbed the back of her neck, trying to ease some of the tightness that was returning.

"Regional man tough to please?" Cable inquired.

"Regional woman," she corrected with a sigh. "She went over that place like a disease-control specialist looking for some rare virus."

"Being unreasonable?"

"Always. She's not married, has no family and simply can't understand when personal matters overlap into work matters. I tried to explain about Mrs. Louis quitting and why that put me behind, but she didn't seem to care. The store has to be open by Memorial Day, no excuses."

"Can you do it?"

Sara nodded with a yawn. "I may have to work around the clock, but I'll do it. What worries me is how this is going to affect Jeremy. All these changes have disrupted his life, and he needs to feel safe and secure. I thought I'd be able to be with him more, but I'm seeing less of him now than when we were at home. Thank God for Edith. She's the only reason I can sleep at night, knowing Jeremy is in her capable hands."

Cable averted his eyes, shifting in his chair. Sara realized she had been confiding in him, when her intention had been for him to do the talking.

Obviously he was uncomfortable discussing her personal matters. She'd have to be more careful in the future.

Strange, though; this was the second time she'd found herself telling Cable about things that worried her. Now she had a new problem to worry over. Why was it so easy to talk to Cable? He was a crusty crab, for heaven's sake.

Glancing down at the dishes, she frowned and then yawned again. Even Wilma Flintstone had a dinosaur-driven dishwasher. Oh, well, the sooner she got started, the sooner she'd be finished. "Guess we'd better get these cleaned up."

"No. I'll do it," Cable said firmly.

"I don't mind, really. It's the least I can do." Sara pushed up from the table too abruptly. The room spun and her legs turned to spaghetti beneath her. With a detached part of her brain she knew she was falling, but she didn't have the strength to even catch herself. Something strong and secure caught her before she hit the floor.

She grasped the support and tried to focus. Cable's dark eyes were boring into hers. It took her a moment to realize he held her in his arms, close against his side. She knew she should pull away, but the warmth of his body, the strength of his arms was too comforting and protective to relinquish. She allowed her head to rest against his shoulder for a moment until she could gather some energy.

Fatigue conquered her resolve, however, and she found she didn't have the will or the desire to move away.

On the contrary, to her shock, she discovered she wanted to go on leaning against him, wanted to feel this sense of belonging, of protection for the rest of her life.

For the first time in years, the hollow spot under her breast wasn't quite so cold and empty. That realization gave her the power to finally push away from Cable. "Sorry. Guess I must be more tired than I thought."

He held her closer. "You need rest."

He was right, but she didn't have time to rest. Memorial Day was only three weeks away, and she was nearly two weeks behind. She'd have to work triple-time to get the store open on schedule.

The only reason she was so tired now was because of Baker's visit. All she needed was one good night's sleep, and she'd be her old self in the morning. She wasn't going to let a little fatigue stop her.

"I'm taking you to your room." He slipped his arm around her again, but she pulled away.

"No. I can walk. I was just a little dizzy for a second. I'm fine now." But her knees buckled at her first step, and she sagged against him once again.

He steered her slowly but firmly down the hall. She must still be dizzy. That was the only explanation for the delicious sensations she experienced as she walked beside him.

With each step their bodies brushed intimately together, hip-to-hip, thigh-to-thigh. The muscles in his legs rippled against her own. His powerful arms wrapped possessively about her waist, creating an intoxicating warmth that spread languidly through her entire body.

She inhaled the scent of him, masculine and earthy. Being in his embrace was like being enfolded in a cocoon of warmth and strength, where no one could harm her.

At the door he stopped and she turned, finding herself in the circle of his arms. Feeling light-headed and giddy, she struggled to focus on his face and ended up with her gaze locked to his. He had such gorgeous eyes, with long black lashes that curled on the ends. His eyes were the color of warm cocoa with marshmallows. The image amused her and she grinned. "You have pretty, hot-chocolate eyes."

"You think so?"

She nodded, letting her gaze travel to his mouth. His full lower lip peeked seductively from under his mustache, the most fascinating thing she'd ever seen. She wondered what it would be like to kiss him, to take it between her teeth and... "Do you have dimples under there?" she asked, touching his cheek and feeling the stiff stubble against her fingertips. It made her giggle. "I'll bet you do. Great big, deep dimples under all that scruffy stuff."

Giggles bubbled up from inside, and she gave herself over to them. "Scruffy the Tugboat." She giggled again, covering her mouth in a feeble attempt to stop. But there was no halting this fit of laughter. "'Cept you don't look like a boat. You look like a cowboy."

"A cowboy?" Cable grinned.

Sara's heart stopped beating. She stared at him, nodding like a plastic dog in the back window of a car. "With a Stetson hat and a six-gun and one of those long coat things."

"A duster."

She snickered. "Silly name. Grandmas wear dusters. You know, the kind with the snaps up the front." Her knees wobbled again and she sagged against Cable, tingling all over from head to toe. She'd never been so weary she tingled before. "Oh, I'm so tired. Have you ever been this exhausted?"

"Yes," he replied, holding her more securely.

"I just want to sleep forever."

Cable was so warm and solid. She closed her eyes, resting her head on his chest. Her thoughts started to drift off on a sea of soft flannel, in a boat made of warmth and light. She could sail like this forever.

Strong, masculine arms wrapped around her body, pressing her close to his lean, hard length. She wanted to be encased in that special kind of warmth only a man could provide. She wanted to awaken slowly with the dawn, to cuddle in luxuriant closeness nothing else could match. A familiar heat rose from deep in her core and she quivered with longing.

"Go to bed, Sara."

With a rude jolt, the hazy dream burst. She blinked and looked at Cable as he set her away from him. He turned and walked off, leaving her cold and adrift upon a foggy, sensual sea.

Cable shut the door behind him and wiped his hand over his face. What the hell had he been thinking of? He should never have touched her. But if he hadn't, she would have collapsed to the floor.

He still burned from the intimate closeness, the softness of her body pressed against him. His head was still dizzy with the seductive fragrance of her hair; his arms still remembered the way she fit so perfectly in his embrace.

The fact that he'd responded to Sara, to her enticing softness, was understandable. After all, she was a lovely, exciting woman. Any man would respond. But for five years all he had wanted was to protect himself. Now he had an unreasonable urge to protect Sara, which was ridiculous. She didn't need protecting. She was strong, independent and capable.

He admired her grit and determination. It must be difficult being a single mother with no one to ease the burden even briefly. She was doing a damn good job. Jeremy was a terrific little guy, bright and inquisitive. Under other circumstances Cable would probably enjoy having the boy around. But right now he couldn't take on the role of daddy, even for a short time. His heart was incapable of withstanding the strain.

But unless he told Sara about Edith, strain or not, he'd be taking on Jeremy full-time and playing daddy again.

He should have told her. He'd had the perfect opportunity. But she'd been so tired, so overworked that he couldn't bring himself to add to her already heavy burden.

The news about Edith would only compound an already bad situation. He could see the effects of the stress Sara was under. When she'd first arrived three weeks ago, she'd been bubbling over with energy and enthusiasm. There'd been a bounce in her walk and a purposeful light in her blue eyes. Over the weeks, especially the week since Jeremy's arrival, he'd seen her slow down, her enthusiasm change to dogged determination.

She needed a good night's sleep, probably more. She'd be able to cope with this crisis when she was rested. He hated that Sara now faced even more stress with Edith gone, but it wasn't really his concern. He only hoped she was strong enough to handle it, and he prayed he was strong enough to withstand the temptation she presented to him.

Sara chewed absently on the cap of her pen, her gaze only partially focused on the list of things to do that day. Her thoughts kept drifting back to last night and supper with Cable.

Each time she thought about her behavior, a new wave of embarrassment washed over her. She'd lost complete control, dissolving into giggles like a schoolgirl and making a complete idiot of herself in the process.

The whole incident was so hazy. She remembered asking him something absurd, but exactly what, she couldn't recall. It had made him smile. She remembered that vividly, because her response to him had had nothing to do with laughter.

Cable's smile had been a bit stiff, as if he didn't use it often, but its effect upon her senses had been like a low-voltage electrical current straight to her heart. There was something tender and special about his smile, which had slipped under her skin and entwined itself around that hollow spot deep inside.

She wanted to make him smile again, to find out if he really did have dimples under the dark stubble. She remembered wanting to taste that firm, exciting lower lip, to rest her head against his hard chest for just a moment.

The next thing she knew she'd been standing alone and shivering in the hall. She didn't even remember how she got to bed.

She'd slept well, though, and awakened feeling human again, if not bursting with energy. At least she would be able to put in a full, productive day at work.

Pouring another cup of coffee, she reached for the sugar, but the container was empty. She lifted the battered metal can with distaste. Lord knew what this had held before Cable had decided to keep sugar in it.

After an extensive search through the cabinets, she finally located an old pink, Depression-glass sugar bowl. She filled it and set it on the table, pleased to find it matched the large bowl in the middle of the table. Cable's junk bowl.

Sara frowned, shaking her head. It was such a lovely old piece, yet he had it filled with letters, bills, pencils, string, nuts, bolts, old batteries, tape and a porcelain doorknob. And those were the things she could see at a glance. She didn't want to think what was buried at the bottom.

If it was up to her, she'd put a dried-flower arrangement in it—some blue hydrangeas maybe, or magnolias. Or she'd just leave it empty and displayed on an antique lace doily.

Sara took a sip of her coffee and smiled at Jeremy. He was scooping up his cereal and feeding his toy dinosaur a bite before he ate himself. She'd been meaning to ask him how he'd liked being with Cable yesterday morning. "Jeremy, did you—"

"Cable!" The boy waved and smiled.

Sara looked over her shoulder and saw her landlord entering the kitchen, his usual scowl in place, his jaw clamped shut in irritation. Sara was reassured. At least some things were back to normal. He must have crawled out of the wrong side of his shell this morning. All that soft and tender stuff she remembered from last night must have been fatigue-induced hallucinations.

At least she understood this reaction. This was predictable behavior. This was the man she'd come to know and tolerate. She met his gaze straight on and smiled. "Good morning."

He nodded stiffly, rolling up the sleeves on his dark blue shirt. He looked rugged, earthy. Without warning, her body warmed with the memory of being held close against his hard frame, of feeling the strength in his arms....

He walked toward the coffeemaker, and Sara took the opportunity to discipline her wandering thoughts. "Look-

ing for something?'' she asked when she heard him opening cupboards and shoving things around.

''Damned sugar.''

Sara lifted the pink bowl. ''Here.''

Cable frowned, his brown eyes darkening. ''What's
that?''

''State-of-the-art food storage. Sugar bowl.''

''I already had one.''

''No, you had a rusty can with sugar in it.''

''It served its purpose.''

''It's outlived its usefulness. Like a lot of things around
here.''

Cable gave her a fierce look, but she merely smiled back.
He was not going to get under her skin today.

''Mommy, I want to go to the sandpile.''

''Sandpile?'' Sara asked, thoughts of Cable temporarily
forgotten.

Jeremy nodded, smiling. ''Cable made it special. It's a big
mountain for my trucks.''

Cable looked away when Sara turned toward him, but not
before she caught the look of embarrassment in his eyes.
''Where is this sandpile?'' she questioned.

''In the yard. I won't go out the fence. Cable said.''

''I guess it's all right.''

Jeremy and Doggie dashed for the door.

Sara was brimming with irritation when she turned her
attention back to Cable. How dare he do something nice just
when she'd convinced herself he was cold and unfeeling?

When would she learn that her judgment of people was
completely untrustworthy? She no more understood Cable
than she had Drake—or herself, for that matter. If she had
known the first thing about human behavior, she would
have seen that Drake would leave her. At the very least she

would have seen that she was making a mistake in marrying him.

Well, she was through trying to figure people out. Especially Cable McRay. He blew warm and cold like an old fuel-oil furnace. She didn't need that kind of roller-coaster ride from anyone, least of all her landlord. Turning her back on him, she started gathering up her work for the day.

A lump of guilt slid down Cable's throat along with a mouthful of coffee. He should tell her about Edith; now was the perfect moment. He watched her stack her materials and brush her hair out of her eyes. There were rings under her blue eyes and a slight slump to her shoulders. She wasn't dead on her feet, but she wasn't the gutsy, energetic woman who'd blown into his life three weeks ago, either.

She needed more rest, but he doubted if she would get it. She was determined to overcome all obstacles and get the store open on time. But what would the obstacle created by Edith's departure do to those already burdened shoulders?

Sara checked her watch, glancing out the back window. He knew she was looking for Edith. Only Edith wasn't coming.

"Go on. You'd better leave."

Sara turned and gazed at him in surprise. He hated that look. As if any kindness he offered was out of character, unexpected and for some reason unwelcome. Was that how she perceived him? As unkind and sour?

He wasn't that way. He merely valued his privacy. He had a nice, uneventful life filled with peace and contentment and work he loved. Or at least he had before she'd showed up.

If he was a bit testy it was because he was being denied that privacy due to Sara and Jeremy's presence in his house. He glanced at her, finding her blue eyes focused on him, curious and probing, penetrating his defenses with delicate skill.

"Go," he repeated, anxious to remove himself from her X-ray vision.

"Are you sure?"

"I said so, didn't I?" What did she want? A signed affidavit?

She picked up her purse and papers and started for the door. "Thanks. Tell Edith I'll make it all up to her."

Cable could hear her saying goodbye to Jeremy as she walked to her car. Why had he let the chance go by? Why couldn't he come right out and tell her—*I can't play daddy again. You don't know what you're doing to me!*

But he'd allowed another opportunity to pass and had sealed his own fate. God help him before he lost his sanity completely.

Something small and soft touched his palm. Cable looked down to find Jeremy holding his hand, looking expectantly up at him with big brown eyes. He hadn't even been aware that the boy had come into the house.

"What are we going to do today, Cable?"

A wave of panic jolted through him, short-circuiting his brain. Dear Lord, where was he going to find the strength to do this? He didn't have it in him. He couldn't be a parent again. Blood roared in his ears, and an overpowering desire to run away seized him.

He couldn't deal with the responsibility of a child, of having complete trust placed upon his shoulders. He couldn't tolerate the closeness and intimacy a child would demand.

"Cable?" Jeremy tugged at his hand, forcing him to function and face the crisis.

Cable glanced down at him, keenly aware of the warm little body at his side. This child was depending on him. Sara was depending on him, even though she didn't realize it. He couldn't run away. He couldn't turn his back, not this time.

He took a deep breath, willing himself to look at the situation logically.

All he had to do was keep it simple. Do what had to be done, but not get emotionally involved. The best way to do that was to keep busy.

The first thought that came to mind was to work, but he didn't want to expose Jeremy to the dangerous machinery. He'd have to make some modifications in his shop before he could work and watch Jeremy at the same time.

Maybe the best course of action for today would be to stay out of the house and the shop. He could run errands and take Jeremy with him. He needed to drive to Ethelton and pick up the lumber for his next project. Then later this afternoon, they might do some yard work and wash the car.

The first half of the day went much as Cable had expected. They drove to the neighboring town, where Cable got a haircut and stopped by the lumberyard. Jeremy had been fascinated. He loved the forklifts scooting about and the stacks of boards and plywood piled high in the sheds. Cable had found an odd kind of satisfaction in explaining it all to him.

He had to be careful, vigilant at all times. He might start to enjoy Jeremy's company too much. Sharing even simple knowledge was too risky. Sharing led to bonding and bonding led to caring, and caring only led to heartache and pain.

"Cable, the wheel is all clean," Jeremy said proudly, dropping the big sponge into the bucket.

"Okay, stand back. Here goes." Cable turned the hose on the hubcap and sprayed off the suds.

The day had passed more quickly and easily than he would have imagined. In a few hours, Sara would be home, and he would be free of the responsibility of Jeremy.

He had to tell Sara about Edith the moment she got home. Many more days of being Jeremy's baby-sitter would destroy him. He could already feel his affection for the boy growing. He had enjoyed his company today, and every now and again he caught himself planning future excursions.

But there would be no more trips, no more need to entertain him, because it would end today. This had gone on too long. Cable had no one to blame but himself, of course, but it had to stop here, today. Sara would have to make other arrangements.

It was only a matter of time, anyway, until Jeremy spilled the beans. Cable was amazed he hadn't done so already. He was bound to tell his mother about the trip to the lumberyard, and Sara would question why Edith had allowed him to go.

He had a feeling Sara wouldn't be happy about his deception regarding Edith or his watching Jeremy for two days.

When the truck was clean and wiped dry, Jeremy went to play in the sandpile and Cable went inside to use the phone. He called everyone he could think of who might know someone to keep Jeremy.

Geri promised to call him the moment there was any kind of opening at all, but she didn't hold out much hope. After an hour on the phone, Cable was convinced there was a conspiracy under way in Carswell. The only candidate for Jeremy's sitter was himself!

But it wasn't going to happen. The deal with Sara had been for rooms only, not room, board and baby-sitting.

"Cable!" Jeremy called, dashing into the house. "Doggie's stuck in the tree!"

Cable took one look at Jeremy and grimaced. His face and arms were streaked with dirt, his knees covered with sand. His shirt had dark brown stains from washing the car, and his hair was plastered to his head. He was filthy.

As soon as he rescued the cat, Cable would have to give Jeremy a good scrubbing. Sara would have a fit if she saw him like this. Though, in Cable's opinion, he looked perfectly normal for a little boy three and a half years old.

After giving Jeremy a speedy, no-nonsense bath, Cable dressed him and took him up to his own room, settling him in the window seat with a book. Then he took a fast shower, pulled on his jeans and looked at himself in the mirror.

He didn't look like a baby-sitter. He looked more like a mountain man—or a cowboy. No wonder Sara had told him he looked like he should be riding the range.

Maybe the news about Edith would go down better if he looked a little more respectable. He wondered if Sara would like him without a beard. And what she would say when she discovered there were dimples under his stubble as she had suspected.

He ran a hand along the scratchy surface of his jaw. Maybe it was time to get rid of the beard. He'd been thinking about it for some time now. His neatly trimmed hair was at odds with the beard. He should have had a shave while he was at the barber's, but it hadn't occurred to him. In fact, he hadn't thought about his appearance at all in a long time.

Cable stared at his reflection as he slowly spread lather over his face. Why did it matter to him what Sara thought? She'd know tomorrow, when Edith didn't come to work, that something was up. He'd have to tell her that the woman was gone, and that for the last two days he'd been the baby-sitter.

"Aww, Cable," Jeremy scolded. "You got soap all over your face."

Cable looked down at the little boy, who had come to stand beside him. The expression on his face said he thought Cable was doing something wrong. "This is shaving cream," he explained.

Jeremy thought about that a moment, then climbed up on the commode and leaned on the edge of the sink. "Why you doin' that?"

"To get all the whiskers off my face."

"Now your face won't be fuzzy?"

"Right. No more fuzz."

Jeremy watched intently as Cable began scraping his face. He left the mustache; no need to overdo things. As he raised his chin to shave his jaw, a memory blazed through his mind like a comet. There'd been another time, another shaving lesson with another little boy.

His heart tightened. This was what he'd been afraid of. Having Jeremy around would only stir up the past, and the past was too painful to endure. This had to end tonight.

"There," Cable said, relieved that the end was in sight. He picked up the towel and dried his face, then reached for the after-shave and splashed some on. The sting on his skin cleared his mind.

Jeremy pointed at him and wide-eyed, announced, "You broke your face!"

"What?" Cable asked. The boy was staring at the cleft in his chin, and he grinned slightly. "No, it's not broken, it's just the way my chin is made. Lots of men have this."

Jeremy frowned, unconvinced.

"Here, touch it and see. It's okay."

Tentatively, the three-year-old reached out and pressed one small finger to the indentation. A smile lit his face. "Where did you get it?"

"My daddy gave it to me."

"My daddy gave me his eyes and his colors."

"His colors?"

"Mommy said I have my daddy's eyes and colors." Jeremy pointed to his hair and then his arm.

"Oh, you mean you have your daddy's coloring. Does your daddy come to see you?"

"No. He doesn't come to my house."

Cable was filled with pity for the child. How could a father turn his back on his own son? He would give all he had to have Todd back with him, yet Jeremy's father apparently never came to see him. Cable's heart tightened with sadness as he thought of the things this little boy was missing.

His own relationship with his father had been special, and he liked to believe he'd given Todd some of that love and closeness. He tried to select a memory, one small moment of time when he and his son had been together. Nothing occurred to him.

He looked down at Jeremy. There would be no special memories for Jeremy, either, without a father in his life.

Losing Todd had cut out Cable's heart. Jeremy's father would never know what a wonderful child he had, and Jeremy would never know the love of his real father. He deserved better. Sara deserved better, too.

Cable almost followed the overpowering urge to scoop the boy up against his chest. He allowed the moment to pass, too fearful of the possible backlash.

"Come on in here," he instructed, heading back into the bedroom.

Jeremy raced past him and climbed up on the bed. "Uh-oh. My book dropped," he exclaimed.

As Cable reached down to retrieve the book, his eyes were drawn to the writing on the inside cover: To Todd from Grandma. An image flashed in his mind. He closed the book and read the title, *Scuffy the Tugboat*. Todd used to like a book about a boat. Was this the one? Cable grappled for a memory. It had to be there in his mind somewhere. Vague recollections glanced off the edges of his mind, but he couldn't latch on to any of them. Were they buried so deep that he couldn't retrieve them? What if he never did? The possibility suddenly terrified him.

"That's a book about a tugboat and he has a big 'venture," Jeremy was saying. "Do you know about the tugboat?"

Cable continued to stare at the little book. Did he have a memory connected with this book, or did he want to have one because he needed something tangible to help him touch the past? "I think it may have been my little boy's favorite."

Jeremy looked at him thoughtfully. "It's my favorite, too." He took the book from Cable's hands and snuggled down on the bed, turning pages and muttering to himself.

Cable moved to the closet, staring blindly at the row of shirts. Why was it so hard to remember? What could he do to unlock the memories in his head? Were they there to unlock? Or had they eroded away into particles too small to ever be reassembled?

He forced a deep breath into his lungs, trying to realign his thoughts. Maybe it was better this way. The past, his memories, only made life more difficult.

Yanking a shirt off a hanger, he put it on, then turned back to the bed. Jeremy was sprawled on the spread, sound asleep.

Cable couldn't repress the smile that came to his lips. It had been a big day for the little guy. He would probably sleep for a couple of hours now.

He picked the sleeping child up in his arms, unprepared for the backlash that resulted. The ache in his chest began the moment he held the child against him. Cradling the warm little boy, so innocent and lovable, unleashed a wave of sorrow that threatened to bring him to his knees.

There would never be another moment like this for him and his son. No closeness, no chance to say I love you, to hug him or to touch him.

Cable's head throbbed unmercifully, his stomach knotted and an awful, frigid emptiness formed in his soul. All he could think of was getting Jeremy downstairs to bed and out of his arms.

He steeled himself against the paternal feelings that bombarded him and moved as swiftly as possible down to Sara's rooms. He placed the sleeping child on the small, antique cot.

His stomach was in knots, his head felt like it was being squeezed in a vice. Doggie appeared from somewhere and settled beside the little boy.

Quickly Cable strode from the room, needing to remove himself from the emotionally charged situation. He'd learned early that the only effective way to combat one of these attacks of sadness was to get busy and stay busy. Working in the shop was out of the question; he had to stay near Jeremy. But the kitchen was close, and it was almost suppertime.

## *Chapter Seven*

"Mommy!"

Sara nearly dropped the binders and laptop computer she carried when Jeremy swooped upon her and wrapped his arms around her leg. "Hello, sweet thing. Did you miss me today?" she asked.

He nodded, a huge smile on his face. Sara couldn't help but smile back. No matter how tired she was, no matter how awful her day had been, seeing Jeremy lifted her spirits and made all the hard work worthwhile.

"Can you help me carry something?"

Jeremy nodded enthusiastically once again. Sara shifted her load and helped him take hold of the computer. He hurried up the stairs and pulled open the screen door, disappearing inside.

She was looking forward to spending the evening with him. She would read him a book or play a game. They might even take a walk around the neighborhood. For a few hours, she intended to forget about being a manager and to just be an ordinary mom.

Of course, after Jeremy was asleep, she'd have to spend the rest of the night working, but with any luck she'd be back on schedule by morning. Continuing up the steps, she shifted her heavy load again. She'd brought a mountain of work home with her. The more she could do here, the more she could see Jeremy.

"Need some help?"

Sara recognized Cable's deep, resonant voice, but the man who stood before her was a stranger. A very handsome, disturbing stranger. She took a closer look, stunned to realize it really was Cable McRay. But this wasn't the same man she'd left Jeremy with this morning.

His dark wavy hair was neatly styled over his ears and along the nape of his neck. The stubble was gone, the skin clean-shaven below his high cheekbones. There was a cleft in his chin that rivaled Cary Grant's and a hint of dimples at the corners of his firm mouth.

The only facial hair that remained was a neatly trimmed mustache that called attention to his brown eyes and lent a devilish cast to his jawline.

He wore a red polo shirt that emphasized his well-developed pectorals and muscular forearms. Light gray trousers rested on slim hips and lay closely against his thighs before tapering downward over scuffed cowboy boots.

Damn if he didn't look like an ad for a brand of yuppie sportswear—handsome, successful, solid and dependable and overwhelmingly sexy.

Sara inhaled the pungent aroma of after-shave, one of those tried-and-true kinds that never went out of style. It suited him.

"Sara?"

"What?"

Cable was holding his hand out, waiting to take some of her load.

"Oh, thanks." Still in a daze at the drastic change in his appearance, she allowed him to take her binders from her arms without protest.

Lagging behind, she followed him into the house. What had come over him? What had caused this drastic change in appearance? Suspicion snaked slowly through her mind. Something was up. Cable the Crab wouldn't suddenly turn into Mr. Yuppie for no reason.

Jeremy trotted toward her as she entered the kitchen. "Mommy, Cable said I could eat with him."

"Oh, well, that's very nice of him, but I thought I'd make you and me some hamburgers for supper."

"I wanna eat his supper. He made noodles."

"There's more than enough," Cable said softly.

Sara wasn't sure spending time with this new version of her landlord was a good idea. Until she had some reasonable explanation for his fresh image, she wasn't about to get too comfortable. "No, I couldn't impose. Thank you."

"Please, Mommy," Jeremy begged, bouncing up and down.

"It's hard to cook for just one," Cable murmured.

She couldn't argue with that. It was far easier to eat a meal that was already prepared than to start one from scratch. It would also save time—time better spent with her son. Giving in was simple logic. Nothing more.

Halfway through dinner Sara began to doubt her powers of logic. There had been little or no conversation, and Jeremy had been fidgety and irritable through the entire meal. Could he be picking up on her own tension?

Everything between her and Cable seemed different now. It was more than the unexpected change in him. Suddenly she was aware of her mussed hair hanging in her eyes and the lack of makeup. Her favorite jeans seemed too tight and too worn, and she noticed that there was dirt smudged across the front of her white sweater.

"I don't like to eat little trees," Jeremy whined.

Sara sighed, fighting her unaccustomed feelings of self-consciousness. The combination of Cable's new image and Jeremy's crankiness was wearing on her patience. "Those aren't trees, Jeremy, that's broccoli. It's good for you."

"I don't want 'em." He pushed his plate away, nearly knocking over his glass of milk.

Sara pushed it right back. "Jeremy, you're not getting down from this table until you've eaten at least two bites."

The little boy shook his head and clamped his hands over his mouth.

Sara pried one arm loose and put the spoon in his fingers. "Eat."

He threw the spoon on the floor.

Stress and fatigue swamped her, robbing her of her remaining patience. "Jeremy Ledon Nelson! You will eat that broccoli, do you hear me?"

He shook his head determinedly.

Sara was on the verge of shouting when Cable reached down, picked up the spoon and handed it to Jeremy. "I like to eat little green trees, just like the dinosaurs do," he stated calmly.

She watched in amazement as her son removed his hands from his mouth, took the spoon, scooped up a "tree" and ate it.

"One more bite," Cable urged quietly.

Jeremy obeyed without hesitation. Sara stared at her landlord, trying to figure out this new version of him. He shaved, put on fashionable clothes, and suddenly Crab Man became Mr. Nice Guy—friendly, helpful and able to coax vegetables into the mouths of children.

Sara took a deep breath, aware of an old, familiar sensation in her stomach. The one that always preceded an upheaval. And she had a really bad feeling about all this.

Jeremy smiled up into her face. "Cable and me had a big 'venture. We went to the lummeryard place and got a haircut and I gotta iscream at the little house."

"Don't you mean you and Edith?" Sara asked, focusing on her son.

"Uh-uh. Me and Cable. We rode in his truck with the big wheels."

A shiver of apprehension chased up her spine. What was going on? It seemed out of character for Edith to let Jeremy go off with Cable. "I wish Edith would have checked with me first," she said, looking pointedly at the man.

He glanced at her briefly, then averted his eyes. "She couldn't."

"Why not?"

Cable hesitated a moment before answering. "Because she wasn't here."

Sara's uneasiness grew. She mentally braced herself for whatever disaster was coming. "What do you mean? Where was she?"

"In Baton Rouge."

"Why?"

Cable fidgeted with the silverware. "Her daughter went into labor."

"When did this happen?"

He met her gaze squarely now. "Two days ago."

"Two..." Sara's mind balked at the information it had so suddenly been asked to digest. Edith was gone? Days ago? My God, how could this happen? How... The implications slammed into her, and she turned an angry glare on Cable. "Then who's been watching Jeremy?" She could tell by the look on Cable's face she wasn't going to like the answer.

"I guess I have."

The uneasiness quickly became dread, sloshing around in the pit of her stomach. No wonder Jeremy was so taken with Cable! He'd spent the last two days completely under his care. Her fear about the closeness that might develop between them took on new proportions.

"You guess you have?" She chewed her tongue, trying to control her fury in front of her son. She didn't want him to see her fighting with Cable. "Why didn't you tell me Edith was gone?"

He didn't hesitate in his reply. "Because you were under tremendous pressure at work. Edith called the morning your regional manager arrived."

"You could have told me that night."

"You didn't need any more bad news. You were exhausted," he reminded her. "You practically fell asleep on your feet."

She didn't need reminding. The night was recorded vividly in her thoughts. Especially being held in Cable's arms. As for her physical state, as much as she hated to admit it, he was right. She couldn't have taken any more bad news that night. But that only accounted for one day.

She momentarily stifled her anger, keeping her voice calm and neutral as she spoke to her son. "Jeremy, why don't you go and play for a while? Pick out a book you want me to read. When I'm finished talking to Cable, I'll read to you, okay?"

As soon as the little boy was out of the room, she confronted her landlord. "Why didn't you tell me about Edith first thing this morning?" she demanded.

He raised an eyebrow. "I planned on telling you tonight."

So that explained the sudden change in his appearance. She'd been right to suspect something. He'd probably figured the news would go down easier if he shaved and spruced himself up. "Well, unfortunately for you, Jeremy beat you to it, didn't he?" Rising to her feet, she picked up her plate and carried it to the sink.

If she didn't get busy and do something, she'd be sorely tempted to knock Cable's block off. But when she realized the full implications of the baby-sitter's departure, her anger turned to genuine alarm. "Did Edith say when she'd be back?"

"No. Her daughter developed complications."

Sara sighed, running a hand through her short hair. "What am I going to do?" she whispered softly to herself. Maybe... She looked at Cable. "Did she mention anyone who might fill in?"

He shook his head. "She couldn't locate anyone. She told me to tell you how sorry she was."

Sara could well imagine how Edith felt, and she understood. But without someone to watch Jeremy, she'd never get the store open. "Maybe that friend of yours at the day care?"

"I already checked," Cable said. "She's overcrowded as it is."

"There has to be someone in town who could watch him," she insisted anxiously. "A retired nurse, a teacher, even for half a day?"

Cable rose and joined her at the sink, setting his plate on the counter. "This is a small college town. Every resource is filled to capacity. Maybe in a week or so, when classes let out, there might be someone available."

"I need a sitter now, not in a few weeks." Sara walked back to the table to gather more dishes. Tired and discouraged, she started grasping for any solution. "I guess I could take him to the store during the day."

"That's not safe or practical."

"I know, but I'm already doing more work at home than I should." There had to be an answer somewhere. She could turn the assignment over to Bud. The majority of the setup was completed. He would be the store manager when she was gone, anyway. Since Bud lived in town, he could work round the clock if necessary.

The biggest blow, however, was losing the opportunity. If she failed in this job, her plans for a promotion, for permanence, would go up in smoke. For the last three years it had seemed as if everything she tried turned to dust when she touched it. Her marriage, her career, her future... She should never have agreed to this crazy situation in the first place.

As she always did when she was frustrated, Sara cleaned. She picked up a handful of silverware and turned, catching sight of Cable. It would be so easy to blame him. But it wasn't his fault. It wasn't anyone's fault. It was just life, and life apparently was out to sabotage her plans. "I guess I should thank you for taking care of Jeremy."

"I didn't have a choice."

Sara pursed her lips at his curt tone. Goodbye, Mr. Nice Guy. "I guess not."

Cable watched Sara agonize over this new complication. She paced between the table and the sink, clearing dishes and stacking them. He didn't interrupt, knowing the activity probably helped her think. He knew it went against her nature to give up and admit defeat. He also knew how much she loved Jeremy and how hard she was trying to balance her dual roles of manager and mother. She would make any sacrifice for her son's sake. But the stress was beginning to take its toll on her physically and emotionally.

He wanted to help, but the obvious solution, the one thing that would help her the most, would destroy him.

Even as Cable wrestled with his dilemma, deep down he knew he'd already made his decision. But he could no more explain his choice than he could his decision to shed his backwoods image for one a little closer to his old self.

He had no idea why he'd wanted Sara to see him the way he used to be, but he knew he'd made a big mistake. He'd realized that fact the moment she'd looked at him. His rugged attire and half-grown beard had acted like a protective shield, a barrier that prevented her or anyone from getting too close.

Now he felt exposed and vulnerable, at the mercy of Sara and her probing eyes. She could get closer to him now and see who he really was, and he couldn't allow her to do that.

Maybe it wasn't too late to repair his defenses. Three weeks remained on Sara's assignment. Taking time away from work to find a baby-sitter would only prolong her stay. But if she was free to throw herself into the job, spend all her time at the store and get it open on time, then she would leave, and his life could return to normal. If all he had to deal with was Jeremy and not Sara, he could manage. One of them he could handle, but not both.

In exchange for a few weeks' sacrifice, he could have his life restored to him. Surely that was well worth the price. Shoving his hands into his pockets, he turned and faced Sara. "There's one alternative."

"What?"

The worry reflected in her blue eyes made it easier for him to make his offer. "I could keep him."

"No. Out of the question." She strode past him to the table.

"I've kept him for two days. He seemed to like the arrangement."

Sara picked up the drinking glasses and headed back to the sink. "I'm not in the habit of leaving my child with just anyone."

"You left him with Edith. You didn't know her."

"I knew her better than you. We'd at least talked. Besides, she's a grandmother, she raised seven children of her own. You're..."

"I'm what?" Cable waited anxiously for her answer. He had a feeling it was going to be important to him.

"I don't know what you are. One minute you're all grim and scowling and the next you're doing something nice."

Is that how she thought of him? As grim? He told himself it didn't matter what Sara thought of him, but his ego stung just the same. "You make 'nice' sound ominous. Call Ken, ask him about my character."

"He's your cousin. Of course he'll say something positive."

An unreasonable need to defend himself possessed him. "He's your friend, too. Would he send you to stay here if I was a threat to you or Jeremy?"

Sara couldn't deny he had her there. Ken had been clear about how harmless Cable was. Of course, there was harmless and then there was harmless. She turned off the faucet and faced him. "This isn't a matter of character, Cable. I'm not concerned about you harming Jeremy. This is a matter of attachment. Jeremy is much too taken with you as it is. Your becoming his baby-sitter would only make it worse."

"It's only for a few weeks."

"Time enough for him to be heartbroken when we leave. No. I won't put him through that again. He's had too many people walk out of his life as it is."

"Do you have any other suggestions?"

She was running out of straws to grasp. "Maybe someone from Memphis could drive down or come to stay here."

"Can you afford that?"

He was right again. Her salary was good, but not that good. Her financial arrangements with Mrs. Louis and Edith had been frugal, to say the least. "No," she admitted sourly.

"Then you'll have to quit."

"No. I'm too close. This job is too important to me and Jeremy."

"Then it seems to me there's only one solution," Cable said. "Both of us want the same thing—a return of the status quo. The quickest way to do that is to get the store open on time. A few more weeks and we'll both have what we want. But we'll both have to make some sacrifices."

"No." She couldn't depend upon Cable. It was dangerous.

"I don't like this any better than you do, Sara, but I don't see where either one of us has a choice."

Sara had to accept the inevitable. Both she and Cable were trapped in a situation neither wanted but neither could avoid. She had to remember her main goal—to get the Dixie Mart open by Memorial Day so she could get the promotion. Surely, in this one instance, the end justified the means.

With a heartfelt sigh, she turned and faced him. "On two conditions. First, I'm going to keep looking for someone else to watch Jeremy."

"Fair enough. The second?"

"I'll pay you what I paid Edith."

Cable shook his head determinedly. "No."

"I insist on paying our share," she said, planting her hands on her hips.

"All right. We'll compromise. You buy the groceries, I'll do the cooking and we'll call it a draw."

"That hardly seems fair."

"Sure it does." The corner of Cable's mouth moved and both dimples appeared in his cheeks. "I've seen the way you eat."

Sara tugged off Jeremy's shirt, creating static electricity that made his hair crackle and stand up.

"Is Cable as big as my daddy?"

The question sent a lump of dread sinking into Sara's stomach. Jeremy had never seen his father and rarely asked about him. But after only one week in Cable's presence, he was starting to compare his absent father to him. What would happen in a few more weeks when he became even more important in Jeremy's life? What would happen when they went home and that bond was broken permanently?

"No. Cable is bigger than your daddy."

"Cable likes to eat little trees just like the din'saurs."

Sara chewed her lip. She didn't want Jeremy to have his heart broken. Cable was being extremely generous and helpful in offering to watch him. Few men would even consider being a sitter full-time. But she couldn't let this one display of consideration and sacrifice give her a false reading on her landlord.

He'd offered because there was no other solution for the time being. She had to remember that her judgment wasn't reliable, and she couldn't let her guard down. Especially where men were concerned.

Cable had already thrown her a couple of unexpected curves. Who knew what he would do in the future? He could change his mind at any moment.

A voice in the back of her mind whispered, *What about Jeremy's judgment?* How much credence could she place in that? Did children, as her mother and Edith believed, possess a special insight into a person's character? Did Jeremy know something about Cable she didn't?

Sara pulled off Jeremy's sand-filled socks and brushed stray grains off his chubby feet. "I'm very proud of you for eating all your broccoli. It'll make you big and strong."

"Like Cable?"

Sara fastened the buttons on his pajama top, wishing she could get his mind off Cable the Crab for a moment. "Did you find a book for me to read?"

Jeremy hurried off, returning quickly with one of the books Cable had given him.

"Which one did you choose? *Scuffy the Tugboat,*" she read when Jeremy held up the book.

"I want Cable to read me 'bout Scuffy Tugboat."

"Mommy will read it to you," she said, swallowing the twinge of jealousy his request had caused.

"I want Cable to read me like he did his boy."

Sara tensed, her heart pounding. "Cable told you he had a little boy?"

Jeremy nodded, opening the book. "*Scuffy* was his favorite book."

What did this mean? First Cable had told her about Todd, and now he'd told Jeremy. Was her dubious ability for drawing confidences from people operating through her son now? She wasn't sure she wanted Cable to tell her his secrets. Her heart was in enough danger as it was. She didn't need sympathy and understanding to further complicate matters between them. "Did Cable say anything else about his boy?"

Jeremy shook his head. "It makes him sad to remember."

Sara's heart twisted in sympathy, even as her conscience smarted. Of course it would make Cable sad. The same way having them here was a constant reminder of what he'd lost. How could she have forgotten that for even a moment?

She slipped her arm around Jeremy, hugging him close and sending up a prayer of thankfulness. With him held protectively in her arms, she sought the words to tell him about Edith leaving and to explain again that someone he cared about had walked out of his life.

"Did you like Miss Edith?"

Jeremy nodded.

"I did, too. But she had to go visit her little girl for a while, so we'll have to find someone else to take care of you."

"Cable?" he asked.

The hope in Jeremy's face only underscored Sara's growing concern about Cable becoming the baby-sitter. She should be relieved that Jeremy wanted to be with him, but all she could see was the potential heartache that waited at the end of their stay.

"Would you like Cable to take care of you?"

"Uh-huh. I like him."

"You do? Why?"

"'Cause he's big and strong like a daddy."

Sara sighed heavily. She was fighting a losing battle. "We'll talk about it some more later, okay? I just don't want you to be sad about Edith leaving."

"Okay," he agreed, and turned another page of the book with the flat of his chubby hand. "Read this page first, Mommy, where Scuffy bumps the cow's nose."

Sara read him the story, with part of her mind puzzling over Jeremy's reaction. He didn't seem the least bit upset about Edith leaving. His only thought was to be with Cable.

Had she made the right decision? After all, Cable wasn't equipped to handle an energetic three-year-old whose favorite question was "Why?"

Who was she kidding? she asked herself at last. There wasn't any other choice to make. She and Cable both hated it, but it was either let him become the sitter or call Ken and tell him to send someone else in to finish her job.

Depending on Cable, however, left her feeling uneasy. His hot-and-cold attitude kept her on edge. He could wake up tomorrow and change his mind. For all she knew, he could pack his bags and steal away in the night like the proverbial thief. Who could predict what a man would do? Doubts about her decision plagued her as she worked the next couple of hours. Tired and stiff, she finally stretched, desperate for bed. But she was still so far behind.

She went to check on Jeremy and found him cuddled up with Doggie. On the floor beside the bed was the little book. Sara picked it up, remembering what Jeremy had said about Cable—how *Scuffy the Tugboat* had been his son's favorite story and how remembering made him sad.

Ken had said Cable never talked about his family. But he'd told her about them, and now he'd told Jeremy. Was that an indication that he was ready to talk? Maybe all he needed was someone with a willing ear. She was willing. After all, she had promised Ken, and she should at least make a genuine effort to help Cable.

But how did she approach this? She couldn't just barge in and order him to bare his soul. That might be possible if they were friends, but they weren't. So how did she let him know she was willing to listen?

She glanced down at the book she still held. Maybe it would help if he had something of his son's to keep, something his son had liked. Opening up the book, she read the inscription, then she went in search of Cable.

She found him on the front porch again. This must be his favorite place to go and think. He turned as she came through the door. "I thought you might like to have this back." She hesitated a moment, then held out the book.

Cable took it from her hand, a deep frown creasing his forehead. "Why?"

"Jeremy said it was your son's favorite book."

"No," he said quietly, handing it back to her.

"But Jeremy said—"

"He misunderstood."

"Oh, well," she muttered, feeling awkward now that her gesture had backfired. "What was his favorite book? If it's one of the others, I'll put it aside so it doesn't get damaged."

"I've forgotten," he said, shoving his hands into the back pockets of his jeans. He leaned against the post and stared out into the dark, ignoring her.

Sara toyed with the book, knowing she should drop the matter, but strangely unwilling to do so. "Well, if you think of it—"

"I won't."

He sounded so hopeless she couldn't help but offer encouragement. "But you might, and I could..."

Cable faced her, his jaw rigid. "I don't want to remember."

His deceptively calm, low tone was more disturbing than if he'd shouted at her. She'd hoped to reach out to him, but instead she'd only succeeded in driving him further into his hell.

His declaration that he didn't want to remember worried her. She couldn't let it drop; she had to push him a little harder. "Cable, you have to remember. It's important."

"Why?" he demanded.

She took a step toward him. "Because it's part of the process of grief. Because it'll only make you hurt more if you don't remember."

Cable stood silently a moment, as if considering her words. "I remember them," he said. "I remember who they are and what they looked like but..." He rubbed his forehead, then leaned heavily against the post.

Now she understood what was bothering him, and she could completely empathize with his dilemma. She went to his side, careful not too get to close. He wasn't ready to share his space as yet.

"But you can't recall the sound of their voices, or the feel of them in your arms. You've forgotten the touch of their hands. Their faces have started to blur in your mind."

Cable turned and stared at her as if she'd just read his mind. "Yes."

"Cable, that's normal when people die or...go away. Their images fade a bit in our minds. That's why we keep mementos and why visiting a grave is often comforting. I gives the person left behind something tangible to hold on to."

Sara couldn't tell if she was getting through or not. He stood stiff and tense, his back toward her. "When you feel like they're fading, take out their pictures and look a them."

"I don't have any."

She wasn't prepared for his reply. Sara had always assumed he had pictures of his wife and son in his room. She recalled her early impression of Cable, and how there was no sign of his personality reflected in the house. She was beginning to understand why. But surely he had brought pictures or some small personal items with him.

"You must have something of your wife's or of Todd' that you cherish. What about the books and the toys?"

"Those were here. I didn't bring them."

Stunned, she could only ask, "Why?"

"Because that's over and done with," he said firmly. "Keeping trinkets and pictures around won't bring them back."

She was at a loss to know what else to say. She couldn't force him to remember, and she didn't have the energy to pursue the topic. Tired and dejected, she sat on the steps. She really should be going to bed instead of trying to play therapist to a crab.

It was a balmy night. A soft breeze rustled the new leaves and the fragrance of flowers laced the air. She could go to sleep right here if she didn't have so much still to do. Closing her eyes, she leaned her head against the post.

"What happened to Jeremy's father?"

She looked up at Cable when he spoke. She was so drowsy she hadn't realized he'd come to stand behind her. "Why do you ask?"

"He mentioned him today."

Sara sighed deeply. "Officially, we're divorced, but he might as well be dead. Sometimes I think it would be easier if he were."

"You don't mean that, do you?"

"No," she admitted, "but it would be easier for Jeremy to understand. Try explaining to a three-year-old that, yes, he has a daddy, but his daddy doesn't want anything to do with him."

"At least you have hope that someday he'll change his mind and want to be with Jeremy. There's no such option with death."

Sara could have cut off her tongue. How could she have been so insensitive? She had been thinking only of herself. She must have wounded him deeply. "Oh, Cable, I'm sorry. That was a terribly thoughtless thing to say."

Cable was silent a long moment before he spoke again. "You must have loved him once."

"I did. But that's when I believed in the forever-after kind of love."

"You don't now?"

"No. It's something that has ceased to be. Like stay-at-home mothers and one-income families."

"You must have seen a lot of failed marriages in your short life."

"No. Actually, my family has been quite lucky. My parents have a wonderful marriage, and my brothers are mostly all happily married. One lost his wife a few years ago, but he's dealing with it."

"Then why are you so cynical? Seems to me you have a lot of reasons to still believe in love."

"I didn't inherit my family's ability to choose the right partner. I have this faulty mechanism in my brain somewhere. I tend to pick the wrong kind of people to trust."

"And they let you down?"

Sara smiled ruefully. "You think you know a person inside out, then they do something unexpected and so out of character you realize you didn't know them at all. I know I made a horrible error in judgment when I married. It gave me a son, but it cost him his father. I should have seen—"

"Mommy!"

Jeremy's shriek pierced Sara's heart like a cold steel rod. "Oh, God." She stood and ran into the house, stopping only when she reached Jeremy's bedside.

"Mommy!"

"I'm here, sweetheart," she said, gathering him close. "It's all right." She pressed his head against her bosom, rocking him gently.

"I had a bad dream."

"I know. But it's all gone now. You're safe with Mommy and nothing can hurt you." She rested her cheek on his head, realizing only then that Cable stood close by. The deep crease in his forehead and the worry in his eyes mirrored her own.

"Does he have nightmares often?" he asked quietly.

Sara shook her head, continuing to rock Jeremy in the age-old maternal rhythm.

Cable stooped down and tentatively stretched out a hand to stroke Jeremy's head. "You okay, sport?"

Jeremy sniffed and turned his head to look at Cable. "Uh-huh." He reached up, took hold of Cable's hand and hugged it against his little chest.

Affection for Jeremy shone clearly in Cable's eyes. His attachment to her son was as strong as Jeremy's to him. For the first time Sara considered the possibility that Cable might be as hurt by their leaving as Jeremy.

"It was a bad one, huh?" Cable asked the child, his voice filled with gentle understanding.

Jeremy nodded, still clutching Cable's big hand in his small one and resting his head on his mother's chest.

Cable's tenderness brought a lump to her throat. She'd never seen him like this—completely vulnerable. He had rushed to Jeremy's side as if he had a right, as if he needed to save him. As if he were the father.

The intimacy of the moment slammed into her with hurricane force. The three of them were bound together, heart-to-heart, hand-to-hand, as surely as any family. They could be a mother and a father coming together to comfort their child.

She was afraid to look into Cable's eyes for fear she would find that he was feeling the unnatural intimacy as well. Playing house was dangerous. Playing mommy and daddy could be disastrous.

Sensing Jeremy was calm at last Sara laid him back against the pillow. He stubbornly clutched two of Cable's fingers, but the big man didn't seem to mind. "You want Mommy to stay with you awhile?"

Jeremy nodded. "And Cable."

She looked up. "Would you mind?" she asked.

The sadness in his eyes siphoned the very air from her lungs. She'd seen many emotions in those deep, thoughtful eyes—tenderness, anger, disapproval, amusement—but never such raw pain. Never such agony of spirit. For a fleeting second she could see deep inside him, down to his soul.

She'd never meant to cause him such anguish. She should never have asked him to stay. "I'm sorry."

He shook his head and looked away, but he continued to cling to Jeremy's hand and Sara wondered who was holding on to whom.

When Jeremy finally fell asleep, Cable gently reclaimed his hand and, without a word, left the room.

Tears blurred Sara's vision as she watched him go. Her heart still ached from the pain she'd witnessed in his eyes. Didn't he see that by denying his grief he was making his life more painful? He was eating himself up inside. She had to do something to help him.

Cable was a sensitive, caring human being. A man like him would be devastated by the loss of those he loved. Perhaps withdrawing had been his only choice at first, but he couldn't stop living.

Inside that shell was a man of infinite gentleness with a compassionate spirit. It was obvious to anyone with eyes that Cable was a man who needed a family, a man who was meant to be a father. Even if he didn't realize it.

Ken was right. It wasn't good for Cable to hold all his emotions inside, denying and suppressing them. One day they might explode and destroy him.

It was time she acted upon her boss's request. She couldn't stand by passively and let Cable slowly destroy himself. One way or another she was going to find a way to pry Cable McRay from his shell once and for all. He had to put the past behind him and pour all that gentle tenderness on people he loved and who loved him.

## Chapter Eight

Cable went directly to the shop and set to work on the gate he was making to close off the drying room. It would provide a safe place for Jeremy to play when he was using the power tools.

But it wasn't Jeremy's safety that had his emotions churning, it was Sara and her beautiful, inquisitive eyes. One penetrating glance from her could pierce his walls and expose the very foundations of who he was. That curious, limpid blue gaze had the power to see through his defenses into places she had no business seeing, forcing him to face unsightly truths about himself.

Who was he kidding? It wasn't Sara, it was him. He didn't want to accept the fact that his life was falling apart. He couldn't sleep, couldn't eat, and the nightmares he'd had after the accident were returning. He wasn't sure he could hold out for the remainder of their stay.

"Cable, are you all right?"

He tensed at the sound of Sara's voice. He tried to ignore her, but knew it was impossible. He hadn't been able to ignore anything about her since she'd first knocked on his front door. But he sure as hell didn't want to talk to her tonight. He was still shaken by the feelings generated by Jeremy's nightmare. The image of the three of them clustered together like a family filled him with more terror and sadness than anything he'd ever known. It had been all he could do to stay in the room until Jeremy fell asleep. "What do you want?"

"I wanted to thank you for your help with Jeremy. I know that must have been difficult."

Difficult? That was the understatement of the year. It had been agonizing torment. Excruciating horror. It had been sheer hell. "You could say that." He made no attempt to keep the sarcasm from his tone.

"Cable, you have to get past this grief," she urged gently. "You have to deal with the past or you'll never be able to go on with the future."

Her soft voice tempted him to open up and share his pain. She had drawn information from him before with her caring nature, her gentle probing—information he'd not meant to give. Not this time. If he opened up to her now, he'd never stop. Once he shared his grief with her, he'd be vulnerable and at the mercy of his pain, and he couldn't stand any more. "You'd better go back to Jeremy," he said, picking up the rasp.

"Cable, you need to face the loss, talk about your family and what they meant to you. You have to stop existing in this state of denial."

"I've never denied anything." He moved behind the workbench, purposely placing a barrier between them.

"Can't you talk to me about them?" she urged quietly. "I'm a good listener and I'm really interested in learning about them. All the toys and books Jeremy plays with were once Todd's. I'd like to know him, to know what he was like and what he liked to do."

He wanted to tell her. Wanted to let it all go. He wanted to let Sara hold him the way she did Jeremy. He needed someone to understand, and Sara would. She'd had a finger on his pulse from the moment their eyes first met. But he couldn't. The consequences were too frightening. "There's nothing to tell."

"Of course there is. You have ten years' worth of memories."

"No, there's not," he persisted, his hand clenching the rasp so fiercely his knuckles whitened.

"Cable, if you'd just give it a try..."

He tossed the tool on the bench. "You want to talk about the past, then let's talk about yours. Tell me about your problems."

Fear flared in Sara's eyes before she looked away. Apparently, she hadn't been prepared for his counterattack. He was playing dirty, but right now, he didn't care.

"My life is just fine," she said firmly. "I have no complaints. I've got a good job and a beautiful child."

Her bravado wasn't very convincing. "You have the perfect life?"

"Yes."

"Then why are you divorced?"

Sara inhaled sharply, pricking his conscience. He didn't have to be cruel to her.

"That was my past life. My life now is perfect."

Cable moved from behind the workbench toward her. "You just told me the past had to be settled before you could live in the present. You don't take your own advice?"

"I've dealt with my past. You haven't," she said, taking a few steps backward.

"Then tell me how you did it." Cable stood toe-to-toe with her now. "How did you overcome your pain so easily?"

"We were talking about you."

"*Now* we're talking about you," he countered.

Sara crossed her arms over her chest and glared at him defiantly. "There's nothing to tell. I was married and now I'm not."

"You left him?" The answer was suddenly very important to him.

"He left me."

Cable's anger evaporated, his heart filled with sympathy and understanding. It must have been awful for a caring, loving woman like Sara to be rejected. His admiration for her strength and determination grew. "I can't image anyone leaving you or Jeremy."

For a moment, he thought she was going to cry. Her eyes glistened brightly before she looked away. But when she met his gaze again, they were dry and hard.

"Well, imagine it. He walked out the moment he found out I was pregnant. He didn't want me and he didn't want Jeremy." Sara turned and moved away a little. "I thought I knew him. I thought I understood him. I thought...we wanted the same things. But he walked away. Without a word of regret. Just turned off the love and left."

Overcome with remorse for pushing her to reveal her own pain, Cable quickly apologized. "I'm sorry."

"Don't be," she said sarcastically. "It was just the single biggest mistake of my life so far. But that's in the past and doesn't concern me anymore."

Sara's attempt to downplay her lingering sorrow touched him. He understood what she was experiencing. Loss was loss, no matter what the circumstances. "It concerns Jeremy," he said. "He needs a father."

"Well, he doesn't have one. All he has is me, and that'll have to be enough."

"You don't plan on marrying again?" It was a question he had to ask, even though he had a strange reluctance to hear her answer.

"No. Do you have any idea what it's like starting a relationship when you have a child? Oh, the men are interested enough, until they find out I have a little boy. Then it's so long, Sara. That's too much responsibility for them."

Cable swallowed the lump in his throat. God, what he wouldn't give to have his responsibility returned to him. "Jeremy is a great kid. Any man would be proud to have him for a son."

"Not his father!" Sara practically shouted.

Cable wished he could go to her and hold her close until the sadness left her blue eyes. But he couldn't. She wouldn't permit it. He watched as she pulled herself together with her customary determination.

"Jeremy and I are doing just fine," she said firmly. "We have each other and that's all we need."

"Is it? I think you want and need something more, Sara."

Fear flashed in the blue depths again. Was it possible she didn't know what she wanted? he wondered. That she hadn't realized she was looking for a man to be a father to Jeremy and a loving husband and friend to herself?

Had he been the only one to sense the intimacy that was growing among the three of them? Was this physical pull that wrapped itself around him whenever he thought of Sara one-sided?

Sara looked into his eyes and beyond his defenses again, stirring a need so strong and so fierce it was all he could do to withstand it. What would she do if he kissed her? Now, this minute? The thought was like a Bunsen burner turned up in his blood, driving him to act upon this all too tempting and powerful urge.

He wanted to taste her sweet, pouty mouth, to ferret out its secrets. He wanted to kiss her until she was soft and pliant beneath his lips, clinging to him and as hungry for him as he was for her.

His desire must have been reflected upon his face or in his eyes, because Sara suddenly broke eye contact.

"What I need is to get this store open, so we can go. That's what I need."

Before he could reply, she turned and walked out of the shop, leaving Cable with an uneasy feeling that they had crossed a threshold tonight. A threshold to what, however, he was afraid to contemplate.

Sara pulled her car to a stop at the end of the drive alongside Cable's truck. Her fears about her landlord watching Jeremy had been groundless. Over the last week he had proved to be more than capable, and Jeremy was as happy as a clam.

She still worried about her son's growing dependence on Cable and how it would affect him when they left. For the moment everything had turned out reasonably well. With Jeremy taken care of she'd been able to concentrate fully on the store, and she'd be back on schedule by tomorrow.

Climbing out of the car, she pushed open the gate, and had started toward the house when something caught her eye. It took her a moment to realize what was different. An old-fashioned tire swing swayed gently from the thick limb of the oak tree in the backyard. It hadn't been here this morning. Cable must have made it for Jeremy.

Her foolish heart softened at the thought of Cable going out of his way to make her son special things like sandpiles and swings. But she told herself sternly to remember the other side of his kindness. When they left, she would have a heavy price to pay. A price paid by Jeremy's young heart.

The aroma of delicious food cooking greeted her as she climbed the back-porch steps. She inhaled deeply and smiled. Coming home to a hot meal each evening was the best part of the day.

Thanks to this new arrangement, she was eating better, sleeping better and, as a result, getting more done at the store.

Sara reached out to grasp the door handle and froze. Through the misshapen screen she could see Jeremy putting silverware on the table. Cable stood at the counter filling glasses with ice cubes. He looked over his shoulder at her and grinned. "You're right on time. We've got dinner ready."

Like a ghostly video, her most-cherished dream had suddenly come to life before her eyes. The scene before her was all too familiar, all too reminiscent of things she kept locked away in a secret corner of her mind.

In a state of shock, Sara could only stare mutely back at him. Until this moment she'd not fully realized the pseudofamily situation that had developed among the three of them. There had been that moment in Jeremy's room when he'd awakened from his nightmare, but that was one isolated incident.

This was different. Somehow they had started to act like a real family. The mommy and daddy roles were reversed, but were terrifyingly clear in their pattern. Cable had dinner ready at the end of the day, the house taken care of and Jeremy scrubbed and clean.

Like the dutiful breadwinner, she came home, ate dinner, helped clean up and put Jeremy to bed.

The scenario terrified her. When had they slipped into this routine? It was the worst thing that could have happened. She'd always longed for a real family for her son, but not like this. Jeremy would experience a family here, the way she'd always hoped, but it was a lie, a trick, and when it ended, he'd be disillusioned and heartbroken. He would never understand.

She did. She knew it was false, created out of unusual but necessary circumstances. Jeremy didn't.

Sara stood at the door, afraid to move. Afraid to play out this dream to its conclusion. It wasn't the fact that they behaved as a family that terrified her, it was the realization of how much she liked the whole idea. She liked feeling part of a family. She liked Cable being here. She liked the comfort and predictability of it.

It was the life she'd always imagined and secretly hoped for. Being confronted with it, however, was another thing. Reality and fantasy didn't mesh. This wasn't real. This man wasn't her husband, only someone who was watching her child. This wasn't her house; she was only a boarder here.

"Sara, are you coming in?"

Slowly she pulled open the door, sharpening her vision and bringing the scene into clear focus. It wasn't too late. There was still time to inject some reality.

Sara waited anxiously in the kitchen for Cable to join her. Supper had been a disaster. In light of her discovery, she'd been tense and uncommunicative. Cable had eyed her suspiciously, but thankfully, he'd not questioned her.

She'd escaped as quickly as possible, and as soon as Jeremy was asleep, she'd gone in search of her landlord. She'd found him on the porch again. They needed to talk, but not out on the porch, with its scented breezes and pale moonlight, but rather someplace neutral and safe. She'd asked him to join her inside.

"Sara, is anything wrong?"

She faced him, determined to explain her concerns no matter how they sounded. "Yes, potentially," she replied.

Cable raised an eyebrow. "Potential trouble. In what way?"

Taking a deep breath, she plunged in. "First, I want you to know how grateful I am to you for taking such good care of my son. But I'd appreciate it if you would keep your distance from him."

"I don't think I know what you mean."

"I'm concerned about Jeremy's dependency on you and how it will affect him when we leave here."

Cable's frown deepened and Sara hastened to explain further. "Don't try and become too important to Jeremy. I mean, watch him, of course, but don't get too close emotionally."

Cable rested his hands on his hips. "How do you suggest I do that?"

"I don't know," she admitted. This was harder than she'd thought. "Stop making things so permanent. Stop making him blocks and sandpiles and swings in the backyard." Even to her own ears her request sounded absurd. "Stop trying to be his hero."

"I'm not trying to be anyone's hero, Sara. I'm just the baby-sitter. I make sure he's fed and rested and safe. That's all."

"No, that's not all. You do all this extra stuff, like building swings and giving him Doggie."

"I'm just trying to give him things that'll keep him entertained. New toys to help pass the time."

"Things that make you look like a superhero." She cringed at how petty she sounded.

"What do you want, Sara? You want me to lock him in his room and shove a plate of food under the door twice a day?"

"Of course not. I'm just concerned about when we leave here. He's become so attached to you so quickly." Sara ran a hand through her hair, struggling to find the words to make him understand. "Jeremy is a little boy. He doesn't understand about why people leave him—first his father, then Mrs. Louis and Edith, and eventually, you, too. How will it affect him?"

"It'll be difficult, and you have a legitimate concern. But you're not giving Jeremy enough credit." Cable came to her side. "Are you sure it's Jeremy's emotions you're afraid of?"

"What else could it possibly be?"

"Maybe this?"

There was no time to prepare or protest. Cable pulled her to him, and his mouth descended on hers in a fierce kiss that set her blood on fire and stole the strength from her body.

His kiss was wild and hungry. His lips devoured hers, tasting, nipping, taking all he could find. Sara couldn't resist. She opened to him, grasping the torrent of excitement he was creating and letting it take her where it would.

Oh, how she missed this—the dark, private world of sensation and passion where nothing else could intrude. She wanted to stay in Cable's special corner of sensual reality. She wanted to feast upon him, to cling to him and become part of him.

Lost in the shock and the exciting unexpectedness of his kiss, she sagged against him, on the verge of surrender—until her mind grabbed control of her senses. As she pressed her hands against his hard chest and ended the kiss, she could feel the fierce pounding of his heart.

She looked up into his eyes and read regret and awkwardness in the dark depths before he stepped back.

"I'm sorry. I . . ." He brushed past her and out the door.

Why had he done that? What had possessed him to kiss her like a desperate lover? Maybe a better question would be why had she allowed him to?

Shaken and disturbed, Sara started back to her room, her fingertips absently touching her lips. There was a truth here that she was trying to ignore, but she'd learned that avoidance only complicated any situation.

In the safety of her own rooms, she took a deep breath and forced herself to ask the questions that were at the root of her confusion. Why had she wanted Cable to kiss her, and why had she been so quick to respond?

Because she was lonely, she admitted. Because he was attractive. Because, dammit, she'd wondered what it would be like to kiss him from the moment she'd returned from Nashville.

There. She'd faced the truth. She found Cable McRay sexy, tempting and very exciting. So what? He was also a man who behaved unpredictably. A man who had no place in her life.

Sara sighed and sat down in the window seat. He was also the man who'd just made her face something she'd been denying: she wasn't really afraid of Jeremy's attachment to Cable, it was her own feelings that scared her. She couldn't let her foolish, impetuous heart drag her into another messy relationship. Cable stimulated every womanly part of her, she realized. He had the capability of becoming someone special to her.

But even with all his potential, he was able to turn off his love and grief. What if that was a pattern with him? What if, whenever love or closeness became uncomfortable, whenever he thought something might cause him pain, he would turn off his feelings?

She couldn't risk that. She'd never withstand that rejection again, and she'd die before she exposed Jeremy to such pain. She had to take control of her life once more. She had to remember this wasn't real and could never be.

This false family arrangement they were trapped in was beginning to affect them all. They were starting to believe they really were a family. If something wasn't done soon, they were all going to be hurt.

The sun was barely up when Cable turned on the coffeemaker. He'd started getting up earlier since he'd become Jeremy's sitter. This way he could get a few hours work done in the shop before Jeremy woke up. He'd fallen behind on his furniture orders, but his customers knew he worked at his own pace, so the delays wouldn't hurt his business.

He'd also moved the computer into the house, so he could work while Jeremy napped. In only a week, his life had completely changed. Without even realizing it, he had adjusted his routine to accommodate a three-year-old child. Strange how easily it had all fallen into place.

Opening the cupboard, Cable reached for a cup, stopping in midmotion when he saw the box of Crackly Grainflakes and the bottle of flavored, dinosaur-shaped vitamins on the shelf.

A quiver of anxiety made his heart beat faster. Bit by bit, day by day, Jeremy and Sara were staking out a place in his home and in his life. If he wasn't careful, they would stake out a place in his heart as well.

He had to guard against that possibility. He also had to guard against his own weaknesses—such as his uncontrollable need to kiss Sara. He'd fought it, of course. He'd told himself it would be a mistake, and it had been.

One taste of Sara didn't satisfy his curiosity and didn't curb his craving. What it did do was stir up all kinds of other needs and longings that had been blissfully dormant. Now that those needs had been unleashed, they were gathering strength and momentum and threatening to get out of control.

Taking a deep breath, he forced himself to calm down. It was only for a few weeks, after all. Though the situation was awkward for all of them, it was completely unavoidable. They'd all have to get through it as best they could. But dear God, where was he going to find the strength to do this?

He needed protection. He needed something to place between himself and the situation. Closing his eyes, he called forth images of Amanda and Todd, willing himself to recall what cereal Todd liked, what song Amanda always sang, what color the damned carpet in their house had been.

He tried again. He needed those memories now to combat this assault from the outside by Sara and Jeremy.

Nothing came.

What kind of man was he that he could forget everything about his wife and son, yet remember in torrid detail each moment with Sara, and with precise clarity, every cute thing Jeremy had done? And why did he find a measure of comfort in these new memories?

This latest realization brought Sara's concerns to the forefront of his mind. Did that mean he was letting this little boy take the place of his son?

Maybe Sara was right. Maybe getting too close to Jeremy was a bad idea. He'd take her advice and keep it cool and distant. Do what was necessary, but no more. Jeremy's heart wasn't the only one likely to be broken when Sara and her son left Carswell. If he wasn't careful, his own might suffer as well.

For the time being, he'd keep such thoughts to himself. Sara had enough on her mind without worrying that the baby-sitter was thinking of jumping ship.

Sara glanced out the window from her sitting room, noticing the waning daylight. She checked her watch: it was almost Jeremy's bedtime. If she hurried, she could finish going over the employment applications before she had to get him to sleep. The ringing of the phone rudely interrupted her concentration. With a sigh of irritation, she answered it.

"Hey, Sara. How's it going?"

Ken's cheery voice was at odds with her own sour mood. "Just great," she drawled sarcastically. "Cable is my new baby-sitter."

Ken's laughter spilled across the wire. "That's great! That ought to shake him up a bit."

His comment about Cable made her unexpectedly defensive. "It did, and it's been very difficult for him. I wish there was some other way."

"Isn't he good with Jeremy?"

"He's wonderful."

"So everything sounds perfect. Has he told you anything more?"

"Not really. You were right, though—he needs to grieve, to talk about his family. But for some reason he's still holding back."

"Give him time. How about you? Are you okay?"

No, she wanted to tell him. She was confused and tired and losing control of her life. "Sure, I'm caught up at work finally. We should be—"

"I meant with Cable," Ken interrupted.

She didn't want to talk about Cable. "We get along okay."

"Just okay?"

"He's not my type." *His kisses are my type,* her mind cried.

"Why's that?"

"Lots of reasons, not the least of which is that he blows hot and cold like a broken furnace. I never know if he's for me or against me. Besides, I'm not getting involved with anyone, so you can stop playing matchmaker."

"You need to be involved."

Sara gritted her teeth. Sometimes Ken didn't know when to stop meddling. "Let me decide that. Right now all I'm concerned about is that promotion."

An ominous silence hung on the other end of the line. "Yeah, uh, Sara, I need to talk to you about that."

Sara knew what that tone signified, and her stomach began to twist into a cold knot.

"Greg Russell got the job," Ken continued soberly. "Baker thought he'd be more aggressive, more flexible. And . . . he was available."

Shock and disbelief washed through Sara. "It was her visit here, wasn't it?" she guessed.

"No," he reassured her. "It was a question of timing, that's all."

"And mine stunk."

"Sara, this is just one position. One opportunity. Something else will come along for you, probably something better."

"Sure, someday. Maybe when Jeremy is fifteen or thirty, maybe!"

"It will all work out, Sara. Believe me."

"Sure, Ken. Goodbye."

She pressed the disconnect button and leaned her head against the back of the chair. She'd been so sure the job was in her pocket. Everything had pointed to her as the best one for the position. Disappointment rose in her like floodwater as she struggled to understand how this opportunity had slipped through her fingers. What had she done wrong? What mistake had she made this time?

"Mommy, will you come and play blocks with me?"

Jeremy's eager voice pierced her dark thoughts. She looked down at his smiling face. Only this time her spirits didn't lift, they just sagged further. The promotion would have benefited him and his future. It would have given her more time with him.

"Will you, Mommy?"

Time. She had time now to give him. Getting the store open on schedule wasn't as pressing as it had been a moment ago.

"Sure, sweetie, I'll play with you." Sara took his hand and they went out to the front porch. The box of wooden blocks Cable had made for Jeremy sat on the floor in front of the swing.

The light rain that fell lent a clean, fresh smell to the early evening air. The soft patter of raindrops created a cozy haven in the broad, well-protected front porch.

Jeremy dumped the box over and started to build a wall, while Sara made a halfhearted attempt to assist him. She wished she could do this more often, but without the promotion, their moments together would decrease.

Wall complete, Jeremy knocked it down and began building a house. Sara went to sit on the swing, her mood darkening. Her plans to get out of their cramped apartment and buy a small house to live in were gone. She'd wanted Jeremy to have a real home, with a yard and a swing like he had here. Without the promotion, she was stuck. She'd either have to change jobs and start over or stay with Dixie Mart and forfeit time with Jeremy.

Obstacles that had once seemed challenging now appeared impossible to overcome. All her efforts for the last year had been totally ineffectual.

A sob welled up from deep inside her, and tears stung the back of her eyes, spilling down her cheeks. She hated it when she cried. It was a weakness she didn't often indulge in.

"Mommy, why are you crying?" Jeremy leaned against her leg, his little hand patting her knee. With a sob she picked him up and set him on her lap, hugging him close to her heart. There had to be a solution somewhere. She'd just have to try harder and juggle faster.

"Mommy's feeling tired and a little sad," she explained, stroking his head gently.

"I don't want you to cry, Mommy."

"It's okay. Sometimes grown-ups cry, but it's a good thing. Crying helps them get out all their sad feelings and then they feel better."

Sara wrapped her arms more securely around Jeremy, swinging slowly back and forth to the reassuring squeak of the chain. She'd pinned all her hopes on that promotion. It would have been the perfect solution to all her problems.

She was so tired, and it was becoming harder and harder to dredge up the strength to face each day. Every direction she looked she could find no way out, no alternative. The future seemed so futile, like fighting a dragon with a toothpick. Feelings of fear and loneliness overwhelmed her.

Crying softly, she wrapped her arms around Jeremy, unaware that he had fallen asleep.

When she finally opened her eyes, she saw Cable standing in front of her. She tried to control her emotions, but it was impossible. The tears refused to stop. She wiped at her eyes with her free hand. "I'm sorry—I . . ." What could she say?

"Here, let me have him."

Sara released Jeremy to Cable's capable hands and watched as he carried the sleeping child into the house.

Cable and Jeremy. She loved seeing them together. Cable was so gentle, so patient with her son. If only he could make the world right for her, too, with a simple pat on the head.

When he returned, he sat beside her on the swing. "Jeremy didn't move a muscle when I put him in bed."

She nodded in acknowledgment but averted her eyes, trying to stop the fresh flow of tears. The disappointment was too overwhelming. She'd worked so hard, had had such faith, but she'd failed miserably.

Cable pulled her near, so that her head rested on his shoulder while she cried. At first she resisted his embrace, but as the warmth of his arms enfolded her, she gave herself over to the comfort she found there. Letting someone else be strong for a moment, being held and soothed by capable male arms, were luxuries she never allowed herself. She needed both desperately right now.

Unconsciously she curled her fingers into his shirt as she let the tears come, venting all the pent-up stress and disappointment, aware only of the comfort and reassurance she found in his warm, secure embrace.

Drake had always been afraid of tears. He'd made her feel ashamed and childish when she cried. Cable knew exactly what to do—hold her close and shut up.

Tired and emotionally drained, Sara felt her tears finally start to subside. She took the handkerchief Cable offered and reluctantly extracted herself somewhat from his embrace. She was still vividly aware of their bodies pressed close together. Each time she breathed, their shoulders brushed against each other seductively.

"Are you all right?"

She nodded, then shook her head. Now that she was thinking more clearly, her disappointment was turning to anger. "No. I'm furious! I'd like to punch someone."

"You can punch me if you think it'll help."

Sara smiled, starting to regain her perspective. "No, I won't take it out on you. I've done enough damage to your shirt." She motioned toward the damp spot on his chest.

"A small sacrifice to be made for a lady in distress."

Sara wiped at her eyes and blew her nose. She wasn't usually such a whiner but she didn't seem to have the stamina she normally did. She couldn't shake this constant fatigue.

She was also feeling totally alone and in desperate need of someone to talk to, even if only to hear herself verbalize her own problems.

For a brief moment she wondered again why it was so easy to talk to Cable, then decided the reason wasn't important. She was simply grateful. All she needed to know was that Cable had a sympathetic ear. Inhaling deeply, she decided to take the risk. But she couldn't do that sitting so close to him. She needed a little space to think. She stood and walked to the porch rail. "I lost the promotion today. They gave it to some whiz kid fresh out of college."

"I'm sorry."

The sympathy in his voice nearly triggered a new flood of tears. "It's not fair," she continued with a sniff. "Why do the ones who do the least amount of work get the prize? It's as if good, honest hard work doesn't count anymore."

"The job meant a lot to you?"

"It wasn't the job itself," she said, facing him. "I mean, I didn't want it for the prestige or anything. Frankly, it would have been more work and more responsibility. I wanted it because it was a steady, nine-to-five desk job based in Nashville. It would have meant more time with Jeremy, weekends free and no out-of-town trips." She sighed sadly. "He's growing up so fast and I'm missing so much. I hate being away from him, but now I'll be away more than ever."

"Could you find another job?"

"That's not as easy as it sounds. I've got seniority with Dixie Mart, fantastic benefits and a good salary. I'd have to take a cut in pay anywhere else."

"Wouldn't it be worth it?"

"Yes, but I have so much invested in this job, in this project."

"Then maybe it's time to ask yourself what you really want."

Sara didn't have to think about her answer. "I want a life outside of the job. I want time in the afternoon to relax before making supper. I want to go shopping, to play with Jeremy or take a class. I want weekends free. I want to come home from work and not feel totally drained. But there's no way I can see to do that."

"There are always alternatives, Sara, if you look for them."

"Right. Like finding some man to help me out, and love Jeremy, too."

"You make it sound impossible."

"It is. Jeremy's own father doesn't want him. Where am I going to find a man who'd love him like his own?"

"There's someone for you, Sara. You just haven't found him yet."

She shook her head. "I wouldn't know where to look."

"They say love finds you, not the other way around."

"Do you believe that?"

"I don't know."

Sara looked into his eyes and saw sincerity and understanding reflected there. "Thank you for listening."

"That's what friends are for."

She realized in that moment that he *was* a friend. But she had no idea when or how he'd crossed that line. "You're really a nice man when you're not acting like a hermit crab."

Cable laughed out loud. "Is that how you think of me? Like a hermit crab?" he asked, standing and coming to her side.

Sara nodded, still in awe of the wonderful sound of his laughter. It warmed the hollowness inside and brought a smile to her own lips. "You hide inside your shop, and when anyone comes close, you pop out, snap your claws and scare them away."

Cable's smile faded, but the amusement still lingered in his eyes. "I suppose I have become a recluse since I came here."

She reached up to lay her palm against his cheek. "You had good reasons to want to hide, Cable. But maybe now it's time to start to heal, and you can't do that alone."

"Am I alone?" he asked softly, taking a step closer.

"No. I'm here. I'll help you if I can. You said we were...friends."

Sara saw the change in his eyes, the shift from uncertainty to decision. She inhaled, and the scent of him enfolded her even as his hands reached out to take her shoulders and draw her near. Her breasts flattened slightly against his hard chest and she tilted her head to receive his kiss. A kiss she both wanted and feared.

But he didn't capture her mouth immediately. Instead he eased his hands across her shoulders and up the sides of her neck, his thumbs brushing along her jaw.

His touch was so gentle, so erotic that Sara quivered with the pleasure of it. She'd never been touched with so much reverence and tenderness.

She looked into his dark, sultry brown eyes and flames ignited deep inside her. When at last his lips covered hers, she was ready, meeting his heat with her own building desire.

She didn't want his kiss to mean anything other than a way to dampen the blaze his look had ignited. She didn't want his lips to control her, to override all her edicts about men and relationships. But they did.

They were warm, gentle, caring, and she clung to him, opening herself to his exploration. His tongue teased the corners of her mouth, gently dipping between her lips to taste her more fully.

His arms held her tightly against his chest, and his heartbeat throbbed in time with her own. She knew she was lost when he transferred his kisses from her mouth to the soft, sensitive area behind her ear.

Cable had known it would be a mistake to kiss Sara again. But it would be a bigger mistake not to. He'd been fighting the urge to taste her lips again since the moment he'd found her on the swing in tears.

When she'd turned to look at him, his heart had melted. Her eyes were wide, moist; her lips quivered. She'd looked small and appealing and he'd ached to erase her sadness. He'd wanted to kiss away each tear, to smother her sobs with his lips and make her forget the unhappiness and the disappointment.

Sara's eyes should never be sad. He wanted her to be happy, to know only joy and passion. Passion under his hand, by his lips and from his body.

He'd pulled her to him, pleased to find how perfectly she fit against him. She tasted ripe and sweet, and he knew he'd never get enough of her kisses. Like a witch's spell, she would hold him from this moment forward. But he didn't give a damn.

He hadn't felt this alive, this vital in five years. Part of him had been dormant, so dead even he hadn't realized it.

Sara was calling to that part of him, awakening a need for something he'd denied himself for too long—the touch of a woman's hand. The soft caress of a caring voice, warm eyes filled with understanding.

The kiss had been meant to comfort, to share his need with her, one reaching out to the other. He wasn't prepared for the sudden bolt of lightning that struck them both.

He could see it in her eyes—the shock, the curiosity and then the desire. A desire so powerful, so compulsive it could devour them both.

Caught unaware, Sara went limp at the suddenness of the need that flashed through her. Curiosity and loneliness had begun this kiss, but suddenly, passion flared like a streaking comet, pushing everything else aside. All that remained was the need and the hunger.

They both felt it. They both feared it.

It was that fear that finally penetrated her passion-fogged brain. This wasn't real. This kiss, this awareness that lurked between them, was part of the illusion. Part of the fake family life they were all living. It had nothing to do with them personally.

Sara pushed away from Cable's embrace, wondering why she had this feeling of disappointment. She had to remember that he was a man in pain. He'd lost his family, and she and Jeremy were a convenient substitute. He'd kissed her because he'd momentarily lost touch with reality.

She, on the other hand, was succumbing to stress. Oh, she found Cable attractive, of course, but for all the wrong reasons. She was at a difficult point in her life. Cable was strong, tender and available, and in a moment of weakness, she'd taken advantage of his strength to lean on.

Cable released her, his arms lowering slowly to his sides. "Sara, I—"

She didn't want to hear him say he was sorry. She didn't want him to say he'd made a mistake, that she'd misunderstood. "Don't say anything, Cable," she interrupted quickly. "Please, don't say anything at all." She turned and hurried into the house, letting the screen door shut behind her.

## Chapter Nine

The kiss had created a strain between Sara and Cable that lasted for two days, and it was driving her crazy. By now she knew his habits. Whenever he was hurting he'd crawl into his shell and retreat to his hideout in the shop, avoiding her completely.

The last two evenings he'd left supper on the stove, and as soon as she'd come home, he'd disappeared. The sound of the table saw had been a steady screech far into the night.

She debated whether to try and reach him again, to encourage him to talk about his family. Her common sense told her to let it be. He was a grown man. How he handled his life was his own business. But then she would remember the pain in his eyes, the way his jaw would flex when he was hurting inside, and she wanted to help.

If he would just talk about them, even a little bit, it would be good. But he volunteered only minimal information, preferring to keep it all locked inside. Sometimes he reminded her of Jeremy. Cable was lost and afraid, needing someone to hold him, to hold on to. He needed someone who cared.

And Sara did care. More than she was willing to admit. She told herself the kiss they'd shared hadn't changed anything between them. But it had. It had changed her. She wanted to help him cut the bonds of the past and become free so he could find a new future.

She wanted it now not because Ken had asked her to, but for her own reasons. Reasons that both scared and excited her. The kiss, the brief closeness to Cable, had resurrected a need she'd denied for a very long time, the need to find the Sara she used to be. The Sara that had been lost somewhere in the struggle to survive.

It had been a long time since she'd thought of herself and her needs. She always came last behind Jeremy and the job, and she'd been perfectly content with that arrangement, until now.

Cable made her remember the passion that could still flow through her, that could ignite her being into vibrant life.

Each time she saw him, each time they talked, she was reminded of that part of her she'd suppressed for four long years. It was getting harder and harder to control her physical yearnings.

Her senses vibrated at his nearness as if caught in a magnetic field of awareness and recognition. Both her body and her heart were being drawn to him on some primitive, sexual level.

Now her imagination had gotten involved in the game. Each time she thought of Cable and the kiss they'd shared, she would start imagining what it would be like to make love to him. His tenderness would enfold her completely, making her feel safe. His gentle hands would explore every inch of her slowly and reverently. His lips would tease and caress her in all her most sensitive places, taking her on a sensual excursion to heaven.

It took considerable effort to rein in her imagination and remind herself that it was her common sense that should control her, nothing else.

Walking to the back door, she stared out into the night. The shop lights were on, but the accompanying whine of machinery was missing. Was Cable out there working or had he merely forgotten to turn off the lights?

When the silence continued, Sara grew uneasy. Maybe she should make sure everything was all right. With all those saws and other power tools out there, he could have injured himself. He was alone. If something had happened, no one would know for hours.

Concern segued into fear. Pushing open the door, Sara hurried down the steps toward the shop, her heart pounding furiously in her chest.

She skidded to a stop just inside the door when she saw Cable standing at the workbench, staring down at his wallet. Something about the slope of his shoulders worried her. She went to his side, laying her hand lightly upon his arm. "Cable?"

He turned to face her, his eyes clouded with sadness.

"Are you all right?"

When he didn't answer, Sara glanced at the open wallet. It held a picture of a lovely dark-haired woman and a smiling young boy. Now she understood the sadness in Cable's eyes. "Your wife and son?"

"Yes."

Sara squeezed his arm gently. "They're beautiful."

Cable nodded.

"You told me you didn't have any pictures."

"Only this one." Closing the wallet, he slipped it into his pocket and moved away.

Sara ached for him. She remembered the deep sense of abandonment, the insecurity and the fear of being somehow responsible when your partner left you behind. She remembered that ever-present fear that the future held only more suffering. But she also knew that with time, those feelings passed.

Walking after Cable she stopped once more at his side, debating whether or not to touch him again. Sometimes the touch of a hand could reassure. At other times a person was so emotionally fragile that a touch could be devastating.

At the moment, Cable looked as if he needed reassurance. "How long has it been?" she asked softly. She slipped her hand into his and he immediately squeezed her fingers, as if desperate to hold on to someone.

It took him a long moment before he answered her. "Five years."

"Five years!" She'd had no idea it had been that long ago. She'd assumed the loss was recent. Had he buried all his pain and sorrow for five long years? No wonder he was so withdrawn and tormented.

"Oh, Cable, why are you doing this to yourself? You have to face the grief. You have to let go of the pain and guilt."

He turned and looked at her, his face contorted with confusion. "How?"

The pain in his eyes scalded her heart and she laid her other hand on top of his in a gesture of comfort. "Start by talking about them. Get angry at them."

"I can't. They didn't die on purpose just to hurt me."

"Of course they didn't, and I know it's painful for you to think about them, but you have to."

Cable pulled his hand from her grasp. "Stop it, Sara. It's no use. Don't you think I want to talk about them? To tell you about all the wonderful times we had?" He stared at the floor a moment, as if gathering strength to go on. "I can't remember any good times, Sara. I can't remember anything at all."

A dreadful churning sensation swirled inside her as a horrible realization began to unfold. "You don't remember any of the things you did as a family? Nothing?"

"No!" He stepped away again abruptly, resting his hands on his hips. "Bits and pieces sometimes, but when I try to call up something specific—" he sighed heavily "—there's nothing there."

"Cable, you must remember something!"

He turned and faced her, his expression a mask of sorrow. "Yeah, I remember one thing. I remember coming home late from work one evening and finding the house empty. I didn't know where they were at first, then I remembered that Todd had soccer practice. I was supposed to meet them there, but I was too tired." He paused, inhaling deeply. "Then the phone rang and it was all over."

Sara could see his jaw working furiously in an attempt to control his emotions.

Her throat constricted as she choked back a sob. How had he gone so long with this emptiness inside him? To be stripped of his family and his memories was a cruelty she couldn't comprehend. Her eyes stung, welling with tears, but she fought them back. Cable needed her now; he needed someone to talk to, someone who understood. Her own emotions were immaterial.

"Oh, Cable." She went to him, wrapping her arms around his waist. He resisted the embrace for a moment, then relaxed and held her close. "I know it must have been horrible," she murmured. "I can't imagine what you went through, but you need to face it and deal with it. Unlock the memories before you destroy yourself. Your wife wouldn't want you to punish yourself this way."

"Wouldn't she? I don't know." He stepped away from her, running his hands through his hair. "God, Sara, why can't I remember anything about her? I try to remember our wedding day, but it's blank. I try to remember the day Todd was born, the day he took his first step, his fifth birthday, our tenth anniversary. Nothing is in here, Sara," he said, tapping his forehead. "Nothing. No dates, no places, no songs. Nothing."

Tears spilled down her cheeks, but she was barely conscious of them. Her only thought was to comfort Cable. She moved closer, went to him resting her hand on his back, massaging it gently. "Cable, did you love your wife and son?"

He scowled at her angrily. "Of course."

"Did they give you pleasure? Happiness?"

"Yes!"

"Then shouldn't you be celebrating those things? Memories aren't something to be ignored and buried along with the dead. They are meant to keep the ones we love alive, to comfort us when we feel alone."

"My memories only gave me more pain."

"I know it seems that way at first, but as time passes and the pain eases, the memories give you strength. Keep them alive, Cable." She could feel his resistance; the fear was too strong. There had to be a way to penetrate it.

She stroked his arm gently. Even through the fabric of his shirt she could feel the fierce tension in his muscles. "Think of your memories like an old blanket. When you're feeling cold and lonely, pull them out and wrap them around you. They'll warm you and give you some peace."

Cable shook his head.

Why was he so stubborn? Why didn't he see she was right? "You can't hold all this inside," she said, trying to keep the frustration from her voice. "It'll eat you up. Do you want to die, too?"

"I already died."

"No. You didn't. You may wish you had died but you didn't, and I refuse to believe that you are alive today just so you could run to this old house and lock yourself away."

"I did what I had to do. It's called survival. There was no other choice I could make."

Cable's words struck deep at Sara's heart. She saw it all clearly now. Ken was right; Cable had turned his back and walked away. She'd assumed he'd come here to grieve in private and take time to heal.

Anger and disillusionment welled within her. She'd thought she understood Cable, but she saw now she didn't know him at all. Her poor judgment had surfaced again. Her heart liked to believe everyone was exactly the way she saw them, but her head knew better. She should have listened to it.

Sara faced Cable, her anger spilling over its banks. "Choice? Are you saying you chose to forget?"

"No!"

His continued denial infuriated her. "I think you did. I think you came here to hide, and you stayed here for five long years because it was easier and safer. No memories, no pain. No pain, no feelings. No feelings, no risk. I don't call that survival, Cable. I call it self-centeredness. You were in pain, so you ran away to Grandma's house. Then you turned off all the feelings and the love, because it hurt too much."

"I didn't turn it off!"

"Didn't you? You ignore their existence. You pretend they never touched your life. You erase all memories because it's more convenient for you that way."

Sara looked at him and realized by the hard glint in his eyes that she'd infuriated him. It didn't matter. None of it mattered.

"I didn't ask for your advice," he growled.

"No, you didn't. You don't need my help, my advice, and you don't need your memories!" She turned to leave, then stopped and looked back at him. "I envy you your ability to shut off your feelings the way you shut off your saws. You apparently have a different definition of the word *love*. Love to me is constant and eternal. It endures through good and bad times. Nothing should be able to end real love. Anyone who can turn love off so easily never really loved in the first place."

"Stay out of my life, Sara!"

"Fine!" she shouted back. "I don't know why I thought I could help you anyway. I told Ken it was a stupid idea."

"What does he have to do with this?"

Sara couldn't believe she'd let that slip. Cable would never forgive her. "Nothing."

Cable advanced on her, his dark eyes burning with anger. "He sent you here. He told you to pry into my life and try and save me, didn't he?"

"No, it wasn't like that." She'd meant to comfort Cable, but instead she'd lost her temper and made things worse. "He's concerned about you. He helped me once when my life was shattered, and he just wanted to help you, too."

"I don't need anyone's help. I was fine until he sent you here. All he's done is stir up things better left forgotten."

"But Cable, don't you see, trying to forget *is* the problem. You hide under that shell and snap at anyone who comes close because you're afraid of remembering and getting hurt. You can't live your life that way."

"It's my life and I'll live it my way!"

"You like living in pain?"

"I wasn't in pain until you and Jeremy came. You've ruined everything."

Sara gasped. His words pierced her heart to the core. She'd been accused once before of ruining a man's life because of Jeremy. Drake had said virtually the same words to her when she'd told him she was pregnant.

The old pain surged into her heart. She really was a fool, making the same mistake again. She'd broken her own rule and allowed her heart to convince her that Cable was different. That Cable was special.

It took all her strength and willpower to pull herself out of the clutches of the past and grasp hold of her pride.

"You're right," she said. "I'm sure you were much happier before we came along. Maybe you are better off without your memories. Since you seem to be so comfortable with your pain, I'll leave you to it."

The moment the accusation was out of his mouth, Cable realized he'd wounded Sara deeply. He shouldn't have yelled at her, but he was scared, scared to exhume the memories and face them. He hadn't meant to blame her. The last thing he ever wanted to do was hurt Sara.

This was all Ken's fault. If he'd stayed out of it, this mess would never have happened.

It was bad enough when his cousin played matchmaker, but Ken had no right to involve Sara in his personal business. Cable paced the workshop, struggling to sort out all his tangled emotions.

Of one thing he was certain: Sara had only been trying to help. But was she helping because Ken had asked her to or because she wanted to?

He longed to believe there was more to her kindness than a promise to Ken. He wanted to think she'd reached out to him because she truly cared. But even if that were true, he'd destroyed any feelings she'd had by being harsh and unfair.

He longed to take back his cruel accusations and wipe away the pain in her blue eyes.

He'd never intended to tell Sara the complete truth about his lost memories. But she made him want to reach out to her, to tell her things, private things.

Now that he had, he felt a strange sense of relief and liberation, as if he'd been freed from some horrible imprisonment.

He should have expected her to comfort him one minute, then kick him in the pants the next. Sara would sympathize down to her toes, but she wouldn't tolerate self-pity.

She'd booted him pretty good, too, forcing him to ask questions he'd been avoiding.

Had he run away? Had he buried his love and all his grief because he was selfish? That hadn't been his intention. He'd simply wanted to stop hurting. Staying in Texas, driving the same streets, living in the same house, seeing pity and sadness in the eyes of their friends only magnified his pain and loss.

But it had been five years now. Maybe Sara was right and it was time to face the past, stop running from it. How would he find the courage to confront it? Too much time had passed, and he wasn't sure he could face it now even if he wanted to.

He needed help. He needed Sara's help. Somehow, he knew she was the only one who would understand. He needed her insight and understanding to show him the road back. But getting close to her was dangerous. The kisses they'd shared had shown him that.

It would be so easy to let Sara become important to him, to let this physical attraction lead to more intimate closeness. But he couldn't afford to reach out to her. He couldn't afford to let her into his heart. What if something happened to her or to Jeremy? He couldn't put his heart and soul at risk again.

But how could he go to her now and ask for help after he'd wounded her with his cruel words?

Looking around the shop, he saw what Sara had seen—a hideout, a place to shut out the real world. Was his refusal to accept the loss of his family the cause of his missing memories?

Sara thought that he'd stopped loving his wife and son. Had he? Had he denied his love, his feelings, because they hurt too much?

Cable ran a hand through his hair. God forgive him if that were true. He'd never intended to become bitter and self-centered. He just didn't want to hurt, didn't want to risk the agony of losing someone he loved again. He couldn't risk caring again because he couldn't risk losing again.

He longed for the numbness that had surrounded him before Sara and Jeremy had begun drawing him out into the light. But he knew now he could never go back. He'd opened himself to Sara and shared his secret fear.

He'd shared something personal and intimate with her. Nothing would be the same between them again.

So what the hell was he supposed to do now?

Sara curled onto her side, staring out the window into the moonlit spring night. A cool breeze gently ruffled the lace panels, bringing the heady fragrance of Confederate jasmine into her room.

She was tired and overworked, but it wasn't fatigue that kept her tossing and turning in the bed. It was a guilty conscience.

She had handled things poorly with Cable tonight. She'd pushed too hard, allowed her own feelings to blur the lines between her pain and his.

She'd taken his comment about her and Jeremy to heart because it was too similar to what Drake had said. She'd confused Drake's rejection of his family with Cable's rejection of his feelings. That wasn't fair.

Cable was hurting. He'd been suppressing his grief for five years, yet she'd expected him to face his problems and overcome them at her command.

She should have been more patient and understanding. Her fuse was short these days because she was tired, but that was no reason to ignore Cable's pain.

Now who was being selfish? Cable had needed her and she'd thought only of herself.

Sara closed her eyes, only to open them again when visions of Cable's pain-darkened eyes filled her mind. She still couldn't fully comprehend his memory loss. He must have been so devastated by his wife's and his son's deaths that he'd blocked anything that reminded him of them.

She could understand why that would have been necessary in the beginning, but it had been five years now. It was time for him to accept the situation and move on, no matter how difficult that was. If he didn't, the stress of his repressed grief would kill him.

How had he survived so long? How had he lived with it gnawing at him, eating him alive? She couldn't let him go on like this. He'd come out of his shell long enough to reveal his reason for hiding, but now she feared he'd crawl back inside and never come out again.

Cable reset the compound miter and collected the molding he needed to finish the armoire. Positioning the wood, he lowered the blade, making a perfect angle cut.

A few more days like this and he'd be caught up on his own work. He'd fallen behind since taking over as Jeremy's baby-sitter. But for the last few days, Sara had been working at home so she could be with Jeremy.

Freedom from his obligations not only provided an opportunity to catch up on his own work, but also gave him a valid reason to avoid Sara.

He'd been reluctant to get too close to her, now that he'd spilled his guts. Sara liked to probe him, peek behind his walls, and he wasn't ready to be examined again too soon. He should never have told her about his lost memories. He'd never meant to bare his soul that way.

But there was something about Sara, about being near her, that made him want to confide in her. Her caring nature reached out to him, wrapping itself around his fears and taking away the sting. Just talking to her eased his burden. It was a phenomenon he couldn't begin to understand.

He told himself he was avoiding her because he didn't want to delve into his problem, but that was only part of it. The truth was he stayed away because of how she made him feel whenever he looked at her. But not being around Sara didn't stop him from thinking about her and knowing where she was every second.

The kisses they'd shared haunted him. Everything about her haunted him, every minute, every hour, awake or asleep, in daydreams and even nightmares.

Images of her played in his thoughts all day—the way she walked; the bouncy little jog that drew attention to her gently rounded bottom and long legs.

The way her hair would move when she talked, brushing playfully against her forehead. The smile that threw light into his dark soul and almost made him gasp with the beauty of it.

The twinkle in her blue eyes that teased him, beckoning him to lose himself in her brightness. The way her lips would purse together when she was irritated with him.

Most of all he thought about her caring spirit and her warmth. She reached out to him, wanting to help him, pulling him out of the darkness of the past and into the sunlight of the future.

Being near Sara made him feel alive; she made him want to live again. She made him hungry, made him yearn to belong, to connect with another person. He missed the cocoon of love and contentment that a family could provide.

He'd started to notice the world around him. Simple things, like the sunset, the flowers in the yard and the sweet peacefulness of twilight. He looked at everything in a different way now. Even himself.

He hadn't realized how cold his life had become until Sara's warmth had touched him. And now that it had, he wanted more. He wanted the two of them touching completely, becoming one in the intimacy of a man and woman. His attraction for Sara went deeper than physical need.

She made him think about tomorrow. But how did he do that? Where did he start?

For five years all he'd thought about was today, the moment, and getting through it with as little disruption and discomfort as possible.

Life for him had been like walking a balance beam. Focus on one spot; move slowly and steadily toward it. Don't look away. Don't let anything distract you, because if you did, you'd lose your equilibrium and crash to the ground.

How did you get past the memory of the pain and loss? How did you find the courage to risk that pain and loss again and remain sane? It was too big a gamble. There was too much to lose.

No. Getting involved, allowing feelings for Sara to develop, was too risky a proposition.

He had to remember there was no place in his world for them. He had to remember that in a few weeks they would be gone and he would be left behind. He didn't need to feel more torn and lonely than he had before.

Cable switched off the saw. In the meantime, he would reassume his responsibilities and attempt to make the remaining time they were here as pleasant as possible. The least he could do was apologize to Sara for his outburst.

The cellular phone rang three times before Sara could tear her attention away from her computer and reach for it.

"Mrs. Nelson, this is Geri Arthur of the Caring Connection."

Sara gave her full attention to the call, her heart filling with hope.

"I have an opening," the woman continued. "It's only two afternoons a week, but I wanted to let you know."

Hope was replaced with disappointment. Full-time care would have eliminated the need for Cable as baby-sitter. Still, two afternoons were better than none. "That's wonderful. How soon can he start?"

"Tomorrow. However, I work on a first-come, first-served basis, Mrs. Nelson. As a favor to Cable I'm giving you advanced notice, but you'll need to come immediately and register if you want this opening."

"I'll be right there."

Sara hung up the phone. The timing was perfect. Now, for two afternoons a week, Jeremy's attention would be focused on children his age in an educational environment and away from Cable.

She stood up, glancing down at the work spread out across the table and the hot coffee she'd just poured. There was no point in putting it all away; she'd just leave everything as it was and go. It shouldn't take more than ten minutes to sign Jeremy up and get back.

"Come on, Jeremy. We have to go to the day care for a moment. Just leave your toys." Sara grabbed her purse, took Jeremy's hand and headed out the door.

Cable stepped into the kitchen and knew immediately that something was wrong. The house was too still.

He moved toward the table where Sara's work was spread out. The computer was still on. A cup of coffee sat beside it. He touched the side; it was hot.

An uneasy sensation moved in his gut.

"Sara?"

There was no response. Why would she go off and leave a fresh cup of coffee, with her laptop on? Her phone was here, too. She never went anywhere without it. She packed the damned thing like a six-gun.

"Sara!"

Silence closed in around him, and his unease became anxiety. As he started across the kitchen, the toe of his boot collided with something on the floor. He winced when his eyes found the object: Jeremy's dinosaur.

"Sara!"

Glancing out the window, he realized Sara's car was missing from the drive. Anxiety grew into fear, accelerating his breathing. He'd lived this scene before—an empty house, a car missing from the driveway.

Damn. Where had she gone? Striding down the hall, he tried to reassure himself that there was probably a simple explanation for their disappearance and no reason to worry. But a thorough search of the house revealed only vacant rooms.

He returned to the kitchen, searching for a note, some clue to tell him where they'd gone and why. There was nothing!

He ran his hands over his scalp, fighting the rising panic, yet aware on some level that he was overreacting. He had to calm down and think logically. There were any number of reasons Sara and Jeremy could have left so suddenly. At least there should be, but damned if he could think of one.

Damn the woman. Didn't she have the sense to at least tell him she was leaving? He was Jeremy's caretaker. He had a right to know if something had happened to him. What was so all-fired important that she couldn't take two seconds to come and tell him she was leaving?

The phone rang.

Cable's heart stopped cold. Blood roared in his ears and his stomach heaved. Like a man in a trance, he walked over and picked up the receiver. He forced his voice through the constriction in his throat. "Hello."

"Good afternoon, sir. This is Sam's Syntho Siding and we'll be in your neighborhood today—"

Cable slammed the receiver down and forced air into his lungs. His hands were shaking from anger and fear. Where the hell . . .

A car pulled into the drive.

Two strides brought him to the edge of the porch. Two more and he was beside the car the moment it came to a stop. He leaned toward the open driver's-side window, his hands gripping the ledge with white-knuckled force. "Where the hell were you?"

Sara looked up at him, her blue eyes wide with surprise. "Excuse me?"

"You heard me," he said between clenched teeth.

Sara's surprise quickly became anger. She pushed open the car door, forcing him to step back. "That's none of your business."

"So you run off without any explanation. Not even a note!"

"That's right," she said, slamming the door. "I don't answer to you."

"I'm responsible for Jeremy," he reminded her.

"No. I am. You're only responsible when I'm not here."

"From now on when you leave, you tell me where you're going."

"I'll do no such thing."

Sara's eyes were sparks of blue fire, but Cable wasn't about to acknowledge her anger in this situation. "I have a right to know when you're going out."

"No, you don't! You're not my husband and you're not Jeremy's father."

"Mommy!"

Cable heard Jeremy's frightened sobs even before he glanced into the back seat. Realization hit and stung. Damn. What the hell was he doing? He was behaving like a raving madman. His shouting had scared Jeremy to tears. He'd never meant to do that.

Sara glared at him. "Now see what you've done."

"Sara..."

Stiff-backed, she ignored him. She opened the door and unfastened Jeremy from his car seat, gathering him into her arms. The sight of his little, tear-stained face, his eyes filled with fear, made Cable sick to his stomach.

Remorse overwhelmed him and he turned and walked away. There was nothing he could say that would justify his behavior. How could he have been so stupid?

Sara was right; he had no authority over them. When he'd found them gone, his mind had projected the worst. Irrational fear, born of the past, had stampeded through him.

Sara had every right to be furious. He owed her an apology—again. He knew her well enough by now to know she would also expect an explanation. He wasn't sure he had one—not even for himself.

God help him, he was becoming more and more possessive of Sara and Jeremy. He had started to think of them as
his. He'd started to worry each time they went out about if
they'd be coming back. If the phone rang while they were
gone he broke into a cold sweat. When had he crossed the
line?

He had to stop. He had to regain some objectivity about
them and their relationship.

Sara and Jeremy weren't his family. They weren't a part
of his life. His family was gone, his life now a solitary one.
He was a man alone, and he liked it that way. Being alone
gave him peace, contentment. But would he ever be alone
again, now that Sara's image was in his mind, now that Jeremy had staked out a spot in his heart?

Cable paced the shop, unable to shake the memory of
Jeremy's little cheeks streaked with tears, his eyes filled with
fear. Fear that he had caused. Fear of him.

No one had ever been afraid of him before, and it left him
with a sick feeling inside. He wanted to go to Jeremy and
hold him, reassure him that he would never harm him. He
wanted to tell Sara how sorry he was, how much he cared for
Jeremy. But how did he find the words? Expressing his
feelings had never come easily for him and had been even
more difficult these last years. Living alone had changed
him, made it hard for him to relate.

Sara would at least understand and accept an apology.
But Jeremy was too young for explanations. He needed
something tangible.

Cable had to make it up to them. He couldn't live with
himself if he saw fear in Jeremy's eyes because of him.

Absently, he picked up a wing nut, twirling it around on
the bolt. He'd have to give Jeremy one of these to play with.
The little boy loved collecting rocks and other odds and ends
to stuff in his pockets.

He held up the wing nut and stared at it as an idea began to form in his mind. What if Jeremy had a special place to store all his treasures? Bigger than pockets, and mobile. Something he could take with him everywhere. He would make Jeremy a special toy. A peace offering designed especially for him.

Now if he could only somehow make it up to Sara...

## Chapter Ten

Sara patted Jeremy's back, making comforting sounds as she carried him into the house. He'd stopped crying the moment Cable walked away. A few sad sniffs and an occasional shudder were all that remained.

"It's okay, Jeremy. Everything's going to be fine."

"Are you mad at Cable, Mommy?" Jeremy asked, wiping his palm upward under his nose.

Sara frowned and dug out a tissue. "No," she said, mopping his face. "He just surprised me when he shouted so loudly. Everything is okay now."

Her words may have reassured Jeremy, but they did little to calm her own feelings. She was mad at Cable, all right. Furious, in fact, but there was no reason to further upset her son by telling him that.

"Cable was scary," Jeremy said, looking into her eyes.

Her heart contracted with sympathy, even as her motherly instincts longed to flatten the Crab. "I know he was,

sweetie. I don't think he meant to be. He was just upset,"
she explained, resting her cheek against his head.

Cable *had* been scary. And intimidating. His deep voice
had rumbled through her like thunder, and lightning bolts
had streaked through his dark eyes. What had gotten into
him? He had often been grouchy and surly, but she'd never
seen him snorting fire like an enraged bull. Not even the
night they'd argued so fiercely.

The gall of the man, presuming he had the right to demand a report each time she left the house. She'd only been
gone fifteen minutes. Next time he came out of hiding she'd
really give him a piece of her mind. There was no excuse for
scaring Jeremy half to death. That was unforgivable.

But the Crab didn't put in an appearance again that day.
Jeremy had recovered and resumed tagging every sentence
with "Cable said." From the way he was gobbling his dinner, he apparently had forgotten about the entire incident.

Sara wasn't finding Cable's behavior so easy to dismiss.
There was absolutely no reason for his outburst or his possessive attitude. It was out of character for him.

Or was it? She wasn't the best judge of anyone's true nature. Her marriage was proof of that. For all she knew, Cable's real self may have shown itself today.

He might be a possessive, domineering and angry man
inside. All that tenderness and sadness she kept seeing could
be a sham.

But as hard as she tried to convince herself, she couldn't
quite believe that Cable was the man she'd seen earlier.
Something must have happened to make him act as he had.
If she wasn't so tired, she'd try and sort it out....

"Can I get down?"

"Sure, honey." Sara watched Jeremy playing with his
stuffed dinosaur and took another mouthful of food. It demanded all her energy to chew and swallow. The run-in with

Cable today had taken more out of her than she'd realized. She was so tired. Even thinking took too much effort.

For the last week she'd been putting in ten- and twelve-hour days.

Of course, all that work had left little time for anything else, like sleeping, eating and being with Jeremy. She barely had the energy to put him to bed at night, let alone read to him. She'd crawl into bed, and no sooner had she drifted off to sleep than the alarm would ring and it was time to start the cycle all over again. Tonight was the first night she'd be able to finish working at a decent hour.

The sacrifices were paying off, though. The planned opening was back on schedule, and in little over a week, she and Jeremy would be going home. Then she could put all thoughts of Cable out of her mind forever.

Who was she kidding? She knew she wouldn't be able to do that. Cable's kisses would haunt her for the rest of her life.

The pestering beep of the alarm rudely yanked Sara from her sleep. It couldn't be morning already!

She started to roll over and look at the clock, but her body refused to obey her commands. Her muscles felt as if they'd been changed into lead during the night. She barely had enough strength to turn her head to the side. Reaching over to shut off the alarm was out of the question.

What was wrong with her? She'd gotten more sleep last night than she had in weeks, but it was as if she'd never gone to bed.

With supreme effort, she pulled herself into a sitting position. Her brain stalled. Her eyelids were coated with grit. She felt at least a hundred years old. Maybe a quick hot shower would get the blood flowing again.

But even extra time under the pulsating water failed to completely dispel the groggy, sluggish sensations that plagued her. It taxed her energy to pull on comfortable clothes and run a brush through her hair.

Slowly she walked into the alcove toward Jeremy's bed. He was sound asleep, and she decided to let him rest a while longer. Maybe a strong dose of caffeine would jump start her back to life.

The walk down the hall to the kitchen seemed eternal. Her body was unwilling to respond to even routine movements. Breathing took a concerted effort.

She paused at the counter, staring numbly into space, unable for a moment to recall where the cups were stored. After retrieving one from the cupboard, she lifted the two-ton carafe and poured coffee into her mug.

Staring into the black liquid, Sara wondered what she was supposed to do next. But suddenly it seemed unimportant. A heavy black shroud drifted over her, and she found she didn't even want to resist it.

"Is she going to be all right?" Cable stood watching anxiously as the doctor finished examining Sara. She'd been in and out of wakefulness since he'd found her unconscious on the floor.

"She'll be fine. All she needs is about a week's worth of uninterrupted sleep. I've given her a mild sedative, and I'll leave you a prescription in case she needs it. She's exhausted. I recommend at least three days in bed with complete quiet. I'll check in on her a couple of times."

Cable pulled Jeremy a bit closer to his chest. "See, Jeremy? Your mom's going to be fine. She just needs to sleep for a while."

Thank God it wasn't anything serious. When he'd found Sara lying on the floor, he'd thought for one bone-chilling moment she was dead. But she'd stirred under his touch, mumbling incoherently.

She'd lain so still and silent in his arms as he carried her to her room that his heart had chilled anew.

Cable was grateful that his doctor lived two doors down. He'd have gone mad waiting for paramedics to arrive. The doctor's diagnosis was reassuring. Rest and quiet was something Cable could provide for her.

"Can I see Mommy?"

Cable set the child down and watched as he tiptoed over to Sara and kissed her cheek. Jeremy looked back at Cable, one little finger pressed against his lips. "Shh."

The scene tugged at Cable's heart. What would the little guy have done if Sara had been seriously ill or worse? The thought turned his blood to ice. "Jeremy, would you stay here and watch your mommy for a moment while I talk to the doctor?"

Cable waited until they were well out of earshot of the boy before saying, "Tell me the truth. Matt, is she going to be okay?"

He nodded. "Yes. She's just worn out. How did she get so rundown?"

"She's setting up that new Dixie Mart and working long hours."

"Well, she'll have to stop working and start taking care of herself. I'm holding you responsible."

"I'll do what I can, but she's a bit hardheaded."

"So are you, and my money is on you. Call if you need me."

Cable said goodbye and returned to Sara's bedside. Lying so pale and still under the covers, she barely resembled the vivacious and energetic woman who had breezed into his life almost a month ago.

And he had to accept part of the blame. He should have seen this coming. He knew she was working too hard, taking on too much. If he hadn't buried himself in his own work this last week, he might have noticed her deteriorating condition. He'd been so concerned with his own selfish problems, things that seemed unimportant now in light of Sara's collapse.

His outburst yesterday had only added to her stress. His anger had pushed her over the edge. Guilt swelled within him. Sara was right: he had been self-centered. It was a sobering realization and one that shamed him.

He looked down at Jeremy, who was playing quietly with his toy dinosaur on the rug beside his mother's bed. Cable would start by making sure Jeremy felt safe and secure. Then he'd see to it that Sara got all the rest and care she needed.

"Come on, sport, let's go out to the shop for a while and let your mom sleep. I have something special for you out there."

Jeremy ran ahead of him outside and across the yard to the shop, stopping well back from the machinery, as Cable had taught him. "Can I play in my workroom?" He pointed to the area of the drying room where Cable had sectioned off a corner for him to play.

"In a minute. First, come and see what I have for you." Cable walked to the workbench and lifted the toy he'd made for Jeremy. After tying a sturdy string through the small eye on the front of it, he handed it to him.

"What is it?" Jeremy asked, his voice filled with wonder.

Cable knelt down in front of the child. "It's a box for you to keep all your treasures in. The wheels and the string are so you can pull it when you want to walk, and the handle lets you carry it if you have something really important inside."

Jeremy squatted down and started exploring all the little doors and chutes and hidden compartments Cable had designed into the toy.

"Can I put my pink rocks in it?"

"Sure. You can drop them right down this chute in the back. You can keep your nuts and bolts in there, too."

"Could Doggie ride on it?" Jeremy asked excitedly.

Cable smiled at the image of Jeremy trying to get the cat to agree to such a demeaning proposition. "Well, I guess you could try."

The delighted expression on the little boy's face warmed Cable's heart. His affection for this child was growing rapidly, and he deeply regretted the way he'd upset him.

Reaching out, he rested his hand on the top of Jeremy's head. "Do you like it?"

Jeremy nodded, demonstrating his new discoveries. "I can turn this thing and open the door, and there's a hole here with a big hook like on the gate."

Cable watched the child a moment longer, then sat on the floor Indian style. "Jeremy, do you remember yesterday, when you were in the car with your mommy and I got very angry and made you cry?"

Jeremy nodded, looking up into his eyes. "You were scary."

The lump in Cable's throat nearly choked him. His gut convulsed as if he'd had a fist rammed into his midsection. If he'd been capable of it, he would have started to cry. "Hey, Jeremy, I'm really sorry. I didn't mean to scare you. I would never do anything to hurt you. You're my little buddy. I was just very upset and I yelled. Do you understand?"

"That's okay. I get scary when I have bad dreams."

It took Cable a moment to grasp what Jeremy was saying. He didn't mean Cable had scared him; he meant Cable had been angry because of feeling scared, the way Jeremy did when he had a nightmare.

Dumbfounded at the child's perception, Cable could only stare into his honest, innocent eyes and marvel. How did this little child understand things a grown man couldn't?

"I was really scary when I couldn't find you and your mommy yesterday."

"We went to day care. I'm gonna get to play in the tunnels and with all their toys."

"Day care?" For reasons Cable didn't understand, he was filled with great disappointment. He'd been so reluctant to keep the boy, yet now that Jeremy was going to day care, Cable didn't want him to go. The idea made him sad.

"That'll be fun. Will you go there every day?"

Jeremy shook his head. "Only two times for a little bit."

Cable's sadness vanished as quickly as it had come, leaving behind a troubling realization. Despite his determination to remain detached from Sara's and Jeremy's lives, he was beginning to like having them here.

Not only had Jeremy claimed part of his heart, but his mother was slowly taking over a section of her own. All he thought about lately was Sara and having her in his arms and in his bed.

"Can I go to my shop now?" Jeremy asked, picking up his new toy.

"Sure," Cable said, getting to his feet.

Jeremy went to the small, enclosed "shop" where he kept the blocks and other items Cable had collected to keep him entertained.

Cable glanced at the calendar. Ten days. In ten days they would be gone. Then he would no longer have to fight his temptation for Sara and this deepening affection for Jeremy. All he had to do was hang on a little longer.

Sara was certain she had died and gone to heaven.

Sunlight flooded the room, and warmth and comfort surrounded her. She closed her eyes and sank deeper into the covers, unable to remember the last time she'd felt so cozy and rested.

Then she opened her eyes and looked at the clock. It was 10:26 a.m. She was late!

She sat up, swinging her legs over the edge of the bed, but dizziness prevented her from standing. Slowly her memory began to return. She remembered waking up and getting ready for work, remembered going into the kitchen for coffee, but after that her mind was blank. What had happened?

Sliding her feet into her slippers, Sara reached for her robe. Her knees were a bit shaky when she stood, but otherwise she was fine, so she wouldn't stay in bed another moment.

Stray pieces of memory flashed in her mind as she walked from the room. Or were they dreams? She seemed to recall Cable cradling her gently in his arms. There was the softness of warm flannel against her cheek and the steady throb of a masculine heartbeat in her ear. It had been like floating on a cloud of contentment and reassurance.

But had it really happened or had she dreamed it? As she reached behind her for the belt to her robe, she glanced down at her gown. It wasn't the one she usually slept in. This was her slinky blue, I'll-never-need-this-in-a-million-years-but-maybe-I'll-get-lucky-someday negligee. Why in the world had she put it on?

As she walked out into Jeremy's sleeping area, wispy images continued to float in and out of her mind. Someone had been asking her questions, but the voice was unfamiliar. Cable had been there, too, his deep, raspy voice she knew well. But there had been a tense, almost fearful tone in it she'd never heard before.

Why couldn't she remember?

She stopped at the side of Jeremy's neatly made bed. There was no sign of her son or his pet, Doggie. He must be with Cable.

Feeling stronger by the moment, Sara ventured beyond her rooms into the kitchen and found Cable was at the back door, doing something to the latch. "I don't suppose you could tell me what day it is?" she asked.

He turned at the sound of her voice, frowning in his old, familiar way. "What are you doing up?"

"Actually, I was going to ask you why I was in bed in the first place. I should be at work."

"You collapsed."

"I did?" Vague images of being smothered in darkness came to mind. "When?"

"Yesterday."

It took a moment for the significance of the time frame to register. "I slept around the clock?"

"Exhaustion will do that," Cable said, slipping his hands into the back pockets of his jeans.

"Me? Exhausted? Ridiculous. Who said?"

"The doctor."

"What doctor... oh, wait, was he the one asking me all those questions?"

Cable nodded.

"I kept wishing he would shut up," she said, brushing hair out of her eyes.

"That's what you told him. Twice."

Chagrined, she could only mutter softly, "Oh. Where's Jeremy?"

"Right outside in the sandpile."

Sara moved to the window, smiling when she saw her son playing contentedly in the sand with his trucks. "I don't understand," she said, turning back to Cable. "What happened to me?"

"You're suffering from stress and fatigue. Too many long hours and not enough rest. I found you on the floor unconscious yesterday morning."

Goose bumps rose on her arms and she shivered. What was wrong with her? She was always as healthy as a horse. She never got sick. Never in her life had she passed out. It scared her that she could barely remember waking up yesterday, let alone collapsing. "That can't be. I never faint."

"Your body shut down because you overworked it. You should be in bed," Cable said firmly. "The doctor ordered three days' rest."

"Out of the question," she replied, crossing her arms over her chest and trying to hide the fear that nagged her. "I can't afford to get any further behind."

"You can't afford anything else."

Cable's tone penetrated her apprehension. It held the same note of concern she'd heard last night. She rather liked the fact that he was worried about her.

Maybe she *had* pushed herself too much. She did have the additional complications of Jeremy and Cable to deal with.

Well, she felt fine now. She'd rested, and now it was time to get back to work. The deadline was staring her in the face and she'd be damned if she'd let it defeat her. If she were seriously ill, she would have woken up in the hospital. "I appreciate your concern, but I feel wonderful. I just needed a little extra sleep."

"No, Sara. The doctor ordered rest and quiet for three days, and I'm going to see you get it."

Worrying about her was nice. Taking charge of her life was another matter. "You and what army?"

Cable walked toward her, stopping only a foot away. She could feel his breath on her face. She inhaled the sharp, earthy scent of him and remembered the silk negligee that she wore. Her insides softened and tingling warmth snaked up from the center of her being as her body responded to his nearness.

"I don't need an army. I'm bigger than you, and if necessary I'll carry you to bed again, Sara."

She squirmed as the implications of his words sank in. It wasn't a dream. Cable had put her to bed, which meant he'd also... She looked up at him, her right hand clutching the robe at her breast. "Did you..." The query stuck in her throat.

"I did."

There was a knowing and faintly amused glint in his dark eyes that weakened her knees and brought a flush to her cheeks.

He had not only carried her to bed, he'd undressed her and put her in this slinky gown. Just the thought of his gentle hands touching her in intimate ways sent quivers of longing through her body.

She could almost feel those long, skillful fingers as they worked the buttons, brushing lightly against her breasts as he removed her blouse. She could imagine his callus-roughened palms sliding along her hips and thighs as he removed her slacks.

The mere idea sent heat rushing into her veins and caused a quivering ache in her center. Her nipples hardened, reminding her of all the reasons she liked being a woman.

Being near him, thinking about him, did strange and wonderfully stimulating things to her senses. Her breath quickened, her eyelids drooped, and she had swayed toward him before she realized what she was doing. She'd better get a grip on her feminine response before she made a very serious mistake.

Getting close to Cable was dangerous.

Sara moved away, forcing herself to ignore the masculine scent of him that drugged her mind like a potent incense. "I appreciate your concern, but I'm fine. Just a little hungry." She sank into a chair at the table, surprised at how good it felt to be off her feet.

Cable followed her. "Go back to bed and I'll bring you something to eat."

"I'll sit right here if it's all the same to you," she announced defiantly.

"No bed, no breakfast." His voice held no hint of compromise.

"Then I'll fix it myself." She started to rise, but found her body strangely reluctant to respond.

Cable's eyes bored into hers. "Bed."

She'd learned long ago that getting your own way was simply a matter of agreeing, then doing what you wanted without telling anyone. Slowly she stood, smiling at him with as much dignity as she could muster. "Fine."

Walking toward her room she lifted her chin. He could bully her into going to bed, but she still had some free will left and she was going to take a shower before she did another thing.

The shower did help, but it also drained what little strength she had left. Wrapping her robe tightly around herself, she walked into the bedroom to find Cable changing the sheets.

Seeing him in her room brought back memories of the last time, when he'd come to fix the window and found her in her towel. Memories of the way he had made her feel, memories of how he had excited her, surfaced as well, but she refused to indulge in them.

Walking to the other side of the bed, she helped Cable arrange the blankets in an attempt to focus on something else. She failed miserably. Straightening sheets and fluffing pillows wasn't the best way to dispel the physical awareness that inexplicably overcame her whenever Cable was around. Her tired brain kept flashing little scenes of her locked in his embrace, his long legs wrapped around her, the cool sheets she was so diligently smoothing tangled and warm from their bodies. . . .

"I thought you were going to go to bed."

Cable's comment jolted her out of her sensual daydream. "I wanted to take a shower first."

"Do you always ignore good advice?"

"Not good advice, no." But she had to admit the thought of crawling in and sleeping, really sleeping, was very appealing.

"You ready to eat?"

Suddenly too tired and too hungry to continue this childish display of defiance, she nodded, sinking onto the edge of the bed. Gratefully she crawled under the covers, and Cable pulled them up over her lap, arranging the pillows behind her back.

"I'll be right back. I'm going to check on Jeremy." There was a softness in his tone that sent warmth through her, despite her mounting fatigue.

As hungry as she was, the need for sleep was even stronger. But she wasn't about to give Cable the satisfaction of being right. She'd eat and then sleep when she was ready, not when he told her to. She wouldn't allow him to direct her life. But right now she didn't have the strength to fight.

He brought her tea, toast and juice and sat in the chair beside her, watching every sip and bite. Had she been more herself, she would have ordered him out, but all she wanted was to close her eyes and sleep.

Fatigue rushed at her so quickly she could barely chew the last bite of toast. Pride and stubbornness vanished when she was forced to surrender to her body's demands. "I think I will rest for a little while."

Cable removed the bed tray, then tugged the covers up under her chin. Her hand touched his and she looked up into his beautiful brown eyes and smiled, she wasn't sure why. It just seemed natural. "Thank you."

Cable gently brushed the hair off her cheek and away from her forehead. For a moment she thought he was going to kiss her, but he only rested his hand against her face, his thumb caressing her skin. He was being so tender and thoughtful, the way he was with Jeremy. Instinctively she turned her face into his hand, nuzzling his palm. "You take such good care of me and Jeremy. That's what I love about you, Cable." Rolling onto her side, she released her hold on consciousness.

Cable steered his truck out of the store parking lot and into the sparse traffic on Main Street. He'd run out to do some errands at Sara's insistence that she was well enough to keep an eye on Jeremy.

Sara had slept for another twenty-four hours after she'd made her visit to the kitchen. He had checked on her frequently, but she'd hardly stirred. Each time he visited, he made sure Jeremy accompanied him to his mother's bedside. Cable told himself it was to reassure the child, but the truth was he didn't trust himself going into her room alone. Having someone at his side, even a small child, was safer.

The thoughts and desires that filled him whenever he saw Sara so vulnerable and so beautiful were intensifying. He wanted to crawl in beside her and hold her while she slept. He wanted to feel her softness along every inch of his body. He ached to feel her satin-soft hair against his cheek and between his fingers.

He wanted to know the whisper of her breath on his chest as he cradled her close. Then, when she'd rested, he wanted to make love to her until they were both senseless.

His hunger for Sara had increased tenfold since she'd drifted off to sleep yesterday with words of love on her lips. His heart pounded each time he remembered. *That's what I love about you, Cable.*

Did she mean those words? Had she intended to say them? Or had they merely been the result of a fatigued mind unable to think clearly?

It wasn't her words that troubled him, it was the hope that had been born in his heart at the prospect of Sara having deep feelings for him. He didn't want to hope. He didn't want to love her. If Sara did care, even slightly, that would force him to examine his own heart, a terrifying prospect.

She was the most attractive woman he'd ever known and he couldn't deny that he had strong feelings for her. But they were feelings he could justify with logic. He admired Sara's tenacious approach to life, her deep compassion and her devotion to Jeremy.

It was his raging physical reaction to her he couldn't understand. His body had developed a mind of its own whenever Sara was near. Not since his teenage years had he experienced such ravenous sexual desires, such an obsessive need for one woman.

Kissing her had been his downfall. It had breached his barriers, leaving behind a voracious appetite for more. He craved her. But it wasn't merely Sara's body he craved, it was all of her—her comfort, her passion, her touch. He wanted to share himself with her, physically and spiritually.

If he didn't know better, he'd think he was falling in love. But it wasn't love he was feeling; of that he was certain. He'd been in love. He'd loved Amanda totally and completely. Love was a soft, deep and steady emotion. It grew slowly and quietly, reinforcing itself with time and shared experiences.

What he felt for Sara had arrived with the force of a nail gun, slamming into his heart, penetrating his every nerve and drilling repeatedly, deeply, into his soul.

Sara had roughed out a spot in his life and framed it with her compassion. He was powerless to stop his growing feelings. Feelings of . . . what?

Maybe what he was feeling for Sara was simple affection and friendship. After all, one of the things he wanted most to do was to help her, to alleviate her stress, to make everything right for her. Whether she knew it or not, she needed someone to take care of her now and then.

He smiled inwardly as he pictured Sara's reaction to such a suggestion. She would be furious. Her chin would jut out, her eyes would turn electric blue and she'd tell him in no uncertain terms that she could damn well take care of herself.

He missed watching the emotions play out across her face. He missed the sparks that appeared in her eyes when she was angry. Missed the way those same blue eyes would soften with a warm glow when she looked at Jeremy and how they'd sparkle like sunlight when she laughed.

But the one expression he wanted to see in her eyes more than any other was passion and desire for him alone. He wanted to bring her to the peak of sexual release, to wrap himself around her and never let go. He wanted to feel her softness enclosing him, her lips parted and inviting his kiss

Every moment they'd touched was still vividly etched in his memory. His senses were filled with her imprint. He could think of little else. Everything he saw or touched in the house, the yard or the shop reminded him of Sara.

He was a grown man. He knew how to control his physical needs. But he'd been celibate a long time. What man could resist a temptation like Sara being thrust into his life?

He had to hold out until she and Jeremy were gone. Then he would again be content to be alone.

Cable pulled into the drive, wondering what Sara was up to with Jeremy. Yesterday she'd been chomping at the bit to get up and get out. It was all he could do to keep her in her room, let alone in bed. He counted himself fortunate that he'd been able to hold her back this long.

So it didn't surprise him when he pulled to a stop near the garage to find her outside playing with Jeremy. What did surprise him was that she was on her hands and knees in the sandpile, rolling trucks down the hill with as much abandon and delight as her son.

With a baseball cap on her head and wearing a T-shirt and shorts, she looked like a kid herself. Except a kid didn't have deliciously long legs and gently rounded hips that invited a man's hands. A kid didn't have softly curving breasts and lips that tempted a man to kiss them until she cried out his name.

"My truck will beat yours this time," Sara challenged, scooping sand higher on the small hill she'd made. "You ready?"

Jeremy scurried over, positioning his truck alongside hers. "Ready, set, go!"

The trucks wobbled down, with Jeremy's reaching bottom first. Sara laughed, and when she did, Cable McRay's last barrier collapsed.

This was the Sara who had greeted him at the door that first day. The Sara whose energy had overpowered him, whose vitality had shocked his long-dead senses to life and made them yearn to live and feel again.

This was his Sara. The woman who possessed every particle of his being. The woman he loved.

Realization exploded in his soul. He loved them. He loved *them*. As if they were his own.

How could he have let this happen? He'd been so careful. He'd guarded his heart so diligently. He'd shored up his barriers and kept his distance. But despite all that, he'd come to love her. His mind reeled from the discovery. Joy and fear mingled with wonder and terror. His heart wasn't strong enough for this yet.

He'd thought he was impervious, that after all this time he'd finally learned to live alone without the need for anything but his work. But Sara had somehow slipped through his defenses, burrowed into his heart and soul and captured his love forever. With her blue eyes and enchanting smile, she'd penetrated his shell and teased him until he came out in the open, exposed, vulnerable and defenseless.

And then there was Jeremy. Cable loved him as much as he had his own son.

This couldn't be! He couldn't love them. But he did. Panic coursed through him, warning him to run and find safety. But he was too stunned to move. Immobilized, he could only continue to stare at Sara. Dear Lord in Heaven, what did he do now?

Sara saw him then. "Cable." She stood quickly and brushed sand off her legs. "Sorry about the sand. I guess we got it spread out into the grass a little."

There was anxiety in her eyes. Was he so fearsome? Didn't she understand? His love had to be written on his face for God and everyone to see. He shouldn't be feeling love for her. He shouldn't be feeling anything! "I don't give a damn about the sand."

Sara took a step toward him and he retreated. If she touched him now he would shatter into a million pieces. He turned and walked away before he said something he'd regret and before she saw the truth in his eyes.

Sara stared at Cable's back until he disappeared into the shop. Now what had she done? One minute she'd been playing in the sand with Jeremy, the next Cable was looming over her, a fierce scowl creasing his forehead and disapproval in his dark eyes.

Like a kid caught being naughty, she'd jumped up, brushed herself off and made a hasty apology. But when she'd looked into his eyes again she'd seen fear and pleading reflected there. She'd started to ask why, but he'd turned abruptly and stomped off. Cable had been so sweet and thoughtful during her illness. He'd seen to her every need and still cared for Jeremy. He'd been very protective of her, making sure she didn't overtax herself. She'd felt herself growing close to him, despite everything.

Now, for no reason she could see, he'd turned back into Crab Man. She replayed the scene once again, searching for some explanation. Was he mad because she wasn't in bed, lounging around like some Victorian lady, or didn't he approve of grown women playing in the dirt?

She glanced down at Jeremy, who was standing at her side, holding his truck and staring up at her expectantly. Didn't Cable understand that playing with her son was resting? She hadn't felt this carefree since she'd first arrived here.

"Crabby old hermit."

"He's scary again," Jeremy said, slipping his hand into hers.

"I know," she said, scooping Jeremy up in her arms, sand and all. "We'll be gone soon and he won't scare you anymore."

"Cable gets scary like me when I have a bad dream."

Scared. Cable McRay, scared? Was that what Jeremy meant? She looked at her son, her mind furiously processing this new perspective. Jeremy was telling her Cable was afraid, not that he was frightening.

"Jeremy, how do you know that Cable is scared the way you are?"

"'Cause he told me. He said he got real scary when he thought we were lost."

Of course! How could she have been so dense? Sara stared at her son in shock and realization. The poor man. He was just reacting to past experiences. He'd come into the house and found her and Jeremy gone, with no explanation. To him it must have been a hellish replay of the day his family had been killed.

Cable had been scared, and Jeremy was the only one who had understood.

But that didn't explain his irritation just now, when he'd found them in the sandpile. "Why is he scared now?"

Jeremy shrugged, and Sara sighed. Even a wise three-year-old couldn't know everything. Perhaps Cable regretted revealing his softer side and found it more comfortable to revert. Or maybe she was listening to her heart again. Cable was what he was and she'd be smart to stop giving him qualities he probably didn't possess. Cable was a crab, end of story. Wasn't he?

## Chapter Eleven

Cable walked out onto the front porch and handed Jeremy his stuffed animal. "Here's your dinosaur."

The little boy smiled, wrapped one arm around Clifford's neck and the other around the ever-growing Doggie. "Is my mommy here yet?" he asked.

"No," Cable replied. They were waiting for Sara to pick Jeremy up for his afternoon at day care. Cable had offered to take him, but she looked upon it as one more chance to be with her son. She loved the child fiercely, which made Cable love her even more.

He knew now beyond a doubt that he loved Sara and Jeremy. How could he not? Taking care of Jeremy, watching him grow and learn, sharing each and every moment had slowly coaxed him out of his dark solitude.

Being close to Sara, wanting her, watching her battle each obstacle so courageously, had given him a reason to seek the sunlight again. How could he defend his heart against two such powerful forces?

But loving them also meant facing the possibility of losing them, and that would be emotional suicide. Surely his instinct for self-preservation was stronger than love.

He walked to the swing and sat down, still struggling to deal with his tangled feelings. He loved Sara. He loved Jeremy. But how could he be free to love them when he couldn't remember important details about his wife and child?

Sara had told him to let go of the past, to grieve. He didn't know how. He'd ignored it for so long he didn't think he could face it now even if he wanted to. He needed help. But his fear and confusion had cut him off from the one person he could turn to: Sara.

Cable dragged a hand across his face, wondering what he was going to do. The question had plagued him since he'd discovered his feelings two days ago.

This love was powerful, all-encompassing, an insatiable beast. He didn't know this side of himself. He'd never before experienced this fierce, emotional typhoon of physical need and soul-searing love.

"Cable?" Jeremy asked, coming to his side.

"What is it, little buddy?"

"Can I sit with you?"

The request made Cable smile. "Sure thing." He set the boy beside him, and Jeremy in turn set his stuffed dinosaur between them.

"I'm gonna leave Clifford here with you."

"Oh? Why's that?"

"So you won't be by yourself."

"Thank you," he said, his heart warming. Jeremy had inherited his mother's caring nature.

"Cable?" the child asked again.

"What?"

Jeremy squirmed around and up into Cable's lap. "Know what?"

"No. What?"

"I love you."

Cable's heart constricted so fiercely he couldn't breathe. He looked into the little boy's face, into the young eyes filled with innocent truth.

From deep in his being, beyond the pain and the sorrow, behind the darkness and the shadows, something flickered to life. Cable could feel his spirit reawakening, pushing through the hard-packed grief, reaching for the life-giving light.

His own love for Jeremy surged through him, warming him, sustaining him. "I . . . I love you, too, son."

Jeremy's expression of genuine, unconditional love had broken the seal on the vault in Cable's soul. All the emotions, all the regret, the guilt and the sorrow broke free as well, rushing through him with a force so ferocious he could hardly breathe.

His soul was suddenly flooded with light. The long-suppressed images of the past flowed out, inundating his senses, filling his emotional reservoirs.

The pain was intense, twisting deep in his heart. His breath caught in his throat and he gasped, knowing tears were coming and fighting with all his might to stop them. If he allowed them to start, they would never stop.

Cable pulled Jeremy into his arms, pressing him against his chest, lifting his eyes heavenward. "Oh, God, help me!"

The emotions bombarding him were too powerful, too fierce to withstand, and he couldn't hold out against them any longer. A sob rose from the pit of his soul, convulsing his whole body. He buried his head in Jeremy's shoulder and unleashed his long-buried pain.

Tears flowed relentlessly down Cable's face as he cried out the loss, the sudden, irrevocable severance from those he'd loved. He cried out the anger and the fury at being left behind, at being robbed of a future he'd hoped for.

The tears cleansed the sorrow and washed away the denial. The astringent sting of acceptance coated his heart, removing the residue of guilt and fear.

From somewhere above the rush of emotions he heard Amanda's voice telling him goodbye. Telling him to be happy and go on....

Sara didn't know what made her stop short of opening the screen door to the front porch. Maybe she'd sensed something wrong; maybe she was just reluctant to get close to Cable again. Whatever the reason, she paused for a fraction of a second, and as she did, she heard his plea to heaven.

"Oh, God, help me."

Cable sat on the swing with Jeremy cradled against his chest. At first she didn't realize it was Cable crying. Then she heard a sob that seemed to be wrenched from his soul.

Suddenly she understood. She didn't know how, but she knew that Cable had finally come to grieve.

A lump of emotion lodged in her own throat, and she quickly covered her mouth to keep from crying out. She wanted to go to him, to hold him, to help him somehow. But she knew this was something best done privately.

She eased back down the hall a few feet, not wanting to disturb Cable and not wanting him to see her observing his pain. But she could still hear his sobs, each one ripping through her like a hot steel blade.

The sight of that strong, indomitable man sobbing uncontrollably tore at her heart. Tears of sympathy welled in her eyes, spilling down her cheeks.

Cable's weeping went on and on, until she thought she couldn't stand it anymore. The scene would forever remain in her mind—Cable holding Jeremy as if his very life depended on it....

From a distant part of Cable's conscious mind he could feel Jeremy patting his shoulder with his small hand, providing comfort the only way he knew how. Cable squeezed him tightly, his heart filled to the brim with gratitude.

The three simple, perfect words Jeremy had spoken had reached inside Cable and done what no amount of rationalizing could. They had set him free.

"It's good to cry," Jeremy assured him with a nod. "Mommy said so."

Cable swiped at his eyes and shifted the boy slightly on his lap. "Your mommy's a very wise lady."

"Are you crying 'cause you got hurt?" Jeremy asked, peering intently into Cable's face. He reached out and patted his cheek. "I'll get you a boo-boo patch."

"No, I'm not hurt," Cable said, taking the child's face between his hands and kissing his forehead. "Not anymore."

"You just getting all the bad feelings out?" Jeremy inquired wisely.

"That's right. I'm getting all the bad feelings out like I should have done a long time ago."

"You feel better now?" Jeremy eyed him closely, and Cable nodded. Reassured, the child climbed down and returned to his toys.

Cable sat on the swing, watching him play, but in his mind's eye he saw another child, a towheaded boy. And he remembered.

He remembered the laughter, the closeness, the special moments. He could recall every day, every precious incident. They were all still framed in sadness, but the sadness had a softer hue now. It was no longer colored in dull, painful black.

Warmth enfolded him as each memory gently touched his soul and chased the chill from his heart. Sara had told him his memories were meant to comfort him like an old blanket. She was right. She was right about so many things....

Sara ached to find some way to ease Cable's torment. She knew the tears were therapeutic, that crying was the best possible thing for him to do. Still, she couldn't stand to see someone she loved in such horrible pain.

Loved? When had she fallen in love with Cable?

Caught in a hailstorm of conflicting emotions, she backed farther down the hall. She was torn between her need to help Cable and the shock of realizing she loved him. What was she going to do?

She couldn't go out there. She couldn't face Cable, and she knew he wasn't ready to face her, either.

She glanced at her watch. It was time to take Jeremy to day care. The ride would give her a few moments to sort things out. Cable needed someone to talk to. Maybe, since they would then be alone, she could talk to him, help him somehow. But could she help him and keep her newly discovered secret?

Right now she had to get through this awkward situation and preserve the privacy of both of them. Sara listened intently for a few moments, catching snatches of soft conversation. Was it safe to go out there now?

Taking a few deliberately loud steps toward the front door, she called out, ''Jeremy, let's go. Time for day care.''

As she'd hoped, a few moments later the screen door opened and Jeremy scurried toward her down the hall.

Sara took his hand, feigning a calm she didn't feel. ''Are you ready for your big adventure? You're going to meet new friends and have lots of fun.''

Jeremy replied, but she had no idea what he said. She made the appropriate noises as she led him out to the car and strapped him in his seat.

''Cable feels better now,'' Jeremy blurted.

A sob caught in her chest as she fastened her own seat belt and started the engine. "He does?"

Jeremy nodded. "He cried and now he's not so sad."

"Good," she responded, trying to hide her own emotions. "Did you help him?"

"I gave him a hug."

"That was very nice of you, sweetheart."

Jeremy didn't say anything for a few moments and Sara bit her tongue, trying not to ask any more questions. Then the little boy asked, "Mommy, could Cable be my daddy if he wanted to?"

Oh, Lord. There it was—the question she'd feared from the day she'd realized her son adored Cable. Only now the situation was complicated with her own feelings. She loved Cable and she wanted him to be Jeremy's daddy, too, but it wasn't that simple.

How should she handle this one? How could she explain to him that Cable couldn't be his daddy because he didn't love his mommy? Where was the chapter in the *Single Parent Handbook* that covered hero worship and interpersonal relationships?

"Would you like him to be?"

"Yep. And you know what I'd do if he was my daddy?"

"What?"

"I'd hug his neck real hard, like this." He demonstrated with a stranglehold on Clifford. "Then he wouldn't be sad anymore."

Sara wished she could hug Cable's neck, too, could hold him and ease the pain, comfort him when he was lost, give him happiness when he was sad. She reached over and stroked Jeremy's cheek with the back of her hand. "You're a very smart little boy. I love you." Smarter than grown-ups, she added silently.

After leaving Jeremy at day care, Sara turned the car back toward Cable's. Things were stable at work for the moment and she needed some time alone to think.

By the time Sara returned to the house, she was no more in control of her feelings than when she'd left. The realization that she loved Cable had been bouncing around in her mind like a supercharged tennis ball. She'd vacillated between rejoicing in the discovery and reprimanding herself for trusting her judgment when she knew it was completely unreliable.

She didn't know when she'd started to fall in love with Cable. It may have been from the first day. Her soft heart had embraced him in spite of her recalcitrant mind. Her heart had always made her choices, and she'd been determined this time to override it.

And yet, as much as she tried, as much as she wanted it to be different, her heart ruled her life. It led her, and her mind had little choice but to fall in line.

Her heart told her Cable was everything she wanted. Her mind still wanted to wait and be vigilant, warning her to keep a piece of herself in reserve. It still bothered her that Cable possessed the ability to shut down his feelings when things got too tough.

A small voice in the back of her mind said she was being unfair and unrealistic. The circumstances for Cable were totally different from what they had been for Drake. Cable had lost his family, and in order to survive the horrible pain that resulted, he had removed himself from his memories. Drake, on the other hand, had made a conscious, calculated choice to walk away from his responsibilities. And the memory of his rejection still encircled Sara's mind like a protective shield against another such betrayal.

But there was plenty of time to sort out her feelings. Cable's emotions concerned her more than her own at the moment. The memory of his torment haunted her.

He'd finally begun to grieve and deal with the loss, but his grief had been repressed so long, she was afraid the sudden return of all those emotions would crush him. He shouldn't have to face it alone. She had to be there to help him understand how difficult the grieving process would be.

She dashed up the steps into the house and started down the hall. Cable met her at the bottom of the staircase. He looked tired, but there was a new light in his eyes and a peace about him that hadn't been there before.

"Are you all right?" she asked anxiously.

His eyes narrowed, and Sara realized she'd have to confess to seeing his breakdown. "I didn't mean to eavesdrop, I just happened to be at the door."

His eyes held her gaze a long moment, but she couldn't find any condemnation there, only relief. Finally he nodded. "It's all right, Sara."

"How do you feel?"

He ran his hands through his hair. "I'm not sure. Tired. Happy. Scared. But I feel alive and at peace, too. Does that make any sense?"

Sara's heart swelled with joy that he was finally facing his loss. Soon he'd be free from the pain and the darkness he'd lived in so long. "Yes." She smiled, going toward him. "That's how you're supposed to feel. You'll never lose that little piece of sadness deep in your heart. Part of you will never be the same. But you can live with it now and you can move forward. Would you like to talk about it?"

Cable shook his head, staring at the floor. "I don't know."

She understood his hesitancy, but she also understood his need to talk, now before the old, comfortable pattern of retreat took hold again.

"Come on," she urged gently. "Let's go into the kitchen. I'll fix you a glass of iced tea and we can talk."

"Sara . . ."

"Please," she said. "It'll be all right. I promise."

Cable followed her, taking a seat at the table while she made the drinks. She sat in the chair closest to him, laying her hand over his, waiting patiently. But when he had taken several swallows of his tea and still remained silent, she took the initiative. "Would you like to tell me what brought this on?"

Cable stared into the distance after meeting her gaze briefly. "Jeremy."

"What did he do?"

"He, uh..." Cable's jaw flexed. "He said... he loved me."

Sara's eyes stung. "He does. He has from the first."

Cable smiled ruefully, moving his hand atop hers now and holding on tightly. "I thought if I could just forget the past it wouldn't hurt so much. But I never wanted to forget completely. I want you to believe that, Sara."

"I do and I understand. You had a lot of pain to deal with."

"You were right about me. I was hiding. I came here and told myself I'd started a new life. I just didn't want to accept that they were gone. It hurt too damned much."

Sara squeezed his hand. "Didn't you have anyone who could have helped you through it?"

"People probably tried, but I was too numb to hear them. That part of it is still fuzzy." He rubbed his forehead.

"That's normal, too," she assured him. "I don't remember much for about the two months after my husband left. I remember him telling me that my baby and I had ruined his life. Then he just left. He walked out and never looked back. I felt dazed and disoriented for a long time. Then one day I was in the obstetrician's office waiting for my next exam. It was like I'd been in a walking coma for a long time and suddenly awakened. I guess when you have a terrible shock your brain shuts down for protection until you're strong enough to face the pain.''

Cable lifted her hand, bringing it to his lips. He kissed her palm, a slow, lingering kiss she felt down to her instep. Every nerve ending vibrated; every cell was alive and tingling.

There was a smoldering invitation in his brown eyes. "Such a small hand to fight such a large battle all alone," he said huskily. "You fight your own battles and mine as well. You saved me, Sara. I don't know how to repay you. You braved the darkness of my seclusion and the thorns of my anger and still refused to let me hide."

Sara's heartbeat quickened at the tender tone of his voice. "I couldn't let you live with all that pain."

"Why couldn't you, Sara?" He reached out, resting his palm against her cheek.

"Because..." His touch sent a slow, seductive warmth spreading throughout her body, making it hard to think clearly. She opened her eyes. Cable's lips were only inches away.

"Tell me why, Sara," he whispered, leaning toward her.

His breath, warm against her lips, mingled with her own and further muddled her senses. "Because..." His lips brushed hers in a feather-light touch that drove all other thoughts from her mind.

"Because why, Sara?" he whispered, taking her bottom lip between his teeth and tugging gently.

"I...care for—" She heard Cable's grunt of excitement as his mouth descended upon hers.

Her whole being answered his kiss, and she knew there was no turning back now. They'd been heading for this moment since that night she'd brought Jeremy back. Neither could deny the attraction any longer.

Cable stood, drawing her against him, and she slipped her arms around his neck, holding on. Sara tried to find some good, solid reason to stop what was happening, but she knew that even if she found one she would ignore it.

His kiss deepened, his tongue slowly teasing her lips apart dipping between her teeth. The invasion shattered her last remaining resistance. She gave herself over to him, to his tender exploration.

Cable raised his head, sucking in air, his eyes caressing her face as his hands cradled her face. He memorized her, then renewed the kisses, slowly mapping and cataloging every inch. He tasted the underside of her chin, the side of her neck, and found the sensitive place behind her ear.

Too weak to stand, she clung to his broad shoulders, sighing with pleasure and burning with sensual fever. He forced his hips against hers, and she could feel his need, hot and hard against her stomach. Like a lighted fuse, flames of passion raced along her nerves, turning her body to fire.

"Sara, I need you."

And she needed him, but his lips covered hers before she could tell him so. Their first kiss had shattered her ideas about attraction. Their second had left her confused and craving. This one took her heart and soul into his complete possession.

She clung to him, knowing that if she let go she'd not have the strength to stand alone. She needed him, now. She needed him with her. She needed him forever.

Cable wrapped his strong arms possessively around her waist, driving his hips against hers. She moaned and gripped his shoulders as his kiss deepened and intensified.

She'd thought of Cable as gentle and controlled in all things. She was unprepared for this wild, uncivilized passion.

But far from frightening her, Cable's fervent appetite awakened hungers deep in her she'd never explored. He'd tapped into a bubbling caldron of feeling so carnal, so feral, she couldn't begin to control it.

They came up for air. Sara looked into the fiery brown eyes and knew he wanted this as much as she did. She'd never reacted to another man this way. No one could touch her like this, only Cable.

"Sara, if you don't want this..." He left the sentence for her to complete.

Sara knew what she should say, but when she spoke, it was to whisper, "I want you."

Cable crushed her to him in an engulfing embrace, feasting upon her lips for a long moment before picking her up and carrying her into her bedroom. He'd barely placed her on the bed when he joined her, pulling her against his chest again. He kissed her as if, in the few moments it had taken to get to the bedroom, he was starved for her again.

Cable kissed her desperately, calling her name between breaths. Her hands reached for the buttons on his shirt, and finding that they were snaps, she yanked them apart. Her fingers burrowed eagerly into the soft, dark hair on his chest and dug down to the warm, smooth flesh beneath.

Cable sucked in air through his teeth, then shrugged off the shirt and stretched out beside her. He pulled her against him, nuzzling her hair.

He didn't think about tomorrow or what might happen. There was only now, this moment and Sara. His Sara, to hold and love. His Sara, who had the power to heal his soul.

She'd given to him from the moment she'd come into his life. He wanted only to give back, to give her pleasure in the most intimate way he could. The only way he knew.

Sara's hands explored Cable's body, the firm shoulders, the smooth, strong back and the soft skin at his sides. His jeans were an obstacle to further exploration, and she tugged at his belt while he rained kisses on her face and throat.

Cable's fingers found the buttons on her blouse and began to unfasten them urgently. Gaining access at last, he slipped his hand inside, tracing the line of her bra before cupping his hand over her breast.

She arched against his touch, needing more, needing his gentle exploration everywhere. Her mind swirled in a kaleidoscope of delicious responses, and she sighed her pleasure.

More buttons gave way and he slid her shirt off, his tongue replacing his fingers at the lacy edge of her bra. She burrowed her hands into his hair, pulling his head down, inviting more intimate touches.

Slowly, systematically, Cable began to search out her most sensitive areas. The spot behind her left ear drew moans of approval. The soft, pale nipple on her right breast was particularly sensitive, so he gave it extra attention.

With each touch he found new ways to stimulate her, and in so doing, tripled his own excitement.

Sara moaned in anticipation as Cable deftly unfastened her bra, tossing it aside. His gentle hands caressed her, massaged one ultrasensitive nipple to an eager, hardened peak. She writhed, unable to stop her stampeding emotions.

Cable's nimble fingers worked the closures on her slacks, then slid them slowly over her hips and down her legs. Cool air caressed her passion-warmed skin and she reached out to him.

When his hand slid up her thigh and under her panties, her body exploded in delicious release. Shocked and embarrassed, she turned her head away. "Cable, I'm sorry. It's been so long—"

With two fingers, he gently turned her face to his, hushing her with a kiss. "It's okay."

Quickly he stripped and rejoined her. Then, slowly and tenderly, he began again. She started to tell him it was useless, that she could never reach that point again so soon. But he touched her someplace magical, and the spiraling coil of desire started to swell once more.

This time the sexual tension grew slowly and with less urgency. But it sprang from someplace so deep inside her, Sara trembled in awe and wonder at its magnitude. Cable's skillful hands carried her on a sensual journey up peaks and down into valleys, each moment building upon the next until she knew nothing but the touch of his hand and the feel of his lips.

Just when she thought she would shatter from the exquisite thrill of his touch, he lowered himself between her thighs and took her into a new realm of existence. Powerless, she could only hold on as he swept them along on a fiery comet, bringing her to the brink of passion again and transforming her completely.

Sara filled Cable's senses to overflowing. He breathed her in and found peace. He tasted her and knew completeness. He heard her call his name and knew pure joy.

He wrapped his body in hers and found paradise.

He took her with as much tenderness as he possessed, but was unprepared for the turbulent, fiery joining that overwhelmed them. It was like standing in the path of a funnel cloud, tossed, wrenched and spun into an emotional plain beyond the confines of reality.

They rode it together, propelled upward with such force, such ecstasy that he wondered if they would ever be sane again.

In the shimmering aftermath of their lovemaking, Sara found a secret part of herself she hadn't known was missing. She'd never made love before, not like this. She'd never been held or caressed with such tenderness. Never been with a man who could create such raging passion in her.

The hollowness in her heart was gone. Cable had filled it completely. He was her other half. Together, the two of them were as one, and she could never be alone again.

With a smile of pure joy, she turned toward him, curling against him and drifting off to sleep.

Watching Sara awaken was one of the most beautiful sights Cable had ever seen. It was like watching spring arrive.

Her eyelashes fluttered open, and her eyes were the hazy, muted blue-gray of a winter twilight. Then she focused her gaze upon his face and her eyes filled with life, turning the bright azure blue of an April sunrise.

Her ivory skin bloomed with a soft pink glow, and he could see vitality and energy infuse her body like a playful springtime breeze.

He watched in fascination as Sara smiled at him, and her smile lit up his heart and soul.

She curled up against him, her hand lovingly stroking his chest, making his body throb in response. Sweet Sara had overloaded his senses. She'd been softer, more exciting and more passionate than he'd ever imagined. In her caring hands he'd felt things stir, parts of himself come to life. She'd opened the final door, unearthed the last, secret part of his soul.

Sara's love blinded him with its warmth and depth. Cable McRay had never loved like this before. In her arms he'd been reborn.

He lowered his head, taking her mouth with all the tenderness he possessed. The taste of her drugged his senses, filling him with a craving that only she could satisfy. He pulled her closer, reveling in the feel of their bodies pressed together. He slid his fingers into the tousled, silken strands of her hair, whispering her name, knowing he would never get enough of her, even if he lived to be a thousand.

The rude, incessant beeping of Sara's watch alarm ripped through his passion-fogged senses, leaving him disoriented and irritable.

"I'm so sorry," she said, stroking his cheek. "I've got to pick Jeremy up from day care."

He nodded and rolled onto his back, draping a forearm over his eyes and trying to reign in urges that had been gathering force with alarming speed.

A few moments later he felt the bed sag, and he opened his eyes. Sara had dressed quickly and now sat beside him. She reached out and laid her hand on his chest. "Cable, something special happened between us, didn't it?"

He nodded and reached up to touch her hair. "Yes, Sara. It did." She smiled, and Cable saw the sun rise again. She was so beautiful, so full of life.

"I've got to stop at the store after I pick up Jeremy, but I shouldn't be too long. We've got so much to talk about."

He lay in bed until he heard her car pull from the drive. Then he sat up, allowing the memories of their lovemaking to wash over him.

Making love to Sara had infused him with life. He'd shared her vitality, her energy and her love. She had so much affection to give, and she'd been suppressing it for a very long time.

He longed to unleash all that pent-up devotion and caring toward himself. He'd forgotten how important it was to be loved, both physically and emotionally. Sara had breathed the very life back into him. Dear God, her love made him feel omnipotent.

Cable rose and began to dress, his gaze traveling around the room as he pulled up the zipper on his jeans.

Sara's robe lay draped across the chair in intimate disarray. Through the bathroom door he could see panty hose hanging over the shower rod. The lingering fragrance of makeup and hair spray hung in the air.

He walked out into the sitting room, taking note of every detail—Jeremy's toys scattered across the floor. Doggie perched haughtily on the windowsill. A half-eaten cookie forgotten on the end table.

The room was cluttered with the unmistakable signs of a home, of a family. Of life!

How had he lived so long without this? How had he believed he would never need this again? His family had always been the most important part of his life.

The magnitude of that realization stunned him. He owed it all to Sara. She'd brought him back to life. She'd taught him to feel again. But feeling was still a risky proposition.

Small fingers of fear began to twitch in his heart. Floods of unfamiliar emotions rushed at him in waves, one overlapping the other until he couldn't sort out the old from the new.

The intensity of his feelings for Sara, the depth of his need, were things he'd never experienced before. He'd never been possessed, body and soul, with the desire for one woman. She made him feel whole and complete for the first time in his life.

Variegated emotions washed over him again. Two elements seemed to ride the crest of the waves high above the others—his love for Sara and a wary peace. An uneasy truce between his past and his present.

Part of him wanted to shut the door on all this emotion. To hide in the quiet nonworld of his denial. He'd come to understand that world. There had been no pain, no grief, no sensations of any kind. Only a dull numbness.

No. He could never go back there. He knew now what he was missing. But being alive again was going to take some getting used to.

He needed time. Time to put everything into perspective. Time for this sudden influx of newly reborn emotions to settle in and reach a manageable level. Then he could look at the past and plot a course for their future.

A future with Sara and Jeremy?

The possibility was still risky. His fear was still there, hovering on the fringes of his thoughts. It had taken five years to accept the death of his family. Did he have the courage and the strength to move beyond the confines of his fear and face that awesome risk again?

Sara had told him once that Amanda wouldn't have wanted him to bury himself. Neither would Sara. She had poked and prodded and coaxed him out of hiding, and once he was out in the open, she'd refused to let him retreat. In her arms he'd been reintroduced to life. Could he turn his back on that now?

The store was almost completed. In a few days she and Jeremy would be leaving. How could he let them go? How could he let Sara leave, knowing that he would never again hold her in his arms? How could he say goodbye to Jeremy, knowing he would not be around to see him growing and changing?

Maybe it was time to let go of the past and try life again. Maybe he could find the courage to take that first step.

Cable had wandered into the hallway when he heard Sara's phone ringing. She must have been in such a hurry to pick up Jeremy that she'd left it behind. He hesitated a moment, then went back into her room and answered it.

"Let me speak to Sara," a voice demanded.

"She's not here."

"This is Russ at the store. Where is she? There's been an accident."

Cable's heart stopped beating. His mind became momentarily blank. *There's been an accident.* He'd prayed to God he would never again hear those four words. He forced himself to respond to the voice on the phone. "She was going to pick up her son before stopping at the store."

"She went to the store? Oh, my God, if she's inside—"

The line went dead.

Cable turned to stone. He didn't know how long he stood there holding the phone. His mind hurled back in time, memories cutting deeply and quickly into his soul. It was happening all over again.

The horror of five years past clawed at him. Fear choked the life out of his body, leaving him a hollow shell once again.

From somewhere far inside he dredged up the ability to move, to grasp at hope, to order his body to respond. His mind filled with endless explosions of fear as he ran to his truck, cranked the engine and backed down the drive.

The store was only five minutes away, but the trip took an eternity. Nearly sick with dread, Cable roared into the parking lot, braking to a halt at the sight of the fire trucks.

Dear God, not again. Was he going to have to bury a second family? Was he doomed to be alone forever? He prayed for mercy, then pushed open the truck door and raced toward the store.

## Chapter Twelve

Sara saw Cable's truck skid to a stop in the parking lot. What was he doing here? How had he heard about the fire so quickly? She started forward, watching him leap out of his truck and race toward the cluster of fire fighters at the front door of the store.

His desperation transferred itself to her, and suddenly she understood. "Oh, my God." Cable thought she and Jeremy were inside.

She could hear him calling for her over the din of employees and rescue workers, but she couldn't get his attention. The fear on his face as he frantically grabbed one fireman after another, shouting in their faces, tore at her heart.

"Cable, we're here!" Tears blurred her vision when she thought of how scared he must be. This was his worst nightmare, learning that people he loved were in danger.

Love? Oh, God, did this mean he loved her? Her heart pounded with excitement as she looked for him again. Of course he did! Why else would he be here, dashing around, stopping everyone he saw in his desperation to find them?

"Cable!" She had to reach him and let him see they were all right. Cradling Jeremy on her hip, she hurried toward him, sidestepping fire hoses and gawking spectators.

He turned at the sound of her voice, his dark gaze raking the area anxiously. The moment his eyes met hers, Sara's heart skipped a beat, then raced wildly. The love shimmering in Cable's eyes told her everything she wanted to know.

He ran toward her, shoving people aside in his haste to reach them. He pulled her close, his eyes inspecting every inch of her and Jeremy before he wrapped them tightly in his arms. "I thought I'd lost you," he said, burying his face in her hair as he crushed her to him.

"We're fine," she said quickly.

Sara started to reassure him, but Cable found her lips, kissing her urgently, desperately, until she thought she would lose her breath.

"Oh, God, Sara, I love you. Thank God you're both all right. That you're safe."

Sara's heart overflowed with joy. Cable loved her. She hadn't made a mistake, after all. She held him as closely as she could, basking in his embrace. "It's okay. We're fine."

He drew back, staring at them again as if unconvinced they were safe.

"Cable, we're all right. We weren't even in the store at the time. I'd already come out to my car."

Jeremy squirmed, holding out his arms toward Cable.

Cable took him from her, inspecting him again, too.

The little boy smiled and hugged Cable's neck. "Did you see all the fire trucks? They had sirens and the firemen ran into Mommy's store and the police came. See all the big hoses down there?" Jeremy asked, pointing to the ground.

Cable smiled and hugged him again.

Sara knew beyond a doubt that Cable loved them. There was love in his eyes when he looked at her. There was love in his touch. They were a family—if not legally, at least emotionally. Being together felt right and natural. Standing at Cable's side, in the small circle of love created by the three of them, felt more natural than anything she'd ever experienced.

She slipped an arm around his waist and smiled up into his still-troubled eyes. "I'm so sorry we frightened you. There was an electrical short that caused a small fire."

Cable captured her mouth again, giving her several quick, comforting kisses.

"Excuse me, Mrs. Nelson, but we need to ask you some questions about what happened here."

Sara pulled out of Cable's embrace to acknowledge the local fire chief. "I'll be with you in a moment."

She turned to Cable, touching the cleft in his chin with her forefinger. "I need to stay and make a quick report. Could you take Jeremy home? I'll be there as fast as I can and we'll talk."

Cable nodded reluctantly, then he laid his palm against her cheek gently. "Don't take too long."

As he and Jeremy walked away, Sara's hopes for the future, her dormant dreams, began to revive.

She had found a man who loved her and Jeremy. A man who would be everything to her and her son. All she wanted to do now was go home and talk with Cable, to tell him how she felt, to plan where they would go from here.

Settling the details of the accident took longer than she'd expected. When she finally arrived home, Jeremy was in bed, sound asleep. She kissed him softly, then went in search of Cable.

They met in the hallway as Cable came in from the front porch. Sara smiled, remembering the last time they'd met here and how they had found their way to bed.

Only this time, something was different. There was a tension in the air, a strained silence that made her uneasy. She was probably imagining it. It had been a harrowing afternoon, and they'd both been through severe emotional stress.

"I'm sorry for scaring you today," she said, resting her palms against his chest.

He looked her over once again. "Are you sure you're all right?"

She nodded and smiled. "I have a feeling everything is going to be okay from now on."

Cable set her away. The coldness in his eyes and the distance in his touch triggered alarms in her heart and mind. What had happened? What had changed in the hour she'd been at the store? "Cable, what's wrong?"

He averted his eyes. "Nothing." Brushing past her, he went into the kitchen.

Sara's stomach knotted as an old familiar feeling started to form. She wrapped her arms around her rib cage and followed him. "Something is. I can tell by the look in your eyes."

"You're imagining things."

Sara chewed her lip nervously. Cable was slowly withdrawing into his shell. But why? "Did I imagine what happened between us this afternoon in my bed?"

"No."

"Then I think we should talk about it."

"There's nothing to talk about, Sara. It happened. It was good."

"That's it?" She could hear the fear creeping into her tone, feel the apprehension snaking along her nerves. "Don't you think we need to find out if what we're feeling is real or if it's just the product of this pretend family life we've been living for the last month?''

"I wasn't aware we were pretending anything."

"I wasn't." A small tendril of hope was reborn in Sara's heart. Maybe she was misreading Cable's signals. "Cable, something special happened between us. We can't just ignore that."

"I'm not ignoring it."

"Well, you're not doing anything about it, either."

"What do you want me to do, Sara?"

She hugged herself tighter as fear swamped her again. What *did* she want him to do? She'd been so sure he cared, so positive that he loved her. He'd even said it. Hadn't he? Or had she only heard what she wanted to hear?

She spun around to face him again. "So I guess you didn't mean it when you said you loved me?"

He turned his back. "I don't know what you're talking about."

Sara grabbed his arm, forcing him to confront her. "You don't remember saying 'I love you' when you found us at the store? You don't remember holding us and kissing me? Did I imagine all of that?"

"No. But sometimes things are said during moments of crisis that . . ."

Sara's heart was being hollowed out with each breath she took. Her dream was slipping away, her love being rejected. "Cable, please." He was changing before her eyes. He was slipping back into his shell, and she couldn't hold on tight enough to keep him out in the open with her.

"Cable, why are you doing this?" She chewed her trembling lip, fighting to hold back the tears. "Don't hide from me now. Don't hide from Jeremy."

"I'm not hiding."

"Yes, you are. Talk to me." She could see the determination in his eyes. They were cold and lifeless again. Like they used to be.

"What do you want to talk about? I'm glad you're both safe. I was worried."

"What about us?" Sara held her breath, hoping for the best, but expecting the worst.

Cable turned his back again, and Sara knew that her last chance to hold on to him was slipping through her fingers. "At least tell me what happened between the time you left the store and when I got home," she begged. "I have a right to know. Was it something I said? Did you get some bad news? Did you have a sudden revelation that you have no feelings for me or Jeremy at all and just can't find the words to tell us?"

"You're being melodramatic."

His indifference increased her fear and anger. "You're not leaving me any other choice. All I want to know is why? Why are you shutting me out? Why are you pretending that there's nothing between us?"

He stood rigid and mute.

Sara clenched her fists and shouted, "Dammit, tell me why!"

Cable spun around so quickly that she gasped and stepped back. "Because I couldn't survive if I lost you and Jeremy, too!"

Sara's heart cried out in sympathy for him. She understood his fear. But she also had a horrible fear that Cable had decided to never risk that loss again. If he was so terrified at the thought of losing them, then he must care deeply. Somehow she had to reach that part of him that cared, that loved them.

"Cable, I can understand why you would feel that way. Today must have been like reliving a nightmare."

He ran his hands through his hair, going to stand near the back door. "The last time I got a message about an accident it meant a trip to the morgue."

Sara wanted to cry. "But don't you see? You've faced your worst fear and it didn't end tragically. Jeremy and I are here and we're alive."

"This time," Cable said softly.

She was fighting a losing battle, but she wasn't ready to accept defeat yet. "So you'll let what we have die because something *might* happen to one of us sometime in the future? That's like saying you won't breathe again because you might inhale something harmful. You can't live your life that way."

"It's my life."

There was a finality in his tone that she'd never heard before. Sara ran her hands through her hair. Her lips trembled as she began to realize that she'd been defeated. Once again someone she loved was turning his back and walking away. She couldn't go through this again. "What do I have to do to penetrate that thick shell of yours?"

When Cable didn't answer, all her hopes died. Her husband had ended their marriage when love became too much of a responsibility. Cable shut his love down when it became too risky.

"Fine. You can have your life back. You've gotten to be very good at turning off your feelings and hiding. And it's so easy. You have everything you need right here at your fingertips. You close yourself up in this small town and in your shop back there because it's a nice safe existence—no decisions, no confrontations, no risks. And God forbid you should take any risks! They might hurt."

Angry tears burned her cheeks. "Well, Jeremy and I won't hurt you any more. We'll be leaving day after tomorrow. You and your shop and your memories can all keep each other company from now on. I hope you'll all be happy.''

Sara turned and fled to her room, shutting the door firmly behind her. She curled up on the window seat, crying out her heartache. When would she learn that her ability to make accurate judgments about people was abysmal? Her talent for choosing the wrong men had triumphed again.

She should have expected this. She knew Cable had a habit of walking away from his emotions when they became too painful. But she'd allowed his gentle ways and his affection for Jeremy to convince her he was everything she'd dreamed.

This was the second biggest mistake of her life, and she had no one to blame but herself. She and Cable had played house to the hilt. They'd forgotten that they were a temporary family, with no ties, no strings, no obligations.

She just hadn't expected his fear to be so strong.

They had both forgotten that their lives for the last month had been only a game of pretend. Some things, however, grown-ups couldn't pretend. Like physical needs and emotional longings that demanded satisfaction. Needs so powerful, so urgent that they completely blocked all rational thought.

She thought of the way she'd felt in Cable's arms, of the rapture she'd known when that cold hollow beneath her heart had been filled at last with his love.

Sara chewed her lip, mentally calling herself all kinds of a fool. Making love with Cable had been an irresponsible thing to do. And in that irrational state of mind she'd interpreted his act of love as a true expression of his feelings.

She saw now that it had been the result of his cathartic experience. He'd been suppressing his emotions and his memories for years, and when they'd returned, it had been with the force of a dam bursting. He'd needed someone to hold, to embrace, and she'd been there, convenient, available and willing.

Sara sighed and wiped the wetness from her cheeks. No. She couldn't hold him totally responsible. She'd needed him, too. She'd needed to be held and loved. She needed to feel special again.

But there was one small difference between the two of them. She'd made love with Cable because she loved him, no other reason. Right or wrong, mistake or not, her heart had made its choice.

Deep down inside she believed that Cable loved her, too. But she couldn't force him to accept it if he was determined not to.

She just hadn't expected his fear to be so strong. She understood how he must feel. How terrifying it must have been for him to be called to the store, not knowing if she and Jeremy were safe. Her heart ached for him. But this time Cable had buried himself so deeply in his shell that she had little hope of prying him out.

The metamorphosis had been alarming. Cable had changed right before her eyes—coiling in on himself, burrowing back into his armor. And there wasn't a thing she could do to stop him. The hopelessness of it all brought her to tears again.

So be it. She'd leave him to his isolation. In a few days she'd be going home. Jeremy would miss Cable for a while and so would she, but they'd get over it. She didn't need him. She'd been alone before and she would survive it again.

Sara shut the trunk lid, glancing back over her shoulder at the house, then reprimanded herself for her foolishness. Cable wasn't going to appear at her side. He wasn't coming to say goodbye or beg her not to go or anything else, for that matter.

It had been two days since they had made love. Two days since the accident that had shattered the joy they'd discovered in each other's arms.

Now it was time to leave, to return to Nashville, put these disturbing, painful weeks behind her and move on.

She'd caught only glimpses of Cable these last two days. He was up to his old tricks. She'd kept Jeremy with her most of the time, trying to wean him away from Cable and help him adjust to their coming departure.

To her amazement, Jeremy was accepting the departure with surprising maturity. Which was more than she could say for herself. For the twentieth time she looked back at the old, run-down house, unable to forgo the hope that Cable would come to his senses and refuse to let them leave.

She stared at the back door, her heart pounding, but no one emerged from the house. No sounds came from the shop. She slid behind the wheel of the car and checked that Jeremy's car carrier was secured in the passenger seat beside her. "All set, sweetheart?"

Jeremy nodded. He'd been quiet and solemn since he'd realized they were actually going home today. He'd said goodbye to Cable last night, but it had been a private farewell, and Jeremy wasn't revealing much about it to her.

She'd expected tears and lengthy explanations. But the only one in the car who seemed to be having trouble dealing with the departure was her.

Cable hadn't sought her out to say goodbye, and she'd been too proud to go to him. Now that she was actually leaving, she wondered if she was doing the right thing. She'd thought on the day of the fire that Cable had finally realized how his fears were exaggerated. But instead it had only reminded him of how much he had to lose.

She'd run out of ideas. She couldn't force him to love her or to risk a life together. Cable didn't want them, and she wouldn't stay where she wasn't wanted.

Sara started the engine, shifted into reverse and backed up, refusing to look at the house one more time. But as the place disappeared from sight, she couldn't help glancing in the rearview mirror, hoping to find Cable's brown pickup coming up behind. She finally gave up hope when she reached the center of town.

Apparently she was incapable of learning from her mistakes. It had been so easy to fall in love with Cable. Each time she'd seen him with Jeremy her heart had melted a little more. Each time she'd seen the loneliness in his eyes, felt the gentleness in his touch or heard the tenderness in his voice she'd believed he wasn't a crab at all. She'd believed that hiding under that hard exterior was a man with compassion, a lost man who only needed to be shown the way back to life and love.

Well, she'd been wrong, and the sooner she got those silly fantasies out of her mind the better. This had been a painful experience but a valuable one. She would never risk her heart again.

Cable stood at the kitchen window watching Sara's small car disappear. He'd thought about stopping her and asking her to stay permanently. Then the old fears had risen up and clogged his mind with doubts.

He turned away from the window, trying to convince himself it was better this way. He hadn't slept all night. He'd spent the time getting reacquainted with memories of Amanda and Todd. It had been equivalent to careening over rapids in a faulty raft, but eventually the turbulent memories had calmed and he'd realized that Sara was right. They did warm and comfort him now.

He wished he could explain his fears to Sara and make her understand. He knew she thought he was rejecting her love and denying the passion between them. But she'd never been through something like this. How could she know what it was like?

He should never have agreed to any of it—not the boarding arrangements or playing daddy to Jeremy. It had only resulted in pain and regret for all of them. He'd hurt Sara, Jeremy and himself for no reason. But he had his memories back now to comfort him, to keep him company. That should be enough.

Cable walked out to the shop, intending to soothe his battered emotions with a little work therapy. But the comfort and security he usually found there were gone. He found he couldn't hide behind his machines and his wood anymore.

He'd been content in his isolation. It wasn't until that solitude had been shattered that he'd started to realize what he was missing.

Sara had changed everything. She and Jeremy had invaded his home, his work, every aspect of his life. Nothing would be the same ever again.

Sara had called him a hermit crab—a species that sets up house in the discarded shells of other sea creatures. That's exactly what he'd done. He'd been living in a house he'd borrowed from someone else.

It was time to examine his life, determine what was real and what he wanted now. When he'd asked her, Sara had known exactly what she wanted. Now it was his turn. What did he want?

He shuffled through all his feelings, his deepest desires and his fondest dreams. Two things emerged: his love for Sara and Jeremy and his love for his work.

Those were the things that defined his parameters now. Good, honest work with his own two hands and a wife and son he'd give his life for. Those were the most important things.

Cable started from the shop, stopping abruptly when he saw a purple dinosaur sitting patiently on his tool bench to the left of the door.

Clifford.

His heart lurched. Jeremy would be devastated without his special friend.

He grabbed up the animal and hurried outside, mentally calculating how he could intercept them before they hit the interstate.

He had his hand on the car door when a sudden thought struck him. He glanced down at the stuffed toy again. How had Jeremy come to leave this in his shop? And on the tool bench, a place forbidden to him?

Cable thought about that day on the swing when he'd cried and Jeremy had comforted him. *I'm gonna leave Clifford here so you won't be by yourself.* Had Jeremy left the toy behind on purpose?

Cable's shell began to dissolve around him as he faced the depth of this little boy's love for him. Jeremy was willing to give up one of his most precious possessions to keep Cable from feeling lonely.

The bravery of this small child humbled and shamed him. Cable had tried hard not to love Jeremy. He had frightened Jeremy to tears on one occasion, and yet the boy was still able to risk his heart and love a man like him.

But Cable was still holding back, afraid to risk sharing his own love again because it meant putting his heart on the line.

Looking up at the old house, he suddenly saw it as it really was—old, decrepit and in desperate need of attention. For the first time he saw his grandmother's house not as a shelter from the elements, but as a vast, empty tomb, a collection of boards and windows, devoid of life.

If he didn't find the courage to risk loving again, to go after Sara and Jeremy and claim them as his own, his life would be as hollow and worthless as this old hulk of a house.

Cable stared down at the toy, feeling his love for Sara and Jeremy filling up his heart, spreading warmth and light into his soul.

Looking back, he could see that their arrival had marked the moment when he'd started to live again. Sara and her son had brought light and color and purpose into his life. They'd given him a reason to get up each day, a reason to work and to look ahead. Before Sara and Jeremy had come into his world, he'd only been existing. He'd been dead inside until Sara came to him. If he let her slip away, he'd be worse than dead.

He loved Sara. Wholly and completely. And while it was a different kind of love from what he'd shared with Amanda, it was every bit as powerful and lasting.

Cable tightened his fingers around the plush toy. He was still haunted by the possibility of losing another family.

He'd survived hell. Now that his memories were back, he could embrace them and enshrine them in his heart forever. But even as he put away the past, he discovered there was plenty of room for Sara and Jeremy as well.

He wouldn't trade a moment of his memories, but they were memories. A piece of his life he'd loved and cherished, but was gone.

He stood at a crossroads. In one direction lay the past, Amanda and Todd. In the other lay the future—life, love and a family. Either way included the possibility of pain. But he couldn't stand immobile forever. He couldn't not choose.

Which was worse—a life alone or a life with Sara and Jeremy that included the chance of losing again? He could have either the comfort of his memories or the comfort of Sara's love.

Cable pulled open the truck door and jumped in.

* * *

Sara paid the gas-station attendant and climbed back into her car. She hadn't really needed gas, but it was a long drive to the next town. Better to be safe than sorry. Besides, she'd been thirsty, and Jeremy had needed to go to the rest room.

She looked back over her shoulder in the direction of Cable's house. No Cable. No brown pickup. She was such a sucker.

Calling herself all kinds of a fool, she cranked the engine, her gaze scanning the interior of the car, mentally cataloging the contents in case something had been left behind.

Suitcases, bag of toys, pet carrier and Doggie. She was surprised when she discovered something actually was missing. "Jeremy, where's Clifford?"

"At Cable's house."

Sara studied her small son curiously. "Why didn't you tell Mommy we forgot your Clifford?"

"He wanted to stay with Cable," Jeremy informed her.

Sara frowned in puzzlement. Jeremy wouldn't go anywhere without the prehistoric purple predator. But he had deliberately left it behind.

"Why?"

"'Cause Cable needed someone to take care of him. Without us he'll be by hisself."

Her son's consideration touched her heart. "You don't want Cable to be alone?"

Jeremy shook his head. "I love him."

Sara caught her breath. "You do?" Tears stung the backs of her eyes. She'd greatly underestimated Jeremy's feelings for Cable.

"I love him this much," he said, spreading his arms as wide as they would reach. "Do you love Cable, too, Mommy?"

Jeremy's question hung poised in the air between them. How should she answer him? *Yes, I do love Cable, but he's*

*afraid to love me back. He's afraid to risk his heart again.*
*So afraid that he was willing to let us walk out of his life*
*forever.*

If only he'd see that love was the answer to his problems.

Suddenly, Sara found herself questioning that statement.
Did she really believe that love was the answer? Yes, but
there was more at stake here than her own feelings. Jeremy's heart was involved, too.

There was no doubt in her mind that she loved Cable, but
how could she depend upon a man who'd blocked his
memories of his family? True, he'd done so out of a need to
survive emotionally, but the bottom line was he'd achieved
complete separation.

What guarantee did she have that if she made a commitment and things became too much for him, he wouldn't shut
down his feelings for them, too? She couldn't risk her heart
again.

But her own words echoed in her ears. That's exactly what
she'd said about Cable. She was scared, too!

She'd made up all kinds of excuses, rationalized ad nauseam but the plain truth was *she* was scared. Maybe not as
much as Cable, but scared none the less.

Was she giving up too easily? What if they ended up miserable because they were both afraid of being hurt? They
could be missing out on something rare and special.

But how did she fight Cable's fear? He'd burrowed so
deep and she couldn't reach him. How could she convince
him that she and Jeremy could heal his scars and ease the
anxiety?

She'd tried shouting; she'd tried understanding. She'd
tried everything she could think of to keep Cable from hiding again. She was running out of time. If common sense,
anger and cold hard facts couldn't drag him from his shell,
what would?

Love!

Of course. She knew how she felt about him, but did Cable know? She'd assumed he knew she loved him. She wouldn't have slept with him if she didn't. But had she told him outright that she loved him? Maybe he was afraid to say so because he wasn't sure how she felt. Well, she could fix that.

She'd come right out and tell him I love you. Then, if he still didn't come around... No, she didn't want to think about that. She would fight fear with love. She'd pulled him out of his shell once and she could do it again. Even if it meant driving back and forth between Nashville and Carswell for months until he came to his senses.

She couldn't leave without one last stand. She and Jeremy were the best things that had ever happened to him and it was about time he realized that. Jeremy was right; without them he'd be all alone and miserable. She had to make him see that he needed them.

With a smile, grim determination and a heart full of hope, Sara turned the car around and headed back.

Sara pulled into the drive and almost ran into the brown pickup backing toward her. She turned off the car and got out, meeting Cable as he stepped from the truck.

"Sara!"

"Don't 'Sara' me," she said, grabbing hold of his shirtfront with her fists. "Just shut up and listen to me. I know you went through hell when your family died and I know that's a terrible loss to adjust to. But hiding away isn't the answer. We are."

"We?"

"Me and Jeremy. We love you. I love you more than anything in the world and that little boy wants you to be his daddy."

"Sara—"

"I'm not done. You need us. I know you don't think so. You think you can do it all by yourself, but you can't. We need you, too. We need you to love us, and I know you do." She shook him slightly to emphasize her point.

"I was coming—"

"I know you're afraid to take that final step. I know you're scared to death to risk it again. But please, Cable, let us love you."

"And if I don't?"

"Then I'll put a cot in your shop and never leave you alone. I'll drive down from Nashville every chance I get until you come to your senses. You might as well face it. I'm not leaving here until you say you love us, too."

"Isn't that backward?"

Sara wasn't going to listen to any arguments. She was gathering steam. "Don't you see it's meant to be? We were all meant to live here together. I'll take the assistant manager position at the Dixie Mart here and enroll Jeremy in school. You can build your furniture and we can start fixing up the house—"

"Stop it, Sara."

Sara clamped her mouth shut. Her heart was racing and she was breathless from her diatribe. She didn't know how to interpret Cable's tone of voice. Had she failed again? Hadn't she reached him at all?

"Stop what?" she asked tentatively.

"Stop trying to complicate a simple situation with details."

"What simple situation?"

Cable held up Clifford. A smile slowly spread across his face, exposing his dimples. He wrapped his arms around her, dinosaur and all. "I love you, Sara. I love your son. It's as simple as that."

Sara smiled, releasing Cable's shirt and slipping her arms around his neck. Her heart was singing now. "And your solution?"

"We're a family. We have been since you burst into the kitchen at one-thirty in the morning holding Jeremy."

Jeremy popped his head out the window of the car. "Can Cable be my daddy now?" he asked.

Cable looked into Sara's eyes and smiled. Then he lowered his head and kissed her possessively. "I don't like disappointing little children."

"Oh, Cable, I knew it would end this way. I love you and I knew you loved us, too, but—"

"Sara, shut up and kiss me."

\* \* \* \* \*

# COMING NEXT MONTH

**#1021 MOLLY DARLING—Laurie Paige**
*That's My Baby!*
Rancher Sam Frazier needed a mommy for his little Lass—and a
wife in the bargain. He proposed a marriage of convenience to
Molly Clelland—but he never dreamed he'd long to call the instant
mother his Molly darling....

**#1022 THE FALL OF SHANE MACKADE—Nora Roberts**
*The MacKade Brothers*
Footloose and fancy-free, Shane MacKade had a reputation as a ladies
man to uphold, and he took his job seriously. Who would have though
a brainy beauty like Dr. Rebecca Knight would cause this irrepressible
bachelor to take the fall...?

**#1023 EXPECTING: BABY—Jennifer Mikels**
An urgent knock at the door introduced Rick Sloan to his neighbor—
Mara Vincetti, who was about to give birth. Next thing Rick Sloan
knew he was a father figure for the new single mom and her baby!

**#1024 A BRIDE FOR LUKE—Trisha Alexander**
*Three Brides and a Baby*
When sister-of-the-bride Clem Bennelli met brother-of-the-groom
Luke Taylor, it was a case of opposites attract. They agreed theirs
would be a passionate, no-strings-attached relationship—but neither
one expected to want much, much more....

**#1025 THE FATHER OF HER CHILD—Joan Elliott Pickart**
*The Baby Bet*
Honorary MacAllister family member Ted Sharpe was carefree and
single. But secretly he yearned to be a husband and a father. And
when the very pregnant divorcée Hannah Johnson moved in next
door—he lost his heart, but found his dreams.

**#1026 A WILL AND A WEDDING—Judith Yates**
Commitment and marriage were two words Amy Riordan never
believed would apply to her. After meeting similarly minded
Paul Hanley, however, she began to think otherwise—and now
the word "wedding" was definitely in her future!

## MILLION DOLLAR SWEEPSTAKES

# As seen on TV!
## *Free Gift Offer*

With a Free Gift proof-of-purchase from any Silhouette® book,
you can receive a beautiful cubic zirconia pendant.

This gorgeous marquise-shaped stone is a genuine cubic
zirconia—accented by an 18" gold tone necklace.

(Approximate retail value $19.95)

## Send for yours today...
### compliments of ▼ *Silhouette*®
™

To receive your free gift, a cubic zirconia pendant, send us one original proof-of-
purchase, photocopies not accepted, from the back of any Silhouette Romance™,
Silhouette Desire®, Silhouette Special Edition®, Silhouette Intimate Moments®
or Silhouette Shadows™ title available in February, March or April at your favorite
retail outlet, together with the Free Gift Certificate, plus a check or money order for
$1.75 U.S./$2.25 CAN. (do not send cash) to cover postage and handling, payable
to Silhouette Free Gift Offer. We will send you the specified gift. Allow 6 to 8 weeks for
delivery. Offer good until April 30, 1996 or while quantities last. Offer valid in the U.S. and
Canada only.

## *Free Gift Certificate*

Name: _____

Address: _____

City: _____ State/Province: _____ Zip/Postal Code: _____

Mail this certificate, one proof-of-purchase and a check or money order for postage
and handling to: SILHOUETTE FREE GIFT OFFER 1996. In the U.S.: 3010 Walden
Avenue, P.O. Box 9057, Buffalo NY 14269-9057. In Canada: P.O. Box 622, Fort Erie,

## FREE GIFT OFFER
079-KBZ-R
### ONE PROOF-OF-PURCHASE
To collect your fabulous FREE GIFT, a cubic zirconia pendant, you must include this
original proof-of-purchase for each gift with the properly completed Free Gift Certificate.

079-KBZ-R

# It's time you joined...

## THE BABY OF THE MONTH CLUB

Silhouette Desire proudly presents *Husband: Optional,* book four of RITA Award-winning author Marie Ferrarella's miniseries, THE BABY OF THE MONTH CLUB, coming your way in March 1996.

*She wasn't fooling him.* Jackson Cain knew the baby Mallory Flannigan had borne was his...no matter that she *claimed* a conveniently absentee lover was Joshua's true dad. And though Jackson had left her once to "find" his true feelings, nothing was going to keep him away from this ready-made family now....

*Do You Take This Child?* We certainly hope you do, because in April 1996 Silhouette Romance will feature this final book in Marie Ferrarella's wonderful miniseries, THE BABY OF THE MONTH CLUB, found only in— Silhouette®

# You're About to Become a *Privileged Woman*

Reap the rewards of fabulous free gifts and benefits with proofs-of-purchase from Silhouette and Harlequin books

# Pages & Privileges™

It's our way of thanking you for buying our books at your favorite retail stores.

**PROOF OF PURCHASE**

SSE-PP118

Offer expires October 31, 1996

## Harlequin and Silhouette—
the most privileged readers in the world!

For more information about Harlequin and Silhouette's **PAGES & PRIVILEGES** program call the Pages & Privileges Benefits Desk: **1-503-794-2499**